Praise for Gustavo Bondoni and his previous work

Of Dark Places

Gustavo Bondoni's new collection of stories *Of Dark Places* is a perfect Halloween-appropriate feast of chills and thrills, but with a difference. Bondoni, an incredibly versatile and prolific Argentinian writer, has a special touch and a unique perspective few others can match.

Global horror can shine the light of storytelling into the dark places we did not know existed. Bondoni's stories range far and wide beyond the confines of suburban America. He takes us to Africa ("What I Never Told Them" and "Shadow of an Ape"), Antarctica ("Frozen Meat"), Mexico ("The Cost of Victory"), the American West ("A Day's Ride from Tarabuco"), and the outer space ("Watching the Stars"). And in every place that we visit, we encounter something surprising, shocking, and unexpected.

The wide range of this collection is not only geographic but also generic. Though Bondoni has achieved popularity with science fiction and fantasy, most stories in this collection have a horror element, which adds a stunning and unique twist to the familiar sci-fi tropes of the colony ship in "Watching the Stars," bioengineering in "A Holiday in Love Canal," or malfunctioning bots in "Garbage In, Garbage Out." Other stories mix horror and noir ("Going for Peanuts"), horror and the Sherlock Holmes pastiche ("A Time for Haste"), and horror and mythology ("Autobiography, Carved in Stone").

But Bondoni's greatest success, in my view, is his historical horror. The stories in the collection will take you to the poppy-bloodied fields of World War I ("Poppies in Full Bloom"), Scotland during World War II where "wights" roam the moors ("Thunder in Old Kirkpatrick"), Mexico City, ancient and modern ("The Cost of Victory"), Romania on the eve of being invaded by the Nazis ("Hobson's Angel"), and even the Etruscan League of Twelve, about to be attacked by Rome ("Aulus Fabius Ambustus"). Historical horror is becoming a very popular subgenre, and Bondoni excels in it.

All in all, this volume is one of the richest, best-written and most rewarding single-author collections I have read in the last year. If you want a fresh new voice in horror, try Gustavo Bondoni."

~ Elana Gomel, author of *Little Sister*, *Black House*, and *My Lady of Plagues*

Previous Work

"Bondoni is an amazingly versatile writer of science fiction and fantasy. His books range from space opera to historical fantasy; from creature features to Latin American mythological fables. In every genre, he displays his mastery of the form and ability to engage the reader."

~ Elana Gomel, author of "Little Sister," "Black House," And "My Lady of Plagues"

"An engaging, impeccably written examination of the way each life touches so many other lives... Although widely recognized as a firmly established science fiction author, Gustavo Bondoni deftly transcends genre with this series of stories in which relationships between and among the characters are viewed and severally related from varying perspectives."

~ Stacy K., Five-Star Amazon Review

"Loved it. For me it was a page turner from the start. Bondoni's narration style combines good storytelling skills, old-school sci-fi plot twists and refreshing creativeness... A great read!"

~ Alex, Five-Star Amazon Review

"All in all, this book gets two huge thumbs up from me and I look forward to reading more from this author. This is a fast paced, fresh, fantastic work of science fiction."

~ Kathryn Bennett for Readers' Favorite

"This is a first-rate piece of writing. The author, whose first language is not English, does an excellent job with the characters and storytelling. It is very much worth the reader's time."

~ Paul Lappen, Four-Star Amazon Review

# of dark places

a horror short story collection by

Gustavo Bondoni

From

Dark Owl Publishing, LLC

Arizona

ISBN 978-1-951716-44-8

Cover design by Dark Owl Publishing

Visit us on our website at:
www.darkowlpublishing.com

Also from Dark Owl Publishing

Collections

The Dark Walk Forward
John S. McFarland

Baby Monster
John S. McFarland

The Last Star Warden:
Volumes I and II
The Phantom World
The Crimson Star Saga Episodes
Jason J. McCuiston

The Brotherhood of Secret Darkness and Other Cults, Cabals, and Conspiracies
Jason J. McCuiston

Professor Wyrd's World of Wonders: Miracles and Monsters
Jason J. McCuiston

Tales from New Pangea
Kevin M. Folliard

No Lesser Angels, No Greater Devils
The Aiphace
Laura J. Campbell

The Tension of a Coming Storm
Adrian Ludens

The Nightmare Cycle
Lawrence Dagstine

The Art of Ghost Writing
Alistair Rey

Bad Dreams and Reflections
Trevor Kennedy

Welcome to Scar Ridge
Jonathon Mast

Anthologies

Something Wicked This Way Rides

Novels

The Black Garden
John S. McFarland

The Mother of Centuries
The sequel to *The Black Garden*
John S. McFarland

The Keeper of Tales
Jonathon Mast

Carnivore Keepers
A novel from New Pangea
Kevin M. Folliard

The Wicked Twisted Road
D.S. Hamilton

For Young Readers

Annette's Books:
Annette: A Big, Hairy Mom
Annette: A Big, Hairy Grandma
John S. McFarland

The Shivers and Scares Series:
Shivers, Scares, and Goosebumps
Shivers, Scares, and Chills
Vonnie Winslow Crist

Table of Contents

Thunder in Old Kilpatrick

The skies came alive with a drone like a disturbed beehive and Richard glanced up at the heavens.

But only for a moment. There were more pressing things occupying his attention on Earth, wonderful things that he'd never imagined possible back in boring old London. Fluttering on the ground in front of him was a bird, red-headed and angry, dragging a broken wing through the heather.

Richard wondered what to do with it. There was no question of just letting it be, not after he'd spent all afternoon trying to bring one down, but he was torn between the sheer delight of tormenting it—taking revenge on all taunting, elusive bird-kind—and nursing it back to health and having it for a pet. These weighty meditations were the reason that Old Tom managed to sneak up on him.

"I see you've got your first grouse, laddie."

"A grouse?" He'd heard some of the men talking about grouses, and sometimes they even went out to hunt them. The guns they carried were so big that Richard had always imagined a grouse would be something huge, with hide, tusks, and a temper to match. The thing wriggling forlornly on the ground certainly didn't look the part.

Old Tom nodded toward the bird. "They're hard to bring down, especially with a sling. You've the makings of a hunter, boy." The groundskeeper's craggy face never showed any emotion, but his voice seemed to radiate approval. "But stones won't save you if Hannah finds you out here. The wireless says the sirens have gone off over in Clydebank, and she's ordered everyone into the cellar."

"The sirens are going all the time. We're too far away for it to matter," Richard replied, half-mutinous. He knew that Old Tom wouldn't report his words, but there was always the chance that Hannah would appear from out of the underbrush. The plump, grandmotherly woman was lightning-fast with a switch. "And I'll tell her I ran all the way back, but I was too far away."

The old man pursed his lips to speak, but suddenly stopped and looked into the air. Richard realized that the drone had grown louder. But he still didn't worry. It was probably just an RAF defender, reaching the scene of the bombing too late to be of any use.

A rough, calloused hand pressed into Richard's shoulder. "Get down, lad!"

Tom pushed him down into the heather, right beside the struggling bird, and lay on top of him. Or at least it felt that way to Richard. Before he'd finished falling, he felt the Earth around him shake. Then he was deafened by the sound of thunder and thrown some meters clear. He hit the ground hard and didn't hear the second bomb.

***

The pain in Richard's hand became more and more urgent, and he came back to his senses with a gasp. A voice, shouting in a closed, unintelligible Scottish brogue, sounded distantly through the ringing in his ears. He turned his head and saw Old Tom brandishing a thick branch in one hand. The groundskeeper's other arm hung, bloody and limp, at his side.

At first, Richard wondered whether the blast that had thrown them across the moor had also finally driven the old man insane. The servants muttered about Tom's lonely life and bleak disposition all the time, not caring that the young master might hear. Now, though, the man seemed to be incoherent, bracing for an attack.

The doubts were short-lived. A lumbering form, wearing rags and some rusted metallic fabric, came into view. The strange figure uttered a low moan, a sound that—even through the buzzing in Richard's ears—felt like the lament of a lost soul. He paused in front of the groundskeeper, and then lowered a shoulder and advanced.

Tom made a valiant effort to stop him, advancing grimly and breaking the branch—a dry, infirm weapon—over the other man's head.

The blow was completely ignored, and the man, moaning continuously, struck once with his hand and sent Tom head over heels to the ground. Then he waited, as if to see what the groundskeeper would do next, until satisfied that his opponent was not going to move again.

With slow, deliberate motions, the man turned to where Richard was lying. The boy felt the fear rushing into his gut and tried to stand, tried to run. But it was impossible. His balance abandoned him, and he stumbled onto the ground, able only to lie and watch as the figure of Tom's assailant advanced.

The man bent and picked Richard up by the shirt. The scent coming off him was of earth and mold. The man pulled him up to face him, and Richard nearly fainted when he saw the eyes: they were white and milky, the eyes of a blind man. The man's skin was gray, almost white—and there was an open cut running across the length of his forehead, but the open flap of skin showed no blood, just more white-gray.

Richard opened his mouth, but the scream came through his deafened ears as a pitiful whine. The man held his gaze for just another second before dismissively tossing the boy to the ground. When Richard's head hit, the darkness descended once again.

***

The next time Richard opened his eyes, he found himself in bed. He was in a wood-paneled room, with sunlight streaming through a window. A glass of water sat on a tray beside the bed.

So, it was all a dream, he thought sleepily, and he decided to go out to see what delights the moors held in store for him.

He never managed it. As he attempted to sit up, a strange bundle around his chest impeded his progress, and it was a good thing, too. Pain shot up from his ribs, and he fell back to the bed with a gasp.

"Richard! What do you think you're doing, young man?" Hannah entered the room, her dark blue uniform immediately filling it, leaving little room for anything else. Hannah was supposedly head of the household staff—not quite a housekeeper, not quite a member of the family—but, in reality, she ran the house with an iron fist, and anyone who wasn't an adult member of the gentry would do as she ordered or feel the sharp sting of her tongue. Richard thought there must be a bit of bear in her makeup. "Near broken in half by the bombs and trying to get out of bed without a by-your-leave. I'll not have it."

He nodded dumbly, as was his custom whenever she asked him

a question, but the tactic—usually infallible—was wasted on her.

"Now tell me how you're feeling. Those ribs all right? Doctor said you'd be feeling the break for a few weeks. No tree climbing for you, lad."

"Break?" Richard said. He was relieved to find that speech was possible, and that the pain had subsided.

"Broke a rib, maybe two. I'm surprised it wasn't more, fool lad, playing out on the moors in the middle of a German attack. How many times have I told you to get inside when the alarms sound? The cellar is the only place to be in a raid. But do you listen? No. No one ever listens to me."

That was so ridiculously untrue that Richard nearly interrupted her but caught himself in time. Even so, it was unlikely that Hannah would have paid him the least attention. She had a full head of steam.

"And that old man is the worst of the lot. Just because the master is fond of grouse hunting and he's the only one who can keep his grouse moors clear, he thinks he's above the law. Well, you see where it got him?" She paused to give Richard a questioning glare, to which the boy could only give a confused look in response. "It nearly cost him an arm—and it did cost him his sanity, not that there was much of it to begin with. Do you know what he's been saying?" This time she didn't stop to ask for Richard's opinion, she just went on. "He's been saying there's a wight loose on the moors. That's Old Tom for you. He'd never be content to be bombed by the Germans. No, he has to bring ghouls and ghosts into his story as well."

Hannah sighed in disgust and left, muttering something about getting the young fool something to eat, if the old fool had left anything at all. Richard ignored her completely.

He was thinking about a wight.

***

The next few days were torture. Even though he hardly felt any pain, Richard was forced to stay in bed, under strict guard and the threat of lost privileges, as life went on around him. That in itself would have been enough to make him chafe. Who knew how long the war would last, how long the German bombs in London would allow him to remain out there in the Scottish countryside? His freedom from the gray limitations of life as the son of a wealthy city merchant might come to an end at any time.

But this was not the main reason for Richard's restlessness. There was a darkness in the house that made the weeks before—when German air raids were a daily occurrence—seem like a light-hearted time of happiness. Maids, whispering as they approached, would immediately fall silent when they entered his room to clean or to leave his meals on the bedside table. Even Hannah, forbidding as she was, seemed to be showing chinks in her armor. Once, during a particularly windy day, a sudden gust closed one of the room's shutters with a loud bang, causing Hannah to start and drop a tray complete with Richard's breakfast. The woman had tried to hide her fear under a veneer of anger, but her face had remained white as a sheet for the rest of the day—and she'd ordered all the shutters on the ground floor to be closed as soon as dusk began to fall.

Frustration mounted as the days went by and no one gave him any indication of what was going on. Day after day he suffered until one afternoon, bored of the illustrated books that had kept him sane to that point, Richard stole out of bed. He reasoned that, if discovered, he would simply say that he was on the way to the restroom—his only permitted excursion—and hadn't told anyone to avoid being a nuisance.

The door of his room was about halfway down the hall on the first floor of the house. Richard made his way silently down the corridor, toward the flight of stairs leading into the entrance hall. He stopped dead. Below him, two of the maids were in earnest conversation.

"They say the wight's not been seen for two days," one said. She was the scullery maid, married to a clerk in town, so she was the source of any and all information in the house.

"Must be hiding."

"No, they say wights don't know how to hide. They're just dead flesh, and they have to keep moving. They have unfinished business, that's why they can't really die."

"But this one was from years and years ago. How come it's just come out now?"

"Old Tom says that they must have buried it under tons of stone and that the bombs set it free."

"Pshaw. Old Tom ain't right in the head since he lost 'is arm. Anyhow, if the wight's gone, the army probably got it."

"No. You can't kill a wight with guns. It can't rest until it does what it has to do. That's what I told Emma when she said that it had probably thrown itself into the sea. I told her that wights have to do what they have to do. It's silly to think they'd go throwing themselves into the sea."

"Why not? Must be an awful way to live, being a wight."

Richard knew these two would not give him any more useful information. They knew less about the monster than he did. Just from looking into its dead eyes for that single instant, he could have told them beyond any doubt that the wight was still out there somewhere. The mere suggestion of it throwing itself into the sea was ridiculous. He moved back to his room, undiscovered.

***

It took the full force of the doctor's command—and Richard managed to overhear the phrase: "I don't care if the armies of Hell itself are out on those moors. The boy needs to be allowed to recover in the fresh air"—for Richard's personal Cerberus to allow him freedom.

At first, the command was taken literally, with supervised strolls along the terrace being deemed sufficient contact with the elements to be going with. But even Hannah quickly realized that this was impracticable. People busy making certain he wasn't being attacked by ancient monsters were often needed in the kitchen or elsewhere. And the fact that they avoided any mention of it was even worse. They pretended to be concerned that he might fall, or that he would move in the wrong direction and hurt himself. Richard fantasized about asking the scullery maid who was with him that day what, exactly, she would do if the wight attacked them.

He kept silent, and on the third day, they simply left him to his own devices.

Richard knew that there was a fine line between freedom and obedience that had to be observed. If he disappeared into the moors for too long, Hannah would cause his freedom to end in a complete way—and besides, he still wasn't in any condition to be overly frolicsome. But there was one thing he had to do, despite the darkness of the day and the fog that hadn't quite burned away, even though it was nearly noon.

The place where the German plane had dropped the bombs was

about half a mile away, just beyond one of the small hills that dotted the estate.

The wight was sitting in the shadows of the crater. It looked up as he approached, and Richard was again surprised by the lack of life in its eyes. He knew what people were saying about it, knew that it was supposed to be the walking dead, supposed to be able to tear strong men apart without even making much of an effort, but he felt no fear. He'd moved on and was no longer the shell-shocked bomb victim the wight had previously encountered. Even injured, Richard knew he could run faster than it could stumble after him.

They studied each other in silence for a moment. The wight's dead eyes seemed to have grown glassier since they'd last met, but other than that, it didn't seem to be worse for wear. It was still wearing the rust-colored shirt whose unused hood fell behind the creature's head. Now that Richard had time to observe more carefully, he saw that the shirt reached its knees and was held in place at the waist by a rotted belt that couldn't possibly hold out much longer. The cloth rags it had been wearing over the shirt on their first encounter were gone.

Somehow, this creature, this dead man from another age, looked perfectly at home standing in a bomb crater in the gloom of the overcast moor. It looked natural, making Richard feel like he was the otherworldly intruder.

Without warning, it emitted the moan again. It wasn't a loud sound, but it cut straight to the boy's soul, passing through his physical body as if it were made of spider silk. Richard nearly turned and ran but held his position until the wailing stopped and they stood facing each other again, with Richard feeling just slightly wave-tossed.

The wight clearly didn't see him as a threat. Whether something had changed since their last encounter, or whether it simply remembered the ease with which it had handled him, Richard had no way of knowing. But the creature simply turned, without so much as a shrug, and began methodically lifting stones that it found in the scarred earth where the German bombs had fallen. There seemed to be no point to what it was doing—every rock it took into its arms was then dropped back into a seemingly random place as it picked up another. It wasn't piling them up, nor was it organizing them in any way. It didn't even seem to know which ones it had already discarded. In the ten minutes that Richard watched it work, he saw the wight pick up one particular stone no fewer than eight times before tossing it back to the ground.

Richard took two steps forward, trying to get a closer look at what was happening. Suddenly, he heard a familiar drone, high in the skies.

He didn't stop to think that it might just be an RAF patrol; he didn't stop to hear if the sirens were going. He just ran as quickly as his battered body could take him for the imaginary safety of the house.

Richard only turned back once, when the wailing of the wight hit him from behind. He turned to see it waving its arms frantically at some unseen enemy above as if it were being attacked by bees. He stood for a second, thinking how much it looked like some of the engravings of old Scottish knights in the books in his father's library.

Then he turned back to the house and ran from the sound of the airplanes.

***

The raids continued around the clock for two days. This time, it was no incidental thing, bombers dropping a load or two on their way back to Germany. This time the target was Clydebank, and Richard could hear the distant rumbling whenever he left the bunker. They were tense times, but all of them knew, at least deep within themselves, that the shelter would protect them. It might have been a false belief, or even completely mistaken, but it kept them from going mad. And the thunder from the bombs never came too close again.

On the third day, the bombing stopped, and thunder of a different kind, full of blowing gales and rattling windows, took over the land. Richard was confined to the house for yet another spell. By the time the storm blew over, he was nearly completely recovered and fit to burst from the combined effects of cabin fever and the secret he'd managed to keep to himself in the shelter. As soon as it dawned sunny, he was off into the moors.

The wight hadn't gone far. It was standing nearly in the same place as he had left it, almost as though it hadn't moved.

But it was clear that it must have. The place where the bombs had fallen had been churned into a muddy mass of deep footprints, and the wight itself had half-dried clods sticking to it as high as its knees.

And it had found a sword.

Well, perhaps the word "sword" is a bit generous for the rusted piece of metal it held in one hand and whose edge lay on one shoulder, but it was clear from looking at the wight that the undead creature at least felt the sword was no less than Excalibur. It seemed to stand taller, prouder, and a sense of calm that hadn't been present in their earlier encounters filled the moor.

It watched Richard approach but made no move toward him. When it was clear that the boy would come no closer, the creature simply turned away, sending its gaze back up into the heavens. It seemed to be waiting for something, and its posture made it extremely clear that it was prepared to wait as long as necessary.

What exactly it was waiting for was more of a mystery.

Richard wondered whether it believed that the noisy, dangerous metal beasts that ringed the sky were dragons—or whether they were angels sent to take him to his promised land. One thing seemed certain: a dead creature from the deep past armed with a rusted sword was unlikely to understand the Luftwaffe. The boy took another step toward the wight. And then another. A third.

At the fourth, the wight turned its attention back to the ground and gave him a look that froze Richard in his tracks. It raised its sword—not at the boy, but at the sky, and grunted. Then it pointed at the countryside, indicating everything around them: the moors, the overcast sky, and a distant copse of trees and tried to speak. The sound that came out was completely impossible to understand, but the message was clear. What was out there belonged to the wight—and all challenges would be met by the sword, rusty or not.

Richard halted but held his ground, anger welling up at the implied message. "All this land belongs to my family. And it has for hundreds of years." He puffed up his chest. "My grandfather said we took it from another clan back when Scots still ruled themselves."

The wight seemed to study him intently, to use its glazed eyes to stare deep into Richard's soul. Then it turned its attention back to the sky.

"I think you're one of my grandfather's grandfathers. Or maybe you were one of their servants. In any case, if you want to stay here, you have to listen to me."

The wight glanced back at the boy for just one instant, then dismissed him completely. Richard tried to get it to respond again, but no matter what outrageous claims he made, it staunchly ignored him.

That night, the boy's dreams were haunted by wights in armor. Every time he closed his eyes, undead from enemy clans chased him through the heather. Each dream ended in a cold sweat, with the feeling of a mesh gauntlet closing around the back of his neck.

***

When Old Tom finally became ambulatory once again, Richard was certain the wight, still standing where he'd left it, would be discovered. But the groundskeeper seemed to have little inclination to leave the house and spent his time drinking broth in the kitchen and telling the maids wilder and wilder tales of undead creatures that made Hitler's armies seem like a thing to be laughed off.

Though the old man stayed away from the moors, Richard still kept him in his sights. He didn't want to find that, in a careless moment, the groundskeeper would sneak up on him like he had that very first day. That would be a true catastrophe.

But Richard's presence seemed to be discomfiting to everyone in the servants' hall. Eyes shifted, and people found other things to do when he walked in. The pall seemed to grow and grow until, late one day, Old Tom, well into his drink, finally spluttered, "Don't you follow me around all day, lad. T'ain't my fault the Germans killed your parents in the last attack. Why if it hadn't..."

But Richard heard no more. Now he understood the freedom he was given, understood why Hannah hadn't even chided him when he'd returned late for dinner the night before. It was no comfort to him that he now owned the house and the surrounding countryside for miles around.

Blinded by tears, the boy ran off into the moor, and whether by design or by accident, he soon found himself face to face with the wight, just as night was falling. Overcome by tears, he had ignored both the sound of distant sirens and the commotion caused by Old Tom's sudden outburst. It was only under the supremely sobering effect of that undead gaze that he realized what was going on around him.

The air-raid siren—a new one that had been installed following the bombing incident—could be clearly heard, its wail only slightly distorted by the distance. And, in sharp barks and cries, the shouts of the household calling his name.

He debated whether to return to the open arms of his own people or to stay there, alone on the moor, surrounded by nothing that was alive.

The memory of his servants' betrayal, of their refusal to do what was right, made the decision for him. As night fell, he stood next to the wight on its seemingly eternal vigil. He wondered what it was thinking about; he, himself, was wondering how long they'd known without telling him.

The darkness was soon complete. If he hadn't known what the thing standing beside him actually was, he could have easily pretended that it was just a silent man. "My dad and mum are dead," the boy said. And with that, the emotion he'd been holding back spilled out. "Killed in this war. I don't understand it, I just want it to end. But now it's too late... too late..." And he broke down completely, even going as far as to lean on the wight's leg.

Shouts in the darkness got nearer, and then farther away as the household staff crisscrossed the moors in search of the wayward boy who was now their master. Richard wondered if he would have to wait to grow up before he could sack them all. He went back to gazing at the sky, tears flowing down his cheeks—starting hot before chilling in the wind.

The air above seemed somehow full of anger, despite the fact that little could be seen save directly above the city of Clydebank, where fires on the ground turned the clouds above unnatural shades of pink, orange, and purple. The distant droning and occasional booms that descended upon them created the sensation of a clash of unseen titans.

But the light was distant and hardly illuminated the boy and his unusual protector; therefore, when the household staff finally stumbled over them, it was as much a surprise to the searchers as to Richard.

Warren, the kennel keeper, a stout fellow of around twenty, faced them in the flickering light of an old-style lamp that hadn't been modified to Blitz blackout standards. Hannah herself held the lamp, trying to keep her face composed.

"It's all right boy, come here," she said. Her attempts at sounding gentle and soothing would have made Richard laugh, had he felt capable of it. Instead, the mere sight of her brought the anger and the helpless sense of having been betrayed back to the fore.

"No!" He turned to the wight and implored. "Save me from these people, kill them for me. I am the lord of these lands."

But the ancient knight ignored him.

"What are you doing, Richard?" Hannah screeched. "Get away from that ungodly thing!"

"Ungodly? Who are you to talk about ungodly? You're just..." But that was as far as the boy got. In his attempt to turn and face the woman, Richard stumbled and fell to the ground.

As soon as he saw that Richard was no longer at the wight's side, the kennel keeper raised a shotgun—the Mossberg, which all his father's friends had told Richard was completely wrong for shooting grouse and was therefore used by the staff—and fired without preamble into the creature's chest.

The wight stopped, raised its head into the air and keened, the sound of eternal torment.

Richard recoiled from the blast. He was close enough that the sound of the gun left his ears ringing, and close enough that the servant should never have dared fire in his direction. The man had shown just how afraid he was.

For a second after the blast, they all stood silent, contemplating each other, before Warren began working the bolt for another shot, and Richard acted. He closed the gap between himself and the wight, placing his own body in the line of fire.

"Get out of the way, Richard," Hannah hissed. "We just want what's best for you."

But the boy remained in place, even stepping toward the gun, hearing the wight come up behind him. He stopped when the shaking barrel was just inches from his chest and looked into Warren's eyes.

It was too much for the man. The kennel keeper broke and ran into the dark moors, ignoring Hannah's enraged commands.

Richard ignored her and looked into the warrior's eyes. "I've done my part." He didn't know whether the creature could understand the words he was saying, and he didn't really care. The words were unimportant. Both knew what had happened, knew what it meant.

Some bonds had to be respected.

"Now, kill them all," Richard said.

This time, the long-dead warrior moved to obey, and though Hannah stood her ground defiantly, as if she believed that God Himself would intervene on her behalf, Richard knew that the rest of the scattered servants would be more difficult to track down among the dark moors.

Fortunately, they had all night.

Miami Style,
Fresh From the Oven

Carlo the Nose burst in just as I was about to blow Jake's head off. We'd finally managed a clean grab, beat the little turd senseless, and dragged him into the unused bathroom on the second floor above the restaurant.

Breaker and Tony held him down. They were big guys, much bigger than I was, definitely much bigger than Jake, but the bastard wasn't going down without a fight. It took forever to get both barrels into his mouth. Hell, I probably broke all the little shit's teeth.

And that was the moment that Carlo decided to interrupt us. It was so unexpected that everyone froze, even the asshole bleeding into the tub.

"Boss," he said. "We got trouble."

"Are you fucking kidding me? I'm kinda busy here," I told him.

But he wasn't having it. "It's the lab on Union Street."

That was trouble. As long as the bosses got their cut, they were happy and didn't ask questions, but I really didn't want to explain to the Bonanno higher-ups that we'd broken their edict against selling drugs. Hell, they'd kill me even if they didn't figure out that we were working with the Russians. They get wind of that, they'd kill me, my family, and anyone who looked like me.

I jammed the gun deeper into Jake's mouth to keep him from getting any stupid ideas and turned to look at Carlo. "What happened?"

"Cops hit it ten, fifteen minutes ago."

"Feds?"

"Nah. Just regular cops. Some in blue, even."

"Shit." We'd really fucked up if the boys in blue were busting our top secret labs. Or maybe it hadn't been our fault. The Russians were useless pieces of crap. They probably leaked like an old radiator. "So why are you here?"

"Needed someplace to lie low. I managed to grab this when I ran." He held up a brown paper bag.

"What's that?"

"Product. Still powdered, not packed into pills yet. I thought the less evidence they could pick up, the better."

"Yeah, whatever. Get it out of here."

"But boss—"

A siren, still a few blocks away but getting closer, interrupted him.

"Out the window, now. Tony, Help him."

Tony opened the recalcitrant pane, and the Nose grabbed onto the drainage pipe and began to shimmy down. I never got to see if the stupid shit made it down because Tony closed it up again as soon as he was out. I listened for the sound of him falling and breaking his neck, but my wish was unfulfilled. The Nose had always been a lucky one. But he wouldn't be lucky for long if he kept doing stupid things like running to our safe house every time he got his panties in a wad.

Thirty seconds later, the cops were banging on the front door.

"Go get that, will you?"

I pulled Jake out of the tub and looked him in the eye. "We're gonna go have a nice conversation with those officers. Then I'm gonna let you go. So consider this your lucky day. Unless you forget yourself and speak to them, in which case, after I get out of jail, I'm going to track you down and kill you very slowly. No quick shotgun blast to the head. You hear me?"

He nodded, all the fight gone.

"Good."

I washed my hands in case I'd gotten any blood on them, checked my hair in the mirror, and turned to leave. Then I saw the bag.

"Little piece of shit," I said quietly. I was gonna break the Nose's gigantic nose for him.

I picked it up, grabbed Jake and the shotgun, and headed down the stairs. In the kitchen, I placed the gun in a cupboard—it was registered to me and perfectly legal—and the bag of powdered pills onto the marble by a bunch of kitchen supplies. The cops would be looking for stuff hidden away, not groceries.

Then I pasted on a smile and walked out to face two cops nosing around the dining room.

"Hi officers, how can I help you?"

Four eyes locked on Jake. The cops knew the score, and Jake being here didn't add up. But they decided to file it away for later and started the dance. "We're looking for Carlo Anderloni," they said.

"Haven't seen him since Howard's funeral."

"Don't bullshit us, we…" And so it went.

***

It was one of those nights. Everything that fucking could go wrong went wrong. First, the cops stuck around, searched the whole place, ran a check on the gun, and only left after the staff began to arrive for the dinner shift. They took Jake with them. After that, Candy called in sick just before we opened. I told her to find a new job. She was a shit waitress anyway.

Then, already shorthanded, we started to get complaints. Mine was one of those joints where most of the patrons were family and friends, which meant that no one complained very loud, so when pizzas actually started coming back, I realized something was well and truly fucked.

"What's happening, Tony?"

He looked pained. A lot of people think Tony's just muscle, and I don't exactly go out of my way to contradict them, but the truth is, he's the heart of our pizza place. Without him, this is just another crappy Brooklyn mob front—the only reason it's full of paying customers every night is because Tony is a magician with flour and tomatoes and cheese. A fucking magician.

"I don't know, boss. Pizza's the same as it always is. Made the dough myself, with my own hands." He held them up as if to show me that they were actually his hands. "But look at this." He pulled on one of the pieces that had come back from the tables, and it stretched like gum.

"So what?"

"That ain't the cheese, boss. That's the crust."

He was right. There was something really, really wrong with the dough. I pulled at it myself and had to pull my arms almost all the way apart before the string finally snapped.

"I've never seen anything like it, boss."

I chuckled darkly. People were so afraid of us that some had actually tried eating that shit before they gave up. One slice of the pizza that came back was bitten down almost to the crust.

"Make some new ones and I'll go out there and smooth the feathers. Don't worry about it."

I made the rounds, and though some tables seemed to be perfectly fine, there were at least seven or eight bad pizzas out there. I smiled a lot, promised that everyone would be eating free that night and that the replacement food would be there soon. The edge of tension in the room subsided, and soon people seemed more inclined to laugh it off as just one of those things than to actually make a big deal of it.

I went back into the kitchen, leaving Breaker at the till. Tiffany was with Ralph, and the morons were actually eating the pizza that someone had sent back and giggling. I yanked Ralph's hair. "Get back out there, you jackass," I said.

Busted, they both turned toward the swinging door that led to the tables, but I grabbed Tiffany's arm. "Not you, babe. I'm having a bad night and need to see you for a minute."

"Now? We're shorthanded."

"They'll wait. I won't."

She made a face, but she came. We both knew the drill. Past the kitchen and into the hall that led to the back door. There was a small bathroom there for the staff. Only I was allowed to lock the door, and I did.

"Make it fast," I told her, dropping my zipper. "You need to get back out there."

I leaned against the wall as she kneeled down. This would be the first good thing that happened to me all afternoon and I planned to enjoy it. Tiffany was an even worse waitress than Candy, but at least she had other abilities.

Suddenly, fire raced up from my leg. I yelled and buckled in pain and got Tiffany in the head with a knee. Her head hit the sink, hard.

I looked down. My right leg, up near the groin, had a huge bloody chunk pulled out of it.

"Did you bite me, you stupid bitch?" I screamed. I pulled my pants back up and kicked her. I never slapped women around, but what kind of crazy slut bit me? If she didn't want to earn her salary, she was free to walk at any time. This shit was nuts.

I'd kicked enough assholes when they were on the ground to know when to stop. I didn't want to kill her. It would be hell to explain that to the cops. I unlocked the door and headed back to the kitchen. There was a first aid kit in there for my leg.

Weird noises reached me from the direction of the tables. Screaming of some kind—someone had probably proposed to his lady or something, and people would be celebrating. I should be out there to congratulate them, but I had to get this bleeding under control. Probably get some disinfectant on the wound as well. I knew just what kind of trouble that girl's mouth got into.

Gritting my teeth against the pain, I was about to turn back toward the kitchen when Tiffany hit me from behind and began to bite my arm through my jacket. "What the fuck!" I turned around, expecting her to yell at me, frothing at the mouth, throwing every little thing I'd ever done to make her mad back in my face. You know how women can get sometimes.

But she was completely calm. "Stop stealing my tips," she said.

"What the fuck are you talking about?"

"My tips. You keep stealing my tips."

I didn't know what she was talking about. "Your tips? Girl, with what I give you for your blowjobs, what do you even need tips for? Get out of here."

"No. Give them to me." And she lunged at me.

I swear she was trying to bite my face off, and if she hadn't been about half my size she would have done it, too. As it was, she fought harder than most of the men I'd ever had to hit back when I was a bouncer. It took all my strength to get her under control and throw her out the back door into the alley. Then I locked that one, too, and put the key in my pants pocket. If she came back, I'd deal with her later. I really needed to get back to work.

I sprinted upstairs. There were a couple of rooms above the pizzeria. I kept one of them for myself. Some days I was too tired to go home. Other nights, I had company—Tiffany when I was in the mood, other girls when I could get them.

I tossed the pants and underwear onto the bed, tried to stanch the bleeding with toilet paper, found another pair of pants, and jumped into them. Then I ran back down the stairs, panting hard. Breaker was always on my case to get back into shape… and fuck it if he wasn't right.

"What the hell's going on?" I shouted as I entered the kitchen. There was no sign of cooking happening, no dishes going out to our customers.

"We're not sure, boss. Tony says we gotta hang tight for a minute. Something happening out there."

"Hang tight, my ass." I stormed past the cooks and headed for the dining room.

Tony came back in at the same time, a bloodied Breaker in tow. We crashed and I went down. By now, I was too angry to even yell at anyone.

"What's going on? What happened to you?"

"I don't know, boss," Breaker said. "Old man Pallavecino just walked up, calm as could be, and started telling me that we were overcharging him. Then he attacked me."

I looked at his face. Two long cuts marred his left cheek. The eye above it was turning purple. "Pallavecino did that? He's what? Eighty-five?"

"You should have seen it," Tony broke in. "The geezer went after Breaker's face like it was made of lemon meringue. It took both of us to drag him off. Then he turned to his wife and said that she was cheating on him and jumped on her. We got back in here to see what you want us to do."

"Get him off her!"

"No need. The sons were taking care of that. They're big guys. But it felt strange out there."

"Strange like what?"

"Just strange. Like half the people were watching us. They all had that face the cops always have. You know, like they know you did it, but they can't prove it yet."

Hoping to calm things down, I went into the dining room and caught Ralph coming the other way. He looked at me calmly. "You're fucking Tiffany, aren't you?"

It wasn't really a secret, but the room was full of my customers. Half of the people here knew my wife. "I don't know what you're talking about," I replied, brushing past.

Or tried to brush past. His hand on my shoulder stopped me. The little prick seemed insistent on signing his own death warrant. "We've been going out. But she never wants to commit. It's because you're fucking her, isn't it?"

To avoid making a scene, I let him pull me back through the doors I'd just come out of. I was watching him like a hawk—I'd already gotten bitten by his crazy girlfriend, and I wasn't looking to repeat the experience. Once the doors had closed, he accused me again.

I turned to Tony. "Take this piece of shit upstairs and introduce him to the pleasures of our bathtub. We'll take out the trash once the people leave." I tried to shake off Ralph's hand, but he was tenacious. He had the expression of someone trying to do long division in his head.

"That's why you always have meetings with her. That's when you do her, isn't it?"

Breaker looked stunned. "Boss, that's exactly the way the old geezer was talking to me. Look out."

There was something about the whole thing that nagged at me, tugging at my memory like I should have known what was going on. But I was too busy wrestling with Ralph's hand to think about it clearly, and Tony beat me to it.

"Holy crap," he said. "The Miami Cannibal!"

"What?"

"You know... the dude who ate that homeless guy's face in Miami and nearly killed him. They had to shoot him five times before he went down. Dude was paranoid, accusing the other guy of stealing his stuff." He looked to see if we were following. My face must have told him that he was right because he went on. "The cops say he was drugged out of his mind, but no one knows what drug it was."

Drug... oh, for the holy love of fuck fuck fuck!

I tore myself free from Ralph and grabbed Tony's arm. "What happened to the bag?" I yelled.

"What bag?"

"The bag of powder from the lab? Carlo the Nose brought it in. I hid it with the groceries so the cops would think it was flour or something. Where'd it go?"

Realization hit him. He slapped his head with his palm. "So that's what ruined my pizza."

"Fuck your pizza!" I shouted. "That was... hell, I don't even know what those Russian bastards had cooked up. And you put it in an oven and fed it to our customers?"

I never got to hear his response because Ralph chose that moment to go for my face. If Breaker hadn't been watching the asshole, he would have gotten me, too. But Breaker was loyal, and the gun in his hand made a noise that filled the kitchen.

Ralph took two steps back. Breaker's bullet had gotten him on the right side, just below the collarbone. That should have stopped pretty much everyone, especially a pigeon-chested weakling like Ralph. But he kept coming.

Bang.

This one hit him right through the heart, at close range. He tried to take another step and sat down, hard. Then he keeled over.

"Well, I guess we know they can't take one to the ticker," Breaker said, grinning in relief.

"What do we do now? They're killing each other out there," Tony said. He was watching through a tiny crack in the door.

Fuck 'em. We had a body to dispose of. "Nothing. We wait for the effect to wear off, just like we'd do with any other junkie. See if we can bar that door."

But the gunshot must have set them all in motion, the double swinging doors suddenly burst inward and a tide of people, ten at least, broke through. A lady I'd never seen in here before ran toward Breaker screaming that he'd shot at her, that he was still shooting at her.

He raised the gun to defend himself.

Big mistake. Half the people threw themselves onto him and buried him under their weight. He got a couple of shots off, but it didn't seem to make any difference. Soon, blood was flying everywhere. Not all of it was his, but I was pretty sure that enough of it was. Breaker was a goner.

The kitchen staff were also fighting for their lives. The three cooks and the girl we'd gotten to wash the dishes grappled with our customers. I heard accusations of spitting in food, of undercooking the dough. I even heard one guy calmly accuse the staff of using non-dairy creamer in the coffee. The customers were winning. It wasn't even close. The blood was already starting to flow.

"The back door!" Tony yelled.

My first thought was of Tiffany waiting back there. But we could take her. Tony was twice my size and strong as a bull. Then I remembered that the key was in the pocket of my other pants. Upstairs.

"No good," I said. "The key's gone. We can use the window in the bathroom. The ones on the first floor are all barred, but we can climb down from the second floor like the Nose did."

He grunted his assent, and we made a break for the stairs. Our customers noticed and came after us.

No zombie shuffle from this crowd. They were just paranoid and had a taste for human faces; they hadn't died and been reborn. These fuckers could *move.*

I was ready to spit out my lungs by the time we made the landing, but at least the door had a lock. I turned it and we moved to the window.

I pulled at the thing just as the pounding started. I couldn't budge it.

"Tony, you're stronger than I am. Get this thing for me, will you?"

He cocked his head at it.

"Come on. Every one of those cocksuckers must be out there by now. That door won't hold them forever."

A look of peace crossed his face. "Boss," he said. "You always paid Breaker better than you paid me, didn't you."

"What? Of course not." What kind of time was this to discuss a fucking raise?

His hand took my shoulder gently. He was perfectly calm. "No. I'm sure you did. That was why he could always afford those good suits and the high-class broads. I'm sure it's true."

"Did you eat the pizza?" I tried to back away.

"That's not what we're talking about now, boss. I know you paid him better, didn't you?"

And Tony lunged.

Watching the Stars

Ander awoke to the knowledge that something was very wrong.

His first clue was that he had been reanimated in software form as opposed to having been printed onto a good, healthy body.

Instead, he was surfing the ship's database to try and figure out why the ship's systems thought they needed an engineer. Short of catastrophic failure, they should have been able to deal with anything.

"What's happening?"

The ship's main processor responded quickly. "I've received an error message from the colonist storage mainframe that goes beyond my operating parameters."

"Let's have a look."

Ander pulled up some visualization ware to see what the data was trying to tell him. "This can't be right. It's saying there's no data pertaining to the colonists. It's as if all that information is gone."

"That's the way I interpreted it as well."

"But that's impossible. Those mainframes are backed up three times, and each of them is in a different part of the ship. No micrometeorite could have taken out all three. Have you checked the wiring?"

"Yes. I encountered more errors. That was when I woke you."

"All right." He studied the data on the wiring checks and concluded that something must have physically damaged both the hardwired and wireless communication systems. That would have taken some terrible luck, but it was still more likely than losing all three mainframes. "Can I get mainframe visuals?"

"No. The video circuits are down to those areas."

Probably the same wiring issue. "Do we have any video that *is* working?"

The computer presented a short list. Most of the internal cameras were concentrated in the control room and living quarters at the front of the ship—both unused during the automated portion of the flight. A couple of the external cameras were promising: one was aligned to show the entire length of the three-kilometer-long vessel. He requested access to that one.

He reflected that it was a good thing that his body was gone because his blood would have frozen at what he saw. The ship was gone. Or at least everything except the tiny area at the front, originally meant to hold only the main computer and the team that was to insert the gigantic colony ship into a stable orbit around Gliese II. The mainframes holding the minds of the colonists, the engines, even the vast fuel containers that made up most of the craft: all gone.

The ship ended abruptly in a dry-frozen molten mess just beyond the crew area.

The stars in the image spun crazily. Whatever had caused the damage had also knocked it into a dizzying spin.

"Can you wake anyone else?"

"No. I can only wake the crew when we arrive."

"We're not going to arrive."

"That doesn't change my instructions."

"Override."

"You don't have access to that level of override."

"Are there any other engineers in your data bank?"

"No. You are the designated troubleshooter."

"Is there anyone else in this mainframe?"

"No. Just you and the crew."

"Crap."

Ander thought about the problem. Then he thought about it some more. He wasn't thinking about the problem of how to land the ship. That was never going to happen. Instead, he thought about the problem of how to avoid going insane.

He asked the computer if he could be duplicated. At least that way, he could talk to himself.

"No."

After some decades of this, and having pretty much memorized the entertainment library, he asked the computer to shut him down.

"I can't do that. I have to keep the engineer active until the problem is fixed."

He raved at it. He threatened it. He tried to appeal to its better nature. But no approach softened the reality of its programming.

Perhaps he could reprogram it himself. He researched programming methods, languages, security protocols. Once again, he was stymied. The system only allowed the most basic access.

Centuries passed. Ander came to see the computer as his enemy. Everything he did was an attempt to thwart its machinations. But he understood that it was a one-sided affair. The computer was unaware of the rivalry, just giving preprogrammed responses to each attempt. Not malicious, but implacable.

Eventually, Ander understood that he had gone beyond insanity. Only the inherent stability of the program built from his thoughts and memories and the data that were his mind had kept him functional at all.

But sane people don't spend a century—timed to the second—staring at the revolving stars. They don't create detailed maps of a colony destined never to be founded.

Most especially, they probably don't spend all their time composing stories of explorers who come upon derelict spaceships occupied by ghosts who kill them in gruesome and imaginative ways.

He did all of this.

Finally, he realized that a ghost ship needed a dead body aboard. After millennia of silence, he addressed the computer.

"Can I print myself a body?"

"Yes. Each colonist is allowed one."

"Can I download myself onto the body?"

"Only a copy. Your primary mission still isn't done. You need to troubleshoot the problem."

He had the ship print a brand-new body. It was beautiful: tall, with razor-sharp features and musculature that would have inspired a classical sculptor. He instructed the computer to download a copy of his mind into that Adonis.

He enjoyed watching the man go mad—first refusing to eat, then bingeing. Running around, yelling wildly that he'd destroy the main computer banks, then hiding in his room for weeks on end. Eventually, he overdosed on something he found in the first aid kit.

It was ideal. In the absence of bacteria, the body didn't decompose, it mummified.

Ander couldn't have planned it any better. Anyone finding them would encounter that gruesome sight sitting there, as if plotting a new course to hell.

He chuckled to himself and waited to be discovered as the stars went round and round.

The Cost of Victory

Bernarda Eztli wiped her forehead with the back of her hand. It came away wet with blood and made her suspect she was covered in gore, but now was not the time to worry about her appearance. The body of the treasurer disappeared in a blaze of fire as the ancient magic holding the vampire together gave out.

Clutching her prize tight against her chest, she hurled herself through the door, sprinted through the metal-lined corridor, bolted up the steps two at a time, hurdled the body of two dead guards—human this time—and burst through the door into the foyer.

Then she skidded to a stop on the marble. "Dammit."

Lord Miquiztli stood before her, hand outstretched. A dozen guards flanked him.

Bernarda turned to see that two more of the armored, plume-helmeted Deathspears cut off her escape.

"I believe that belongs to me, young lady," Miquitzli said with a voice like the desert wind over cactus spines.

"It belongs to my family."

The slightest hint of a smile, as bitter as the emaciated vampire was old, hinted at the edge of his lips. "And your family belongs to me." The smile widened. "And now, so do you. Take her."

She didn't even try to resist. No one resisted the Deathspears.

***

As far as Bernarda could tell, the training complex was in Polanco, the noblest of the regions in Mexico City. Her family—the few of them that survived, hidden from their vampire enemies—insisted that the modern city was an abomination, an atrocity built on the bones of the regal city the Thirteen Families had ruled for millennia. But Bernarda, barely twenty-five—less than an infant in vampire terms—had grown up a creature of neon-spangled night and open rooftop bars. She'd heard the stories of the old town and wanted absolutely no part of it.

To her vampire senses, the underground complex smelled of sweat and blood. Not the appetite-inducing charnel house smell of human blood, but that of vampire blood lost in training. Old blood that would only attract those of her kind too ancient to be able to nourish themselves on human food.

Other odors, less intense but permanent, wafted into her tiny cell. Moist earth. The distant scent of a storm drain. All the little cues that reminded her that she was underground, training for...

...for what, she wasn't sure.

She heard a new rumor every day, every time someone disappeared and every time someone new spoke to her, but nobody knew any more than she did.

"Up!" a voice boomed.

Gerardo was one of the Deathspears, a grizzled veteran of a million skirmishes and even of the war against the Conquistadors—a war that was lost on the battlefield, but then won through immortality. The armies of the Thirteen Families might have been vanquished, but time allowed the vampires to reposition themselves in the new order.

After all, a musket ball through the heart might make an ignorant Spanish soldier think you were dead, but after he left, any vampire so wounded could simply get up and go about his business.

At least that was what the old ones always said.

"What's on the schedule today?" she asked.

Gerardo cocked his head at her. "Do you know you're the only person in this whole complex who hasn't given me a moment of grief since they arrived? What's wrong with you?"

"I'm not stupid. I know you can kick my ass. I've never been in a fight," Bernarda replied.

"You are in here because you orchestrated a daring raid on House Miquitzli's largest treasure store. You killed two guards and a curator."

"That wasn't a fair fight. It was a surprise attack."

The Deathspear captain let his look linger on her. "And now you're trying to make me think that you want to lull me into complacency. Which means that's not it either. I know you're up to something. And I'll find out what."

Bernarda took a sudden decision. "What if I told you that I'm being a model citizen because that way I'll have the best chance to survive. Because I can tell all this training is going somewhere, and I want to do as well as I can in whatever you're building us up for. Because I know what happens to vampires who fail in our compulsory tournaments. I've seen the ceremonial bones."

"Those bones are only from the ones who earned the honor." His voice hardened. "And no one from your clan should have been in the Palace of the Depths to see them."

"So I snuck in on a feast day. Are you going to rat me out?"

Gerardo stiffened. "I'm a Deathspear, not a spy. Get moving."

There was almost no light in the corridor, but that wasn't a problem. She could see in almost pitch dark, in places where cats would be utterly helpless.

The arena, on the other hand, was lit by four torches, one in each corner of the pitch. The yellow, flickering light made the place look forbidding.

Though it had evidently been rebuilt in the high-tech underground complex, the field itself was original. Magic emanated from the ancient stones. Even vampires with much less affinity for ancient sorcery would have been hard-pressed to miss the pulsing power of the place.

It was also difficult to miss the brown stains on the rectangular altar at one side of the stone playing field. Blood—and not all of it human—stained that eroded block. The field wasn't flat. The middle, perhaps five paces wide, was a long straight section of flagstones. Outside of that, the flanks of the field were set at an angle—perhaps another two paces. These ended at stone walls. In the center of each lateral wall, a vertical ring of stone was set in the rock through which the teams had to thread the ball.

The trainer wasn't a vampire. He was a gnarled and bent old human with a mustache who glared at her and growled. "Let's see if you can finally understand how to score." He held a ball slightly smaller than a soccer ball. She could smell the human-skin leather from where she stood.

The man threw the ball in her direction, waist high. Instinctively, Bernarda jerked her hips and connected with the ball, sending it on a high arc toward one side. To her complete surprise, it flew straight through the stone ring without touching the sides.

"I did it!" Bernarda said.

"It's about time," the trainer responded. "I've seen humans do it faster."

Bernarda had grown used to the trainer's insults, but the man must have been held in high esteem indeed to have been shown the location of this complex and entrusted with balls made of human leather. If his discretion and worth weren't considered absolute, he would have been killed long before.

The risk he represented was not trivial. Before the arrival in the glorious Aztec Empire of men bearing crosses and holy water, the power of the vampires over the people of Mexico had been absolute. They'd had their every whim attended to and bred an entire race of slaves to do their bidding. No human dared stand in the way of one of the masters.

But the Spaniards, far from being cowed, had simply fortified their position and called for reinforcements in the form of a band of black-robed priests. Apparently, these were experts in vampire lore because wherever they went, nightwalkers fell in vast numbers.

Mexico had converted, becoming a country of believers shepherded by the men in black and their legions of successors.

The Thirteen Families had had no choice but to retreat into the shadows and fight amongst themselves for the vast wealth they'd accumulated as lords of America's largest and most advanced empire.

But the hold of the Catholic Church was slipping. Scandals, materialism, and just the ever-changing tides of history were weakening the hold that traditional religions once had, even in bastions like Mexico.

Which meant that many activities that had been confined to the shadows were coming forward again. The survivors of the inter-clan wars were now in the news—owners of industrial conglomerates, shadowy lords of drug cartels, and leaders of powerful political parties.

Even with the sudden openness that prevailed, allowing a mere human to know the secret that the leather for the balls for the great game must be made from the flesh of a young human male, skinned alive, was not something she would ever have thought possible.

And yet, here was this man, his scowl somehow even deeper than before. The trainer watched the ball bounce into the distance, then sighed. He turned back to her. "It appears that determination can be stronger than talent. Or perhaps I'm simply the greatest teacher of the game of pok-ta-pok to ever walk upon the Earth." He nodded sagely. "Yes. That must be the reason."

"I did it," she said. "What now?"

"Get the ball. If you can do it again, we'll talk."

Fifteen minutes later, the ball went through the ring a second time.

She laughed delightedly. The trainer frowned.

"Do you think this is a game, young lady?"

She glared at him. "You know what I am?"

"Yes."

"And you dare speak to me that way?"

"I dare. And I dare more than that. Because I know what you really are. You are a mere pup, hardly worthy of the name you carry, even if that name is now forsaken. You're not even my own age, and yet you attempt to cow me with the glory of vampires a thousand years old?" He sneered. "I dare because without me, you will die. Not of violence because of my absence, but because without me, you will die without achieving glory. You will come to the true arena of which this is a mere shadow, and you will fail."

No one needed to tell her that failure and death were synonymous. She replied more respectfully. "So. I did it again. What now?"

"Now? You become part of a team. I've had someone chosen for you for some days… but I was half expecting you to fail to grasp the movements needed before the time came to assign partners."

Bernarda didn't ask what that would have meant. She didn't need to.

The trainer clapped, a noise that echoed in the enormous hall. A door on the other side of the chamber opened.

"Bernarda?" the voice was thin, tremulous, young. She knew it well.

"Cuitlahuac," she said. "I told you they'd get you eventually."

The man—still looking like a boy at twenty—actually smirked. "They got you first, though."

She approached the other vampire—a young bastard probably born of a human mother, a woman who'd died in agony as the beast within crawled out, fully intelligent and aware, and who would never have been content to feed on mother's milk—and hugged him with more emotion than she expected. A familiar face, even that of someone she'd always seen as a slightly ridiculous inferior, was an unexpected pleasure.

"Enough," the trainer said. "You will be facing the best players of this game to emerge in five hundred years. Perhaps the teams are nothing compared to the glorious players of old, but some will have innate talent that both of you lack. Every team will be playing to survive and to achieve the highest honor. If you want to live long enough to play for that… you will need to get to work."

The training to that point had been nothing, merely basic preparation, honing her superhuman strength and reflexes to perform the unnatural movements of the game. Now she understood why. Any imbecile—even a human—could strike a ball with their foot, or throw it with their hand, but to put a ball through a little stone ring, one of which was set high above the pitch itself, by hitting it only with your hip while another team was doing their best to give you bad angles… that took a vampire.

It was strange to think that people who saw the fields and the rings displayed in museums had not realized the sport was incompatible with human limitations.

The training proved that beyond any doubt.

Vampires don't sweat. Vampires don't need to sleep.

But they can, after uninterrupted days of rigorous training, feel a weariness deep within the unholy bones of their bodies, a pain that mere mortals couldn't imagine.

It took her a few days to understand why the trainer had chosen Cuitlahuac as her partner. She expected a virtuoso, a man who could score through the ring from any position, with the ball coming in at any angle.

Instead, he had even more trouble attacking the ring than she did. She found herself being the one who brought greater skill to the table.

But not for long. If Bernarda's great strength was that, when she failed, she would try again a hundred times, Cuitlahuac would try a thousand. He was indomitable, refusing to quit, refusing to rest, refusing to even acknowledge that stopping was an option.

He forced Bernarda to match his intensity.

They improved. Then they improved more, and when they felt they could beat all comers, the trainer came back in, accompanied by several workmen with heavy equipment.

"You are doing very well," the trainer said as the men unbolted the rings. "And now, we will use the goals as vampires do."

The rings, which had been set close to the ground, were repositioned ten feet in the air.

The trainer looked at them with satisfaction. "Now you know why the fields had two goals. The lower levels were so that the humans could imitate their gods… but the games that matter have always been, and will always be, played in the upper goals."

Just like that, much of their progress evaporated and they had to start over, adjusting their play and their tactics to the new position. Again, Bernarda managed to learn faster, but soon, Cuitlahuac's sheer force of will had him working at her level.

Then Gerardo returned. "Go to your cells. You'll be called when it's time to play," the Deathspear informed them. "Expect to wait three days."

"We need more practice," Bernarda protested.

"You need to rest," the aged trainer said. "You won't improve enough in three days to make much difference. But the rest… It will work wonders."

Bernarda wanted to argue, but Gerardo's expression convinced her not to try. "All right."

***

Bernarda was in deep rest, that state in which vampires could heal after a battle or other rigors. Time passed unheeded, but when a scratching sounded at the door of her cell, she jumped into a defensive crouch.

"It's time," Gerardo said. "Put this on."

A bundle of clothes, red and green, landed on the stone floor beside her, and the Deathspear turned away. She stripped down to her underwear and then realized that the attire she'd been given consisted of a sort of loincloth of the kind she'd seen the Royal Guards wear on ceremonial occasions, deep under the city.

It took her a few moments to figure out how to tie it, and another couple of moments to build up the courage to abandon her panties and bra, but she wasn't going to fall at this hurdle. Not after all she'd been through.

"You can turn around now," she said.

Gerardo looked approvingly at her attire. "Now, you look like a real vampire." Then he pulled a small clay pot, about the size of his fist, from the depths of his robes and handed it to her. "Use it sparingly."

Gingerly, she removed the tightly clamped lid. The smell of earth and blood and spices and paint hit her like a memory of childhood. Her mother had shown her a pot like this one once: sacred unguent.

"This..." she began

"This is a sign of my favor. I've overseen dozens of dissidents in training, and an equal number of loyalists who volunteered for the honor. None of them deserved to be here as much as you do."

Bernarda dipped her finger into the thick salve and placed three stripes on her face, two below her eyes and one running up from the bridge of her nose to her hairline.

Gerardo nodded in approval. "I knew I made the right choice. A worthy design. Humble but unafraid."

He led her through tunnels that opened into a parking garage and then an elevator where Cuitlahuac joined them, dressed in a loincloth of the same color as hers. He did a double-take when he saw—and more importantly, smelled—the lines on her face.

The elevator finally opened onto a black tunnel that ended in a tiny chamber with windows tinted just enough to keep the fierce daylight at bay. They sat on black leather seats and the door to the tunnel closed behind them.

A roar shook the little room, sound and fury and vibration.

"Helicopter," Gerardo shouted needlessly.

They rode for about twenty-five minutes before the aircraft descended.

"Stay away from that door until I tell you to," Gerardo said. "It's noon out there."

A clanging noise from outside was followed by four raps in succession. Gerardo opened the door.

Another tunnel had been attached to the side of the helicopter.

"Where are we?" Cuitlahuac asked.

"If you can't figure that out for yourself, you might not have been the best choice for this," Gerardo said.

"Choice? I was arrested for protesting the Miquiztli Cartel."

"Well, then I'm right about how smart you are," Gerardo replied.

"It's Teotihuacan," Bernarda said. "We're going to the ceremonial fields under the Pyramid of the Moon."

Gerardo nodded. "An enormous honor."

Teotihuacan was one of the largest tourist attractions in Mexico, but tourists were never allowed onto the sacred fields. The curators of this section were all vampires. Old ones. Even an outcast from a forsaken clan like Bernarda knew that.

She felt the energy, the hum of voices, long before the stone corridor had finished its descent into the bowels of the earth. There were more vampires in there than she'd ever sensed in one place.

The field was exactly like the one they'd been practicing on, but instead of ending at the walls, there was an arena above, lit only by four torches hanging from chains in the center of the playing field. Air currents moved in the enormous space, causing the flames to sputter and flare. Visibility would be an issue.

Cuitlahuac and Bernarda waited. They'd been presented first, which meant they were the less important team. The crowd sat in silence as they waited to learn whether the training had been a cruel hoax and that they were to be sacrificed without ceremony.

Bernarda breathed a sigh of relief as two figures walked into the arena.

Then she tensed. She didn't know who the young man on the other team was, but she knew Silvana. Silvana was bad news. She was a little princess from the Yaoyotl clan. She hadn't been arrested. She was there because she wanted whatever honor was available. And she would have had the best teachers gold could buy.

Without warning, a ball fell from the sky. Bernarda smelled it before she saw it, before it entered the pale of the light. It smelled like freshly tanned human leather.

She didn't stop to think. She ran to where it would fall and put her hip out.

A single strike sent it through the ring.

A deep gong sounded, the reverberations losing themselves in the dark space.

They played for hours. Strike and counterstrike, but it soon became evident that though the enemy was slightly faster and stronger, they just didn't work well enough as a team to have a real chance. And when things got difficult, they didn't really bear down and grind to close the gap.

It wasn't close. When horns sounded up above, Bernarda and Cuitlahuac were up by five scores.

"Contestants, face your judgment," a voice boomed from the stands. It was a voice of power, a command that no vampire or human could disobey. It was the voice of the highest of the blood.

Helplessly, Bernarda fell to her knees and pressed her forehead against the flagstones of the arena.

Footsteps, heavy and ominous, pounded the stones, and she saw feet in the war sandals of the Deathspears. A piercing cry sounded, and the iron smell of vampire blood filled the air, followed by a muffled grunt and more smell.

"Rise," the voice said.

Bernarda and Cuitlahuac stood to see their opponents lying dead in pools of their own blood, expertly staked through the back in a way certain to pierce their hearts.

"You have earned a single string," the voice said. One of the Deathpears held out a bracelet of blue beads to her and to Cuitlahuac. "Retire to await your next bout."

The Deathspears marched them off into a chamber with a stone bench. They waited in silence, sharing none of the banter they'd enjoyed during training. What could they say to one another? They had to keep winning until they'd earned whatever the maximum prize was.

Hours passed before the sound of marching feet reached them again.

"It's time," a Deathspear told them.

They returned to the arena and again arrived before their opponents.

They're more scared than we are, Bernarda thought. Though the other team also wore the blue beads of a winner, they walked unsteadily, clearly frightened of what would happen if they lost. *Our advantage is that we thought we were dead meat as soon as they caught us.*

The match went pretty much the same way as the first, with Bernarda and Cuitlahuac pulling into the lead. The only real difference was that at one moment, the woman on the team—a girl Bernarda had never seen before—jumped close to try to dispute a ball. "Please," she said in a whisper that only they could hear. "You're prisoners. *Please.*"

Bernarda didn't reply, and the young woman cried and begged most shamefully when it was time to meet her end.

Four more rounds went the same way, and though it was obvious that some teams had greater skill than they did, the way Cuitlahuac and Bernarda played together brought them through match after match, often by the slimmest of margins, and they accumulated beads… but were never introduced first.

After five bouts, they arrived in the arena to find a bright bonfire in the center of the pitch and their opponents being marched in at the same time.

"This is the call to glory," the voice from above said. "To the winner shall fall eternal rewards. Play well."

The ball was falling even as he spoke. The hush grew even deeper.

From the very first ball, which fell on the other side of the bonfire, Bernarda knew they were in for a desperate fight. The team across from them, composed—as they all were—by a young man and a young woman played not only with skill and coordination, but with a desperation that none of the others seemed to be able to bring forth, not even after they learned what befell the losers.

It was a back-and-forth affair. The enemy played so well that the only way to keep them from scoring was to land the ball on their side of the court at difficult angles and with unfavorable spin. That was Cuitlahuac's specialty, so when a ball arrived that they would obviously not be able to shoot toward the ring, she let him take it. When a favorable one bounced their way, she took the shot.

Unfortunately, if she missed, it gave the opponents an easy strike.

Despite the skill on both sides, the game was limited to only three goals, two for the opponents and one for them, and Bernarda was convinced that the final trumpets were about to sound.

So when a low ball bounced their way, a ball she would normally never have attempted a shot with, she yelled, "I've got it!"

Cuitlahuac almost didn't give way. He almost went for the ball, and she had to shoulder him aside as she slid desperately along the stones and managed to get a hip onto the ball. She thought something had wrenched inside her, but the savage twist she gave was the only way to give meaningful force to the ball.

The ball was too low to attempt to get a decent arc, so she banked it off the slope, and against the wall—a panic-driven shot if ever there was one. But it bounced just high enough to roll—actually roll—over the vertical inner lip of the ring.

The trumpets sounded before the ball hit the ground, before the gong finished marking the score, and both teams looked up to see what would happen now.

Did I just kill all four of us? Bernarda asked herself.

A man in ceremonial robes walked onto the pitch and picked up the ball. He disappeared into the stands.

"Play!" the voice thundered, and Bernarda smelled the ball descending again.

It was about to land almost in the center of the pitch, just to the left of the bonfire. Bernarda attempted to reach it to bank it into a difficult corner, but her opponent reached the ball first and placed a wonderful shot into the back of the court, with spin that made the return shot impossible.

Cuitlahuac did his best, giving a quick twist and bouncing the ball against two corners to return it.

It was hugely skillful... but not good enough. The second bank and the spin dropped the ball into the center of the court. The woman on the other team actually smiled as she took the easy shot and put it through the ring.

The gong and the trumpets sounded at the same time.

Bernarda's heart fell.

"Kneel to receive your due," the voice said, and all four contestants, winners as well as losers, prostrated themselves.

Determined not to embarrass herself as she'd seen so many of her opponents do over the past interminable hours, and also certain that by trying to fight, she'd just lose any honor she'd gained from getting this far, Bernarda bit her lip, awaiting the sharp stab of the stake between her shoulder blades signifying that the eternal life she thought would be her birthright was being taken from her.

Strangely, Cuitlahuac's stoic silence beside her made her prouder than his performance on the field. Theirs was the only doomed team to face their fates completely silently, as vampires should.

"Winners, rise," the voice said.

Bernarda lifted her head just enough to see that the man and woman who'd doomed them stood to receive a ceremonial headdress. The Deathspears around them knelt in deep respect and Bernarda gasped; she'd never seen Deathspears kneel to anyone, not even to Lord Miquiztli.

Then, suddenly, the same royal guards got up from their crouch and grabbed the winners by the arm. Bernarda heard their protests, growing more alarmed as they were dragged to one side of the playing field.

"The highest honor a vampire can attain has been earned today. Now it shall be imparted to the victors."

"No, please! We won! It's not fair!" It was the man's voice this time. There was always one of the two who couldn't face their fate.

But the screams soon turned to gurgles, and the pitch suddenly became crowded. The spectators had decided to come for their portion of blood as the young vampires—too young to know what the games had meant—gave their lives to the vampire lords who'd organized the sports.

And still, the death from above didn't come. Bernarda barely dared breathe, hoping that they'd simply be forgotten.

"And what should we do about you two?" a voice said. "You can rise, by the way." Lord Miquiztli, red eyes glowing from the massive infusion of young vampire blood, stood before them, surrounded by his guards. "You played very well to make it this far. You displayed more teamwork than anyone else… if, perhaps, not as much talent. And then you managed to keep your honor in the face of certain death. It's depressing, really."

"Depressing?" Bernarda asked, managing to find her voice. She supposed it meant their reprieve was over, that Lord Miquiztli was lamenting the talent that would be lost.

"Most depressing. That damnable Gerardo is always right. He marked you for greatness." The overlord pointed at her forehead. "And he was right. I'm going to have to kill him soon. Either that or make him a general before he comes for my job." Miquiztli shrugged. "But then, everyone is after my job. Have been for three hundred years. How would you two like to go into training?"

"As what?"

"Deathspears." Lord Miquiztli said.

"Deathspears killed most of my family," Bernarda replied.

"I'm well aware of that. I sent them, after all. My question wasn't whether you had an annoying family history to regale me with. My question was whether you preferred to go into training as Deathspears or die here in forgotten ignominy."

"I'll train," Cuitlahuac said in a quiet voice.

"Very good." Lord Miquiztli's red eyes turned to her. They

seemed to pulse and glow.

"I'll train too," Bernarda replied. "But I'll be coming for you."

Lord Miquiztli laughed, an evil sound. "You have no idea how many people you will have to go through to get to the front of that particular line. But I will be delighted to watch you attempt to progress as long as you do your duty in the meantime."

The ancient vampire, too powerful to attack directly, turned and left. Every Deathspear, including the two newly appointed novices, watched him leave, greed and envy in their eyes.

Autobiography, Carved in Stone

"By the amount of wear, I'd say it's from the twelfth century," Benoit said, running his finger over the pitted surface of the statue.

"Impossible," Terry replied. "Look at the detail work; look at the skill. We don't have any evidence of a master sculptor working in this area back then… and precious few anywhere else. This looks like it was made at the height of the Golden Age."

"I wish Vittoria could be here. She would likely tell us who sculpted it and the exact year just by looking at the hands. Those fingernails are just perfect."

But Vittoria wasn't there, and she wouldn't be coming. The dig was located on the Greek peninsula of Mount Athos, a place where females of any kind were not permitted. It was an edict dating back nearly a thousand years, and the Greek government was not in the least bit interested in changing it. It extended to human women, of course, but also to cows and sheep and everything else that was practical to police. The monks who ran the place only allowed female birds and mosquitoes because it was impossible to do anything about them.

"Well, take as many pictures as you can get onto the card and send them to her. She can make us feel like idiots when she wakes up and sees them."

Vittoria was back in Texas, running the show from her office at the university despite being forced away from the actual dig by medieval misogyny. Her presence—and her absence—were felt in everything the expedition did.

With the help of one of the graduate students, Benoit pushed the life-sized carving into better light. The team had mounted it onto a wooden sled to make it easier to move… as long as that movement was headed generally downhill from where they'd found it.

The statue had been buried at the bottom of a ravine that cut its way up the side of a wooded hill. A monk happened to step on something after some hard rains and, when he looked down, he saw what appeared to be a stone finger.

The statue depicted a slightly hunchbacked man with a bushy beard, wide eyes, and one hand stretched out in a gesture of… what? Alarm? Salutation? The expression on the man's face, the look that might have answered the question, was concealed behind a shaggy beard.

But there could be no doubt about the skill of the artist. As the statue moved into sunlight, Benoit reached out and touched the beard, half expecting it to flatten under his touch like real facial hair. He was disappointed to find that it was unyielding rock… but so fine it was almost impossible to believe someone had carved it. The rough-woven cloth, likewise, was exactly the right texture. He thought he could almost see skin underneath.

"How has no one ever heard of this guy before?" the student, a rosy-cheeked kid called Andy, asked.

"The sculptor? I suppose it's because nothing this fine would have survived the elements. The detail work on any of his statues that stood outdoors for any length of time would have eroded until they looked like every other statue in every museum. Hell, there are probably dozens of his pieces scattered around the world's museums, and we have no clue what they looked like originally. This one must have been buried almost as soon as the guy put down his chisel."

He began to take picture after picture of the sculpture, wondering what the subject had been. A peasant? A monk from an order with a vow of poverty? Other than the humble clothes and the stooped posture, a testament to endless grinding work, there was little to go on.

Well, Benoit thought, *whoever you were, you're famous now.*

***

Marcos took a long pull on the cigarette.

"You want to get turned to stone?" Adrian said.

"She won't turn me to stone for smoking."

"She will if we're spotted."

"Those guys on the hill can't see anything. They'll be blinded by the spotlights."

The presence of the archaeologists from the American university on that particular hill had caused quite a stir among the crew of the *Gorgon.* As smugglers, their livelihood depended on having a good place to quietly drop off and pick up goods. Mount Athos had always been ideal: policed only by monks and ignored by the outside world, it was the definition of the perfect stretch of coast. And the mistress' deal with the monks to keep women away from it meant that no one was tempted to set up a seaside tavern. That inspired idea, more than anything else, was the reason for the peace and quiet that allowed them to fulfill their illicit tasks unmolested.

And now this.

They drifted in, motors off, lights extinguished. Men with stout poles stationed around the small craft—a converted fishing boat—kept it off the rocks and on a straight path to the tiny inlet they used as a harbor.

It was a well-practiced exercise that created little sound. Marcos leaped from the prow onto an ancient wooden platform placed there to keep people from breaking their ankles and secured a rope to a rusted ring that looked like it had been drilled into the rock in the days of Homer.

Perhaps it had.

"Only you and I will be going up today."

He hadn't seen her step from the ship, hadn't heard her walk up behind him. It made him shudder, as always. He'd been a boy on the docks of Patras back when they were still awash with fishermen and dock workers as opposed to empty wastelands populated only by the occasional tourist. He knew how she moved, could tell the sound of her footfalls from half a block away.

But she still always managed to sneak up on him.

He nodded. She shouldn't have been able to see the movement in the dark, but a hand on his arm told him that not only had she seen what she needed to, but that he was to lead the way.

A well-worn path led to the edge of the illuminated area. There, hidden in the trees, they watched five men ranging in age—from a barely bearded youth just entering his third decade to grizzled veterans Marcos's own age—go about their business.

Voices carried in the night; these men were unconcerned with stealth. They spoke English, a language which grated on his sensibilities. They were apparently in conference with someone at their home base.

"We dug up two more this afternoon," the eldest of the men said. "There are at least eight remaining farther up the hill, all executed to the same level. But..."

"But what?"

The woman's distorted voice came in over a computer, probably via Skype or something similar. The younger sailors were always using that stuff to talk to girls. This was also a woman's voice, one heavy with age and authority.

"The ones higher up are different."

"Different how?"

"I've just sent you the latest batch of pictures. Maybe it's better if you see for yourself."

A long silence ensued. The five men onsite—at least the ones the laptop's camera couldn't see—exchanged worried glances. Marcos almost laughed; they thought they had an academic problem to worry about.

But he didn't make a sound; that would have been both unprofessional and lethal.

"The clothing on those last pictures..."

The men around the computer nodded among themselves. "Exactly. The clothing gets more and more modern the farther we go up the hill."

"How modern? The last one you sent me looked like someone from the eighteenth century."

"There are a few more farther up. There's even one carved to look like a German SS officer. The very last one is wearing jeans."

"So this is all a false alarm, some sort of hoax?"

"Well... I thought so, too, but Terry is adamant that the wear on the statues at the bottom really is exactly right for a stone statue buried for hundreds of years."

"Then..."

"Your guess is as good as mine. We think this is something the monks do, a tradition passed from one supreme master to another over the course of the centuries. They must have tools and techniques that I've never seen before, though."

"That doesn't make any sense. The monks were the ones who called us in. They wanted us to dig and to try to see what we had. They thought we might have found a site from the Classical Age. They're not stupid: a good dig would bring money to their coffers... almost enough to cover their ridiculous decision to exclude half of humanity from their peninsula. But just in case, talk to them again." The voice on the laptop didn't sound happy. "Tomorrow. As soon as they wake up. I'll be waiting for your answer, because we may need to cancel the project. I have a feeling the governors are going to be after my ass in a big way when I tell them."

The sound of a call disconnecting echoed through the forest.

Marcos turned to his mistress, seeking instructions. The hood turned to face him, and he held his breath even though it was much too dark for her magic.

"I'll take it from here," she whispered and stepped past him.

Her cloak fell onto the floor, and he watched her stride, naked as always, into the center of the circle of men.

Other than her hair—a tangled mass of serpents that writhed furiously in a futile attempt to detach themselves from her head and strike out on their own evil agendas—Medusa's body looked like that of a perfectly formed twenty-year-old. Most men would have been unable to turn from that view.

Marcos shuddered and looked away.

***

Benoit cursed as Vittoria broke the connection. He knew better than to try to call her back, to try to smooth things over. She had an Italian temperament: quick to anger, but equally quick to calm down... if you gave her the chance. By tomorrow she would have constructive ideas aimed at salvaging what they could from the fiasco. He'd worked with her long enough to admire her ability for lateral thinking. Vittoria had an almost magical capacity to turn calamity into career advancement for herself and her team.

Terry turned to one of the grad students. "Give me a cigarette. I don't care if it kills me. I need one of these." He turned to Benoit. "So you'd better not say anything."

Benoit shrugged. He was French, a nationality that prided itself on letting people kill themselves however they wished without overthinking it. Besides, after listening to Terry's story of how hard it had been for him to quit, there was a certain perverse pleasure in seeing the American cave. "I need to pee," was his only response.

He walked up the ravine to their latrine, just a clump of trees far enough from their workspace and the main path that odors wouldn't disrupt their concentration.

Business done, he descended, but a rustle in the undergrowth stopped him. He froze; the monks had warned them that there had been some wolves in the forest the previous winter. Then he relaxed; wolves wouldn't come anywhere near humans, especially considering the abundance of sheep—all male, of course—in the surrounding fields.

Then he heard it again, closer this time. He turned toward the origin of the noise and peered into the darkness.

A rough hand closed over his forearm.

Benoit jumped and turned, ready to fend off any foe.

"I'm sorry, my friend. I didn't mean to startle you."

"Tassos?" The stooping figure of their guide, a middle-aged monk from the St. Timiou monastery on the southern tip of the peninsula, could be made out in the light from the spots that filtered through the trees. "What are you doing here?"

"I came to warn you that we saw a ship approaching. It would be best if your team stayed in the monastery tonight."

"Smugglers?"

"Probably. We don't ask questions... some of these men do not care that we're doing God's work."

Benoit nodded. They knew about the peninsula's history. It would be a good excuse to sleep on a real bed. Vittoria had been so furious when she found out she wasn't allowed to come that she'd told the team to ignore the monasteries and camp and made it very clear that anyone who disagreed was welcome to stay behind.

Even under her edict, running into criminals in a semi-deserted wilderness wasn't Benoit's idea of a good time.

"Are they coming this way?"

"No. The crew is still on the ship. Even if they started up right after I looked, it should take them ten minutes to get here. Your team has time to gather its things and get clear."

But when they reached the camp, his team was gone. The lights were on and the cluster of statues stood to one side, but nothing moved.

Benoit was just about to call out when he remembered that making noise would attract unwanted attention. So he tiptoed through the camp until he came to the carved figures. Then he shrugged and turned to Tassos. "They must have gone. But where…?"

His companion wasn't listening. The man's eyes grew wide, his face turned pale, and he took a single, trembling step back. A hand pointed feebly to the statue beside Benoit before Tassos turned and ran like the devil himself was after him.

"What the…"

Benoit looked where Tassos had been pointing. Just one of the statues. This one appeared to be one of the ones in modern dress.

Then the bottom dropped out of his world.

Terry looked back at him with stone eyes. The statue was the spitting image of his friend and colleague.

Benoit reeled. He checked the cluster of statues and found that four of them, sprinkled among the figures they'd already dug up, represented members of the expedition.

He ran his hand over one of the carvings. It was brilliant, perfect.

Not one line was wrong. The representation of men he'd spent the past week with was utterly flawless, and Benoit thought that he had to meet the sculptor. Anyone who could create such masterpieces in the short time they'd likely had to work was a genius of a kind the world had likely never seen since Leonardo.

Maybe he'd been working from blanks—human-shaped blocks of stone awaiting only the final details of faces and clothing—but even so, the work was amazing. And it was repeated four times.

Another possibility was that someone out there had some kind of scanning machine, and they fed the data into automated carving equipment. Maybe something with lasers. If that was so, he still wanted to meet the party responsible. Something like that would make creating reproductions of priceless artifacts a doddle.

Yeah. That was probably the best explanation; this was a marketing gimmick from some auto-carving company, a demonstration of just how good their products were. By dropping the results of their efforts right in the middle of their target audience, they could hope for immediate sales.

"Now where am I, then?" he wondered and chuckled. Tassos's reaction and the story about smugglers was clearly part of the script. The monks wouldn't turn down donations from an ad agency... he'd heard enough about how hard it was to get maintenance done on the colossal monasteries to know that.

Well, they'd be along to tell him the story in a minute or two, and likely to bring the statue representing Benoit himself, so he studied the image of Terry. Yes, it was flawless, right down to the cigarette he'd been smoking.

Benoit froze.

Terry had started smoking that particular cigarette no more than five minutes before. He'd quit years before and had bored everyone with the story of how hard it had been. There was no way anyone could have carved the statue in the time it had taken Benoit to answer the call of nature, no matter what machinery they had.

Then how...

He heard the rustle behind him again and thought it must be Tassos returning, but his greeting caught in his throat.

Something pale approached through the undergrowth. He couldn't see it clearly enough to tell what it was, but it was definitely too big to be a fox.

Benoit ran.

It wasn't a conscious decision. One minute he was trying to identify the creature stalking him, the next he was running up the path as fast as his feet could carry him, branches cutting into his face. Terror made stopping, even to check whether his face was all right, unthinkable. The light dimmed as he left the floodlit area, but he didn't care. Every step took him further from the thing behind him.

Benoit barely felt the root that tripped him. He certainly never saw it. One moment he was running full speed, the next he slammed into the ground, rolled into the underbrush and down a few meters of hill.

He lay panting in a hollow that appeared to consist of half dry leaves and half sharp edges and took stock. He was scraped and bruised, but the sharp pain that denoted a broken bone was absent.

Relief was short-lived, however. Something moved in the shadows, making its way slowly along the path he'd just left.

It stopped, searching. He could hear it breathe, but it was much too dark to see what it might be. The impression of size still dominated. Even bigger than a wolf. A bear? Could he really be that unlucky?

"Hello, little man." The voice spoke Greek, but even this short phrase came through in the archaic tongue of the classroom, not the modern language spoken by people on the street.

The voice was a hissed whisper that cut through the forest and through him. He felt his blood freeze and thought that he wouldn't have been able to move even if he wanted to.

"I know you're out there. I know you can hear me. Do you know what I'm going to do to you?"

Turn me to stone. The thought came unbidden from somewhere deep in the primeval hindbrain, but he didn't doubt it. When you were lost in a forest, miles from civilization, sundered from all aid, you believed what your ancestors believed. This was how myths were created, woven out of fear and the things that only seemed real in the night.

And now he knew the origin of one of them.

"I'm coming, little man." It was somehow a woman's voice... well, a woman's hiss.

The rustling he'd been hearing earlier reappeared. To his relief, it moved away from him.

Think, he admonished himself desperately. *What can you do?*

The problem, he realized, was that he was refusing to accept what was happening. Sure, the primal, unevolved remnant of his mind knew the answer, but the civilized, rational being was resisting.

This was no place to listen to reason.

"Are you she?" he asked, in his best attempt at the ancient tongue.

The rustling stopped. "You know of me?"

Excitement, the intellectual challenge of holding up his side of the sparring session, surged and had its usual calming effect. The sense was that of being thrown a curveball in an academic discussion; it was something he was used to. Suddenly, the forest around him disappeared and he was in a paneled exam hall.

"Know of you? I teach students about you. We analyze all the versions of the myth... of your story, I mean. We discuss what you represent and how you've been used as a symbol of what is done to powerful women and a servant of a male-dominated world."

She made a sound he couldn't quite identify for a second. Then he realized what it was: the Gorgon was laughing.

"Spare me your petty political analysis. You academics are all the same, always trying to find the pattern in meaningless things. My life is what it is because of the same forces that mold every person's existence. Lust and pride, selfishness and power games. Sometimes love and mercy."

Inspiration hit. "But that's not what people hear. It isn't what they learn. I can rewrite your story with you as the protagonist, not Perseus."

A loud hiss filled the dark woods. "That lying bastard. If you ever mention his name in my presence again, I'll kill you the way I should have killed him."

Which, of course, left the door open to the possibility that she wouldn't kill him otherwise. If he talked fast enough.

"I understand how you feel, but he's the guy standing between you and a rehabilitated image."

The long pause that ensued could have meant anything. He hoped it was a sign that she was thinking about his proposal, and not sneaking up behind him. His heart thumped like a drum, filling the silence with its tattoo.

"You think you can change perception?"

"Not immediately. I'll write the book. You can help me with the scholarship and tell me the real story, which I'll then justify using historical sources. The tangled myths can be made to tell any story, really... I think they'd be best served telling the truth, don't you?"

"Perhaps not the whole truth."

And now he was on the homestretch. "Whatever version you prefer. I'll sign my name to it."

"And why should I trust a man who would put his mere survival ahead of keeping his honor intact?"

"Because if we do this right, clearing your name will make me a very famous and very wealthy man."

The hissing laugh returned. "Stay there. I need to get some clothes." The voice turned to ice, sibilant ice. "If you run, I'll hunt you down like a dog."

***

It was a warm night on the Aegean. Stars blinked brightly overhead, and Benoit looked out over the water, hearing ripples break against the bows and a few insects chirping in the grass on the desolate islet behind him.

He'd been on board for two weeks, a prisoner in all but name. There was always some member of the crew there to watch him, to ensure that he didn't try to run, although where he could run when the boat spent most of its time at sea or moored to tiny islands, he couldn't imagine.

He felt her presence behind him. As always, he'd heard nothing.

"You were always planning to let me live, weren't you?" he asked.

"Why do you say that?"

"Because, back on Mount Athos, you allowed me to hear you coming."

A soft hissing laugh.

"You might be smarter than you look."

"Not hard to do, in my case."

"But important if you want to stay alive."

"Oh, yes, I do." Then he turned to face her. It was safe: Medusa always wore a veil when she was aboard. "I'm the foremost expert on Greek mythology in the world."

"No, you aren't. You're just the only one I was able to lure here."

Benoit was stunned. How much of this had she planned?

"Well, I will be the foremost expert once the book is published. Everything would be much easier if the team I was with hadn't disappeared, though. That's going to raise so many questions.... Isn't there any way to bring them back?"

"Only the gods could do that, but I haven't seen any evidence of them walking the Earth for two thousand years. The world doesn't need them anymore. There was a talisman, once, the Golden Malak, but it's long lost."

"I've never heard of that."

"And you call yourself an expert. You know nothing."

He bristled, and she laughed again.

"Come," Medusa said. "Let me show you something. Perhaps you'll learn a skill that will serve you well."

"What?"

"Humility."

That didn't help his mood, but he followed. What choice did he have?

The Gorgon led him along a path that was little more than a game trail. He lit the way with the flashlight from his phone—even if he'd wanted to call for help, there was no service out here and no internet on the boat—but Medusa didn't seem to need the light.

They came to what looked like a small grove that turned out to be a ring of trees around a central clearing.

The clearing wasn't empty. Eight statues were arrayed inside. Now that he knew what they really were, Benoit stared with fascination.

"Who were they?" he asked.

"Glad you asked." Though he couldn't see her face, fortunately, Benoit could hear the smile in Medusa's voice. "This one here," she laid her hand on the shoulder of a bald, overweight man in a toga, worn down by the elements, "is Aeschines of Knossos. He was the first." Then she stepped lightly along the line until she came to a mustached man wearing what looked to be a British uniform from World War II. "And this is Sir Alex Whitham of Oxford. He was the last. Well, the last so far."

"Why are they here? What did they do?"

"Ah. That's the question, isn't it?" She looked at each of them. "They were learned men. Scholars. Each, in his day, was... how did you so eloquently put it? Ah, yes, *the foremost expert on Greek mythology in the world*." She patted Whitham's arm. "And each received an offer equivalent to the one you got: tell the world the right story and live. Otherwise... well, they certainly lasted longer than they would have otherwise, don't you think?"

"So that's why the myths are all mixed up..."

"Partly. You also need to remember that when I was young everyone lied about everything, so a lot of the confusion dates from the very beginning. But my point is that these men, every single one of them, thought they could do what you're tasked with. Each failed."

Benoit said nothing. He just stared at the stone figures.

"I thought it would benefit you to sleep here tonight. Perhaps you'll find their company inspirational."

With a hiss of amusement, Medusa walked back towards the boat.

A Holiday in Love Canal

They sprinted across a vacant lot, sirens barely audible in the distance. Tina stopped at the edge of the trees, allowing Shawn to catch up. They crossed 100th Street, trusting the advanced twilight to hide their movements.

"No cops," Shawn said. "Go!"

The fence was only about seven feet high. They scrambled over it without difficulty and ran across the open grass until they reached the nearest clump of trees.

The police cruiser that had picked up their trail on Colvin had lost them again. The siren receded.

"How much did we get?" Tina asked.

Shawn pulled the bills from his pocket and counted. "Fifty... no, sixty... three."

She held out her hand for her half, and he handed over thirty dollars. "Now what?" she said. "Bastards had a camera. Behind the register."

"I know. But I saw it too late."

"You're a shithead," she replied. "You should have checked before we showed the gun." She threw the old revolver, a useless, rusted-out paperweight they'd found in her grandfather's basement, into the darkness. "Every cop in the city will be out for our heads. For sixty-three fucking bucks."

"I know." Shawn tried to gather his thoughts, but everything was going too fast. He needed time to think things over. He wasn't fast like other kids.

He looked over at her face, barely visible in the fading light. She was pretty, with dark, curly hair, and she'd already turned eighteen. What she wanted with a lunk like him... he'd never understand it.

The robbery had been her idea, to buy drugs with. She'd thought of it as soon as she saw the gun.

He hadn't been sure. He didn't like the drugs she made him try. Most of them made him feel dumb. Dumber than usual. Even less in control. One time he'd itched all night.

But Tina talked fast, made him think it was easy. He was nearly convinced when she used her ultimate weapon. "Say yes and I'll let you do anything you want tonight."

He'd said yes.

"So now what do we do, genius?" she said.

"Let me think!" he shouted.

"Yeah, like that's gonna happen," she replied. Then, looking around, she snorted. "At least you were smart enough to think of running for the containment area. No one ever comes in here."

Shawn knew it. He walked past the empty space in the middle of the neighborhood every day. His parents were too poor to move away, so they still lived in the same house as always, the cheapest house in Niagara Falls, right across the fence from the Love Canal Containment Area. Whenever anyone at school asked him where he lived, they'd tell him that Love Canal didn't exist anymore, that it had been evacuated. But his house was in Love Canal. There were still a few houses there. The government said they were safe and far away from all the poison—but no one wanted to live there anymore.

Suddenly, Shawn remembered why he'd run in this direction.

"I think I know where to go," he said. "There's people here. They live here. They can protect us."

She blew a raspberry. "That's your idea? There's nothing here but grass and a couple of trees. If there was anyone around, the cops would see them from a mile away and send people in to arrest them. That's what they'll do to us if we stay, too."

"No. I mean it. I see them sometimes from my window at night. Hiding place. Underground. Over there."

"I can't see where you're pointing in the dark, Einstein," Tina said. "But no one is going to hide underground here. They'd be right next to all the chemicals and shit."

He felt the anger rising and clenched his fists. "I know what I saw."

"Whatever."

"I'll show you." He grabbed her hand. She tried to resist, but he ignored her feeble efforts and dragged her across the grassy plain that had once held houses and playgrounds and roads.

"You're hurting me," she said in the voice that meant she was pissed because he wasn't doing what she wanted.

"I'm going to show you."

"All right. I'll come. No need to tear my arm off."

He let her go. She knew it was no use running. His legs were much longer than hers.

They came to a small circle of concrete where grass grew between long cracks, barely visible in the moonlight.

"Well, where is it?" she sneered.

"Lend me your phone."

"What's wrong with yours?"

"I forgot to charge it."

"Of course."

"Besides, your flashlight is better," he finished lamely.

She handed the phone over with a snicker. "You know the cops'll see that light, right?"

"They won't. They aren't looking for us anymore."

"They'll be looking for us forever. Don't you understand? We robbed a store. We're fucking criminals."

He ignored her. He'd found something. Footprints. The whole grassy area was trampled. There was even an imprint of a large, bare foot near the concrete disk, where someone must have stepped when a grassless spot was wet. It was dry now, but the foot was right there.

Most of the footsteps seemed to be right at the edge of the cracked cement, around the stem of an old hose fountain.

He tried to turn the knob, but it was rusted solid.

"What the hell are you doing? Trying to get some poisoned water out of the ground so that our kids will have three eyes?" Tina said. "Well, I've got news for you. You're a loser, and we're never going to have kids."

Again, he ignored her. He would think about what she said later. One thing at a time. "I'm trying to find the entrance."

"To what?"

In frustration, he tugged on the rusted faucet. Hard.

To his surprise, it moved, pulling up a large square of sod. A trap door pivoted right at the base of the faucet.

"What the fuck?" Tina exclaimed.

"I told you," Shawn said. "I see them some nights. Just walking around right here."

"What the hell are they doing here?"

"Hiding. They're probably just like us."

He stepped into the hole under the door. The steps were made of metal grating, but they seemed solid, barely flexing under his weight.

Halfway down the first flight, he turned back. "Aren't you coming?"

"No way," she replied.

"The cops'll get you," Shawn said. "If they do, don't rat me out."

He kept going until he reached the bottom. Footsteps ran down the stairs after him. "You left me alone up there."

"You said you didn't want to come."

"I had to. You've got my phone. Besides, you left the door open. If the cops saw that, the game would have been up."

He smiled, happy she'd come. He didn't like the idea of Tina being stuck in jail.

The space around them looked wide enough to be a tunnel for cars, not people. Lights on the roof illuminated concrete walls stained with damp patches and pools of water on the floor.

"Wow. This place goes on forever," Shawn said. He couldn't see the end of the tunnel in the distance.

"We should leave," Tina replied, nervously. "I thought we'd find some hole in the ground full of junkies. This is something else. We need to get the hell out of here."

Shawn hesitated. "But what about the cops?"

"Look. Even if they nail us, we're first-timers. They'll go easy, especially on you; you're not even eighteen yet. I think getting caught down here would be much worse."

"You sure?"

"Hell, yeah."

"All right."

He turned back toward the stairs. A figure separated itself from the shadows and stepped toward him. It looked like a man, but bent and crooked, like an old tree. The guy moved sideways, covered in an old overcoat, and Shawn never got a chance to talk to him. The overcoat parted and he saw a baseball bat rise.

He wasn't quick enough to get out of the way and it fell onto his head. It hurt like hell, and he saw stars.

The second blow knocked him out.

***

The place reeked like a badger's den. Like something had died in there. Like a homeless guy who hadn't been near soap in a hundred years.

Shawn sat up and his head slammed into something.

It didn't quite put him out again, but the pain was so severe he threw up. Or maybe it wasn't the pain—he was pretty dizzy.

He remembered why. Someone had whacked him in the head with a bat. They must have dragged here and tossed him into this hole.

The light was too bright to keep his eyes open. So he opened just one, a little bit. The light came from a lantern. Not a flashlight, but one of those old kerosene jobs you saw in cowboy movies. It was yellowish.

But it wasn't that bright. He could barely see the space around him.

He saw that someone had shoved him under a sink. That's what he'd slammed into when he tried to get up.

Shawn turned onto his side and tried to crawl out, but there was something wrong with his hands. They'd tied his wrists together with enough duct tape to hold up a house. He wasn't going to bite his way through that any time soon.

Also, they'd taken most of his clothes. They'd only left him his boxer shorts. And those were torn, and wet from the vomit.

"Tina?" he said. He couldn't see her anywhere.

"Oh, God. You're alive. Thank God. Thank God."

It was her voice, but those didn't sound like her words. She was half-crying, and she never talked about God. She didn't believe in any of that stuff.

"Where are you?" he said, struggling to his knees.

"Over here. Behind the toilet," she sobbed. "Help me."

He turned around. Behind him was a toilet stall with the bowl full of pieces of concrete and old brick and dirt. He could see her hair, dark in the weak light, behind it.

Standing was a trial. He nearly fell over because he was too dizzy, and he couldn't use his hands for balance. Even though he desperately wanted to comfort her, he had to ignore Tina's crying while he got his bearings. Finally, he lurched over to where she was.

They'd taped her to one of the posts holding up the stall.

And they'd taken her clothes, too.

He knelt beside her. "Are you all right?"

"No. I'm not. They..." She cried. "It doesn't matter. Just get me out of here. Get me out of here."

"My hands are tied up."

"I don't care. Do something. Please. Please. Please."

Shawn thought. What could he do? Then he noticed the metal pole that held up the stall was thin and rusty. He slammed his shoulder into it. Spurred by Tina's sobs, he slammed into it again and again, ignoring the dizziness and the stars in his vision.

"That's enough," Tina said. She slid up the post, which had broken in half, and freed her hands. "Let's get out of here."

"You two aren't going anywhere." The voice was barely a whisper, hoarse and pained.

Shawn turned to see who'd spoken. Movement in the darkest part of the room gave him a hint. A moment later, someone shuffled out of the darkness and into the yellow light.

Tina gasped.

This guy wore jeans and a t-shirt that showed off every twisted limb and misplaced angle in his body. His knee joints looked like they were in the wrong place, too low. His waist was twisted, so his legs walked toward them while his torso seemed to be heading in a different direction. The man's head sprouted from his neck at a low angle, and his eyes—one much larger than the other—gave him an almost comedic effect.

There was nothing funny about the shotgun pointed at them, though. The twisted-rope hands were rock steady.

"Now you can walk. Walk."

"Which way?" Shawn said. Tina appeared to have withdrawn into a shell.

"The way you're going. I'll tell you if you need to turn."

The man herded them into the long tunnel, and then into a hallway that bisected it at right angles. The light here was really bad, and the smell was nearly as disgusting as it had been in the bathroom. Not a sewer smell—that would probably have been preferable—but the smell of unwashed bodies and human despair.

They arrived at a room that must have once been a storeroom: gray walls, racks of rusted shelving pushed off to one side, rotting cardboard boxes. It had been turned into a shelter, with blankets and pillows and discarded clothing covering most of the floor. People—men and women—ate and smoked or just lay still in the middle of that refuse. They were the source of the smell.

Everyone looked at least as deformed as the guy with the shotgun. A guy with T-rex arms mumbled to himself, clutching a metal cup close to his face. Whatever the cup held must have let off powerful fumes, because the guy would occasionally take a deep breath and then start off on another bout of mumbling.

Tina stopped. "What the fuck is this?" she screamed.

"Your new home," the guy with the gun said from behind them.

Another person approached. A woman in her sixties. Her tunic must once have been white, but it had been stained to almost the uniform brownish gray of everything else in the netherworld around them. Her eyes, in contrast, were completely milky-white. "Welcome to Love Canal," she said. Her voice was little better than that of the man with the gun. "We can always use strong bodies here. And they tell me one of you is a healthy woman." She nodded. "Good. It's been a while since the boys had one of those."

Tina turned to run, but a hand grabbed her before she went three paces. The hand was too big for the arm it was connected to, but more than strong enough to keep Tina immobilized.

She looked like such a tiny thing that Shawn took two steps toward her. But the butt of the rifle to the back of his head sent him to his knees. He knew he was in bad shape; he nearly passed out from the blow, and the feeling of wanting to throw up returned.

"As I said," the woman continued. "We need strong bodies to help us out down here."

"What are you freaks?" Tina said between the tears.

"Freaks. We're what happened in Love Canal."

Tina glared at them. "No, you aren't. Love Canal was evacuated when they discovered that the stuff from the chemical plant was poisonous. People died of cancer and stuff. It wasn't like everyone was deformed. I read about it in school. Every. Single. Grade. Until I graduated."

"You can't believe everything you learn in school."

"They showed us the newspapers."

"It's a cover-up. Trust us. We've been down here long enough to know."

"And how long is that?"

"Ever since the government paid our folks the cover-up money. I think most of them were glad to see the back of us."

Shawn worked his way back up to his feet. "Well, we're not staying."

He headed towards Tina again. This time, the butt of the shotgun put his lights out.

***

Waking the second time was even worse than the first. It felt like his head would explode. At least he was lying on something warm and soft. He opened his eyes to see Tina staring down at him. One eye was red-rimmed. The other was swollen nearly shut. She reeked of the people around them, but he couldn't bring himself to try to understand why.

"Water," he croaked.

She poured it into his mouth, using both hands, which were still duct-taped together.

"I thought you were going to die," she said. "We all did. That's the only reason they let me near you."

"I've been bumped on the head before."

"You were out for a long time, Shawn. I thought you were dead. I wish I was dead."

"Well, we're not. We're too strong to kill."

He worked his way to his knees, and then to his feet, little knowing his nightmare was only beginning.

***

They worked them like slaves.

Carry this.

Lift that.

Hold the other thing.

Bring me water.

The days rolled into one another, each one the same as the last, but there was a clearly defined night cycle where everyone but the guards assigned to them slept. They told them what had happened to the other slaves they'd had before. Though the lost people down here seemed to have a tenuous grip on time, the one thing everyone agreed on was that the life expectancy of a slave was measured in months at best. They either died of the contaminated water—the monsters there had their own water, from bottles, that the slaves couldn't drink—or from other dangers.

That wasn't the worst part of the night. The worst part was that they took Tina away. He could hear them, grunting and insulting her. And he could hear her whimpers. Fortunately, the handcuffs that had replaced the tape allowed him to cover his ears.

What he feared most, though, was when they had to go to what the locals called the drugstore. This was a place a couple of hundred yards down the tunnel where, once every ten days, a bag would be dropped off for the monsters who claimed to be what was left of Love Canal.

The guy with the shotgun—they'd learned his name was Ralph—herded them to within twenty yards of the spot and forced them to go the rest of the way alone.

"You try to run, and I'll shoot your little pecker off," Ralph would say to Shawn before turning to Tina. "I'll shoot you in the foot. I don't want the boys to be mad at me for ruining their toy."

She'd spit at him, and Ralph would laugh. Every single time.

There was a reason he had them do the last few yards alone; the wall where they left the bag was warm—not warm enough to burn, but Shawn had gotten blisters the one time he'd touched it. Every hair on his hand had fallen off.

The blisters had turned to sores that didn't heal.

Ralph had laughed. "You don't wanna do that, slave boy. That's radiation. You'll have two-headed kids."

"As long as they don't look like you, I'm fine with it," Shawn replied.

That had earned him a shotgun butt to the head, but it had been worth it.

Then they'd had to hide from a large black SUV that thundered down the tunnel.

"Who are those guys?" Shawn asked when they emerged from

the tiny cross-corridor they'd huddled inside. He normally would have left the talking to Tina, but Tina had grown silent, skittish, afraid to open her mouth. She didn't even like Shawn to go near her.

"Government," Ralph replied. For once, he sounded shaken as opposed to arrogant. "Bad juju. They won't stop for you. And if they do, no one will ever see you again. They're the ones running the real experiments here. The chemical thing was just a coverup." He shuddered. "Bad juju."

They trudged back in silence.

Shawn's vision was starting to turn blurry. He was getting weak and his hair—all of it—was beginning to fall out. So was Tina's. The sores on his hands hurt all the time, and he thought he felt hard lumps forming under his skin. He knew they'd die if they didn't get out of there. Soon.

Days went by. He barely had the strength to do what he had to, much less think of escape.

He knew he was dying, knew it was the end for him if he stayed. It didn't take a genius to figure that out.

Even so, he was too scared to run until the night Tina crawled back so badly hurt that she couldn't walk and actually went to sleep in his arms. He decided they were leaving. For her.

He waited for a night after they'd been to the drugstore and everyone was less alert. Then, pretending to roll over in his sleep, he pounced on the only guard who was awake and strangled him with the chain of his handcuffs, delighting in feeling the life flow out of him.

Then he woke Tina, with a hand on her mouth.

"We're leaving," he said.

She had tears in her eyes, but she nodded. She probably would have agreed if he'd proposed walking into hell itself.

He pulled her to her feet, appalled at how little she weighed. She'd always been a delicate thing... but now, she was little more than skin and bones. He held her up as they went.

They walked down the tunnel, past the drugstore, trying to stay as far from the warm wall as possible.

They must have missed the staircase. Or maybe they came the wrong way. The tunnel went on forever.

Finally, when Shawn felt he could support her no further, they came to a door.

The yellow double door was different. It didn't lead into a dirty storage room or emergency cabinet.

It led into a brightly lit corridor with a floor so clean Shawn would have eaten off it. Doors with glass windows in them opened off into equally antiseptic rooms, all empty and locked.

"In here," he said. "There have to be people in here. Someone has to clean it sometime. They'll find us and help us."

Their footsteps echoed.

A man with a clipboard exited from one of the rooms and did a double take when he saw them.

"Who are you?" he asked.

"Thank God," Shawn said. "Please help us. We're being held prisoner by the... monsters back there."

"The Love Canal crew?"

"Yes. Help us."

"You're too young to be from Love Canal. They're all in their fifties."

"They grabbed us. They make us work for them. And Tina... they..."

The man glanced at Tina. "I can imagine," he said. "But that's all over now. You came from the neighborhood?"

"Yeah. We were running from the police," Shawn said.

"Ah. Excellent. But you don't look too good. Come with me, I'm a doctor."

The man led them into the room across from the one he'd emerged from. Beds lined the walls, and he helped Tina into one and strapped her arms and legs down. "There, she won't fall, now." He pointed to another bed. "Could you lie on that one?"

Shawn did, not sure if it was a good idea. But the man had said he was a doctor, hadn't he? Only when his arms were strapped down did he say, "Wait, can't you leave my arms free?"

The man patted his arm. "Don't worry about that now. I need to call my boss."

He left the room and returned a few minutes later with a gray-haired man in an olive-green uniform.

"I found us two new subjects," he told the soldier. "They're pretty far gone. Looks like radiation sickness, but we should get some valid results for bioweapon toxins."

The soldier nodded. "Good work," he said, studying Shawn and Tina. "They don't look like anyone will miss them. Carry on." He left.

The man beamed down at them. "I'll get my syringes. And don't worry, this won't hurt too much." He smiled. "Or rather it will, but not for very long."

He left them there and Shawn pulled on the straps.

They were like iron.

For the first time in his life, Shawn screamed.

Only Tina heard him.

And she was too far gone to care.

Poppies in Full Bloom

Mud surrounded them on all sides. Trees were mere blasted trunks, none taller than his waist, all splintered by the shells that had fallen on every open spot. What had once been a thick stand of trees was now just a pockmarked ruin of abandoned trenches, deep craters and stumps.

Erich Ludendorff turned to his driver. "I will take a walk while you repair the car."

The driver nodded and turned back to the open hood of the Daimler. The man disappeared almost all the way to the waist, and only muffled swearing confirmed that his upper body was still there.

Ludendorff had seen his share of bodies without legs and of legs without bodies, so the driver's voice was a comfort.

"Come, Janzen, let us walk."

His aide was little more than a mere boy. How officers could be so young, so beardless and innocent, was something he couldn't understand. But they'd been getting younger, seemingly, with every passing day of the war. And the war had lasted forever and ever. The newspapers said it had been four years, but Ludendorff knew the truth; it had started at the dawn of time and would end with the end of the universe.

"I'd like to get closer to the lines," he said.

"Yes, sir," the young lieutenant replied. "Our artillery is right over the next ridge. We can be there in ten minutes, as long as the mud doesn't get any worse."

There was still danger, of course. The gunners on both sides knew it was all to end at eleven o'clock, but there was still fighting in many sectors. The British were still doggedly advancing to the south of them, although doing so with caution, smelling the armistice. The French were too tired for caution and too tired for advance—but some still struggled for sweet revenge.

Here in this tiny strip of occupied Belgium, the front was quiet. It's possible the Belgians weren't aware of the coming armistice, but then again, it's possible that they were still wary of the retreating German army. They had been brave in 1914, but they'd learned the price of valor. Valor had few arguments against high explosive shells.

"Were you at the front, Janzen?"

"Yes, Sir. I fought in Bulgaria and was stationed in Vienna when the Empire broke apart."

He seemed too young to have been in Bulgaria. That must have been centuries ago. "But you have never been in the trenches?"

"Thankfully no, sir."

"Ah. The trenches are what this war was about. Testing the bravery and resolve of three great nations against each other, day after day, night after night. Never has humanity shown greater courage than here! Here, one loved one's comrades and respected the enemy. There was no hate, no personal animosity, just duty and courage. Just duty and courage."

The aide remained silent. Ludendorff knew he was much too young to remember when war was about mobility, about encirclement and cavalry charges. The poor fellow had missed all that and couldn't appreciate how beautiful it was to watch war go from an art to a science.

A big gun broke the silence, and a shell whistled shrilly toward the Belgian position. It was the first they'd heard all morning. A distant thunder announced its landing, and Ludendorff hoped it would bring a response.

They arrived at the artillery position to find a single gunner struggling with a huge shell, cursing as he rolled it from a small pile, through the mud to the gun.

"How are you going to lift it into the gun?" Ludendorff asked him.

The surprised man turned, startled. He looked Ludendorff up and down, taking in the clean uniform, the polished buttons and medals. The man's own attire bore little resemblance to the uniform he'd been assigned. Tattered, stained, and patched, it was almost impossible to recognize as German. The man's rank was a mystery, too. "With great difficulty, Herr General."

"Let me help."

Ludendorff was not a young man, but he was still strong. Food rationing had not applied to the general staff, and he'd virtually been running Germany for the past few months, or at least until October. They managed to lift the shell, align it, and fire the gun.

The gunner covered his ears, but Ludendorff let the sound wash over him, and then the smell of it, which momentarily overpowered the stench of mud, waste and death. How glorious was this instrument of science, this colossus of steel that would rain death down on the enemy, no matter how far, and no matter how deeply dug in?

"Why are you here, alone?" he asked the man.

"I am covering the retreat of what's left of our unit. They hitched the other guns to horses before dawn. We hope the Belgians won't figure it out until they get to safety."

"That is heroic," Ludendorff replied, nearly overcome by emotion. This was what war was about. "I don't think the Belgians will come today, though."

"We shall see," the man said.

So, the man hadn't heard the rumors of Armistice. Ludendorff removed one of his medals. "What is your name?"

"Roland Ratzenberger, sir."

"Well, Ratzenberger, I award you the Iron Cross of Prussia."

The man looked at the medal. "I am not Prussian, sir."

"But you act like one and therefore are worthy of it. Wear it with pride." He looked the man in the eye. Unless Ludendorff was mistaken, the man was as young as the aide—but with much older eyes, proof that the war had lasted forever, at least on the Western Front. "What will you do when the Belgians come?"

The man shrugged.

"Just remember that a Prussian does not surrender." He turned and walked away, leaving the man holding the cross and staring at the mud in front of him.

He didn't believe that the man would do the right thing, fighting the enemy until death if they charged up the hill, but he could hope. War was everything, and it would disgrace the man to meekly surrender, leaving a heavy Krupp field piece in enemy hands without a struggle. Perhaps the medal would be enough.

"Come, Janzen, let us go this way. I'd like to see the trenches once again before we go. What time is it?"

"Ten fifteen, sir."

"All right, go back to the car. I'll meet you there shortly." The man saluted and walked the other way.

A mere three-quarters of an hour before the armistice. Even the personal danger he'd so recklessly courted by coming to this place was now essentially moot. No army on this battlefield could move across the mud quickly enough to pose a threat to him in that time. And he hadn't heard a single Belgian gun all morning.

He walked into a ruined trench and followed it until it reached a crater. Then he turned toward Germany, into a stretch of plain that had once been part of the no man's land between two opposed trenches. Here there was little, save mud, abandoned equipment, and shell holes. He strode forward, imagining the area to be active, the machine gun bullets to be buzzing around him. The battle cries of determined men.

He realized that he was facing the wrong way. When this place had been a battlefield, the Germans had defended the side he was approaching. He turned back, to face the Belgian frontier.

He froze.

Standing before him was a single man holding a rifle, bayonet mounted, across his chest. The man wore the khaki of the British Expeditionary Force, and his uniform and helmet were of the type worn in 1915, not seen on the Belgian front for two years.

Ludendorff took a step back as he contemplated the figure before him.

The man's uniform was riddled with holes. Dozens, hundreds of tears dotted it. They were tears that the old general had seen before—machine gun holes. The gray, sallow skin of the man's face was likewise punched through ten or twenty times. Many bodies in no man's land looked this way. Riddled once, twice, ten times by machine gunners who didn't know that the movement was caused by a different gunner hitting a man long dead.

Even the barrel of the rifle was splintered and perforated, and Ludendorff turned to run—even the animated dead would have difficulty moving with muscles shredded by lead.

Facing him was another man. Another dead man.

This one was dressed in the remains of a German army uniform, the gray visible in places beneath the crusted mud. He was not riddled with bullets, but missing one arm, and had a large piece of shell shrapnel caught in his neck. Half the face was exposed bone, the other half unmarked, one baby-blue eye looking at Ludendorff. The filmed gaze of a dead fish was insufficient to hide the fact that half of the face was much too young to be dead.

Instinct took over, and Ludendorff moved to his left, first checking that there were no more of the apparitions. Now that he was no longer directly between the slowly advancing wights, he calmly pulled his revolver out of its holster and fired twice, once into the head of each corpse. The German soldier's skull bone fragmented around the hole, while it was impossible to tell where the Brit was hit—just another round entry wound in a head full of them.

The corpses didn't bleed; they didn't drop. And they didn't stop.

Ludendorff didn't bother using the rest of his bullets on them. His aim had been true, and it was possible that he would need a bullet for himself. He turned to run.

But the mud made running impossible. It was mud that had swallowed thousands, mud that had meant that falling into it while wounded could be a death sentence. It was mud that, somehow, favored the slow gait of the dead over the frenzy of the living.

He was bogged down, and then he was caught. A hand landed on his shoulder, colder than the mud, colder than the November day. He felt it through the thickness of his uniform and overcoat.

The hand on his shoulder turned him around to face the British trooper who'd tracked him like a hound a hare. To stare into the face of death. A hand moved toward him.

Ludendorff steeled himself for the blow that never came, closing his eyes despite himself.

But when he opened them, there was just a single red flower in the corpse's grip. It was proffered to him, as if the dead man was fraternizing with its killers, celebrating the peace that was just minutes away. Beside it was another, held in the single hand of the poor, dead German boy.

Numbly, Ludendorff took them.

The corpse released him and turned. The two dead enemies walked away, through the mud, side by side. Within moments, they'd disappeared over the ridge.

***

"Where did you get the poppies?" Janzen asked when he returned to the car.

Ludendorff looked around. The Belgian countryside was one solid mass of gray. Gray mud, gray trees, gray hills in the November distance. Red flowers such as these would have been visible for miles.

"What time is it?" he asked, in lieu of an answer.

"It's eleven ten. The war has been over for ten minutes. We've survived." The man actually looked happy, and younger than Ludendorff had ever seen him. He continued to speak in a most unmilitary fashion. "It's Armistice, a day the world shall remember—the end of the war to end all wars! What will you do now that we have peace?"

Ludendorff looked at the two poppies in his hand. "I don't know if I believe in peace."

"Of course you do. It's just too sudden. You'll see."

"Perhaps," Ludendorff replied. He dropped the poppies to the ground, driving them into the mud with his boot. "And perhaps not. Tell the driver that I would like to go to Potsdam."

He walked toward the car—driven back but proud, unbowed, unbeaten.

Going for Peanuts

Mikey slammed through the kitchen doors. "One spaghetti and meatballs," he said. "Oh, and do you have a couple of peanuts?"

"Peanuts?" Lou looked up from his pans. It was just four in the afternoon on a Monday—there had been no lunch service, so the two cooks wouldn't be in for another couple of hours.

"Yeah. Some Midwestern farmer out there who doesn't have the sense to know you can't have dinner at four o'clock in the city went on and on about his peanut allergy and how he couldn't eat here if the food had any peanuts in it. I told him that neither spaghetti nor meatballs have got any peanuts in them, but he still repeated it like ten more times."

"So he's worried."

"Well, I'm gonna give him something to worry about. A night on the toilet should teach him not to bug people when they tell him there's no peanuts in his food. You got them or don't you?"

Lou pulled a can out of a cupboard to the right of the range and popped the lid. Mikey ground the nuts into a fine powder and, when the steaming dish landed on the counter, he carefully mixed the dust into the sauce. "There. Jackass won't know what hit him."

***

They stared at the body on the floor. The guy was well-fed and dressed in khakis and a yellow polo shirt. His face was dark red, his features frozen in an expression of panic.

"Whatcha bring him in here for?"

"I couldn't leave him out there, could I?" Mike retorted. "I didn't want anyone to see him. He was just sitting there, looking like that."

"You sure he's dead?" Lou asked.

"Don't you start on me, now. I've seen enough dead guys to know when one is in my restaurant. Yeah, he's dead."

"Crap. You did it this time."

"Me?"

"What do you think? The peanuts must have killed him."

Mikey blanched. "What do you mean?"

Lou wiped his hands on a dishcloth, abandoned the pasta he was flattening with the rolling pin, and pulled his phone out of a pocket. He typed a search and scowled. Then he handed the phone to his brother.

"Oh, damn. How was I supposed to know the allergy would do that to him? I thought he'd just get the runs."

"Well, with your record, the judge ain't gonna be too impressed with that defense."

"What am I going to do?"

Lou sighed. "We're going to do what we always do when you screw up. I'm gonna pull your nuts out of the fire. This body is going to disappear. Go get some trash bags—and look out into the dining room to see that no one is going unserved. Last thing we want is for people to come in here wondering why the waiter disappeared."

Mikey left, and Lou frowned down at the dead man for a couple of moments. Slowly, his frown disappeared and turned into something that wasn't quite a grin, but which held a measure of speculation.

"So," Mikey said, returning with the bags. "We gonna put him in the trunk and take him to the woods?"

Lou let the grin loose. "Nah. I thought of something better. Help me take his clothes off."

Mikey fell into the pattern they'd always followed, both in their life on the street as well as in those years they'd spent behind bars: he shut his mouth and didn't ask his older brother any stupid questions as they lifted the dead weight onto the countertop where meals were prepared.

They stripped the guy down all the way, removed a gold crucifix from around his neck, pulled out the wallet, phone, and a hotel card key, and tossed the clothes into a garbage bag. Mikey cracked the guy's phone open and removed the battery.

"Bring me the big cleaver," Lou said with a wicked smile. "And lock that door. How long before Raul and Sergio arrive?"

"It's still early."

"Good." The cleaver descended with a whistle right onto the guy's neck, lodging in bone halfway through. Lou pulled it out with a grunt and brought it down again and again until the head rolled free.

"Well, we can't use this, can we? Toss it in a bag. We'll bury it tonight."

Then they quickly allowed the blood to flow down the drain and tossed hands, feet and other protuberances in the bag. They removed the arms and legs—making sure to conserve the buttocks—from the torso and put that in another bag.

Lou paused and Mikey looked at him. "What about the arms and the legs?"

"Skin 'em."

"You gonna put them in the meatballs?"

"Nah. Too obvious. I've been thinking of revamping the menu, and this is perfect for it. Everyone loves carpaccio."

"What's carpaccio?"

"You'll see. Now help me skin this stuff."

***

"The trick," Lou said, decked out in a brand new chef's outfit he'd bought especially for the occasion, "is in the marinating sauce. You've got to leave the meat in the sauce just long enough to have it absorb some of the flavor, but not to overwhelm the taste of the meat."

"But this… it tastes so different." The critic took another bite. "I suppose you're not going to tell anyone the recipe."

Lou smiled. "Does it really look to you like I want to lose the customers?"

The critic returned the smile. This was going better than they'd expected. When the *Post* had called to say they'd heard about the new dish and would be sending someone over, Lou thought the man would be snooty and look down his nose at just another neighborhood Italian place. But the critic had turned out to be a guy who could have walked in off the street without raising any eyebrows. No starched white shirt and demands for wines that weren't on the list—just a guy who liked to eat. "And you seared the outside."

"Yes. That's just to seal the meat, though. It's not cooked."

"Oh, of course not. But it's my job to speculate on the secret of the raw meat everyone is talking about."

"I wish everyone was talking about it. I'd be a rich man."

"Well," the critic replied after the last bite disappeared into his mouth, "they will be when they read my article. This was truly excellent."

"Thank you."

Lou had served the pasta dish personally, allowed the man to have his coffee in peace, and watched him leave. Only then did he return to the kitchen.

Raul intercepted him when he entered the kitchen. "Hey boss, we're running low on the carpaccio meat," he said.

"How much do we have left?"

"Probably until the end of tomorrow night. Maybe a little more." Raul paused. "Unless the article comes out first."

It was Saturday night, so Lou just nodded. "Don't worry about that. The food section goes out on Wednesday."

"Well, get in touch with the supplier. We need to ride this train as far as we can. I don't remember ever having a week this good."

"Yeah. I'll do that."

***

"You okay, big guy?" Mikey asked on Monday, just after they finished setting up the tables, and just before they opened to the public.

"Yeah. Just worried about the supply situation."

"The special meat?"

"Yeah. We're all out. I checked the stuff that was left, and it's just the offcuts. We can't use it." They sat in silence thinking about the consequences of that. Most people who'd heard of the dish didn't actually want to eat raw meat, but the restaurant had filled up anyway and they bought other stuff. They were buying the same spaghetti as always, except now they were buying the stuff by the tub-full. If the article was as positive as the guy said it would be...

They sat in silence for a couple of minutes before Lou got up and sighed, the sound of a man about to do something he was pretty sure he'd regret.

"Mikey?" he said.

"Yeah?"

"You still in touch with Johnny Balls?"

"Yeah. Haven't seen him in years, but I'm in touch. Why?"

"We might need his help on this one."

"You want me to call him?" Mikey asked. "Maybe tell him that we can make his bodies disappear if he'll bring 'em over?"

Another sigh. "Not yet. I'm still thinking this through, but we ain't got much time."

The front door opened, and they lifted their heads to see a big blonde woman enter and sit at a table beside the window.

Mikey grunted and stood, grabbing his dishcloth and a menu on the way to the table. It was always a drag to get early customers, especially on Mondays when they had the restaurant to themselves.

Lou chuckled.

"What?" Mikey said.

"Ask her if she has any food allergies."

Mikey shrugged and walked out of the kitchen.

A couple of minutes later, he was back. "She'll have the vegetarian lasagna. And no, no food allergies."

"You actually asked her?"

"Wasn't I supposed to?"

"Not really. It doesn't matter. I know what she's allergic to."

"What?"

Lou brandished a small transparent plastic bottle that held a clear liquid. "This."

Mikey peered at the label. It looked like something you'd get in a pharmacy. "How do you know she's allergic to that?"

"Because everyone's allergic to cyanide. Now, you said vegetarian lasagna, right?"

Lou hummed as he worked, happy to have solved the supply problem for the time being.

Mikey shrugged and took the woman her water. Instead of pouring from the jug of iced tap water, he opened a Perrier and gave her that.

A last meal deserved decent water.

A Day's Ride from Tarabuco

"We ain't in Peru, Henry," Butch Cassidy told the Sundance Kid.

"We don't need to be in Peru. The Incas were all over the place. Here in Bolivia, and even farther south in Argentina," Sundance replied. "And if these injuns know what they're talking about, there's a burial chamber just up the trail."

Cassidy shrugged. "If they know about it, there won't be anything left to take. Old bones won't pay Gómez's monthly bribe."

"Tulu says the injuns won't go in there because they're too scared. They say the Incas left magic behind to keep anyone from trying anything." He grinned. "And you know what else the Incas left everywhere? Gold, that's what."

Cassidy leaned back on his chair and, lifting his hat out of his eyes, peered at his companion. "You shouldn't take those injuns seriously. Have you ever seen any gold in Bolivia?" He gestured at the dusty landscape around them and the mountains in the distance. They'd ridden through most of the country, and they'd found two kinds of places: poor and poorer. It had come to the point where they didn't even bother holding up travelers anymore. No one had any money.

"It can't hurt to look, can it?" Sundance replied. His mustache, which he liked to keep neatly trimmed, was lost in the beard he'd grown out over the past few weeks. "Besides, we've either got to get something for Gómez or we've gotta get out of here. He knows where to find the Pinkertons, and if he ever finds out how much the reward is, he'll sell us in a minute flat."

Gómez was the local law, a retired army lieutenant who'd been made a *Juez de Paz* and given a pension and a minuscule budget which, in the tiny outpost of Tarabuco, gave him the capacity to raise a posse big enough to respect.

"He'll take our money until we run out," Cassidy replied. "He doesn't trust gringos he can't control."

"Well, we're out of money, and he's a day's ride away. If we don't pay him, he'll come for us. Or he'll send the Pinkertons."

Cassidy spat. The detectives were implacable, capable, well-paid, and well-fed, and as long as the reward was as big as it was, they wouldn't give up.

The Kid stood. "Well, I'm off to have a look. If I'm not back in a couple of days, it's because I found El Dorado and bought myself a pardon."

Cassidy grunted and followed him across the dirt-floored yard beside the yellow adobe house they'd holed up in. It belonged to Gómez, too, which might have seemed ironic if it weren't always the same story: the local law in South America went both ways. If you kept them happy, they were the ones who would protect you. But only until a better offer came along. It was much better than up north, where lawmen would hunt you for the honor of it, or where the reputation of an agency depended on them finding you—like the blasted Pinkertons.

They saddled up their horses, loaded the pack mule with water, and started out into the hills. It wasn't worth the trouble to lock up the little house. They'd left nothing inside worth stealing, and the *peones*, the natives who kept the property for Gómez in exchange for a place to live, would come at you with sticks if you tried—not defending the gringos' stuff, but Gómez's property.

The land they rode through had once been a sheep farm, suited for the hardy arid-land sheep brought in from Patagonia, but the farm had long since gone under and the house was the only thing left.

A trail led to the east. Up.

The hills looked just like the lands below: yellowish-gray dirt dotted with short green scrubs. Not quite a desert, not quite farmland, but that lonely kind of land that could support a few hardy souls and a few rugged animals.

"Did the *peones* say which of the hills is supposed to be the haunted treasure place?" Cassidy said.

"Of course. Half a day that way. Over and between four little hills and across a dry creek. A mountain shaped like a bird."

Cassidy snorted. "Like a bird? They're always saying things look like one animal or another, and it's always impossible to see it."

"I guess we'll need to look for the dry creek then," Sundance replied.

They rode in silence for four hours. When two men had been partners for so long, there wasn't much they wanted to talk about.

Cassidy broke the silence. "Creek," he said, pointing to the right.

A slight depression filled with rounded stones and slightly grayer dirt wound between two hills.

"Reckon you're right," Sundance said. He spurred his horse up a rise and looked around. "And that's the bird mountain over there."

Cassidy didn't need to see for himself, and since he was leading the mule, he simply headed in the direction Sundance was pointing.

The wind picked up as they crested the last rise to find a single triangular peak in front of them, the last lonely mount before the hills beyond became even higher and rockier.

A gust nearly pulled Cassidy's hat from his head. He looked up. "I think we'll get some rain soon."

"Just our luck," Sundance replied.

It rained occasionally in the dry hills. Clouds full of water coming up from the Pacific would hit the hills and get pushed up or something. Since it was cold up high, they lost their water.

A fat raindrop landed on his shoulder, but Cassidy ignored it. They'd been wet before, and it was best not to hurry when climbing narrow paths in the mountains. That was a good way to lose a horse.

An overhang let them watch the worst of the shower without getting too soaked. Cassidy inhaled deeply, breathing in the smell of wet dirt.

After ten minutes, the rain hadn't stopped, and the wind, if anything, appeared to be picking up. It hissed between stones and made a sound like a train.

"The injuns say the cave's just on the path that leads up the mountain," Sundance said. "I think we should leave the horses here."

Cassidy studied the rocky climb. It looked like it had been worn into the stones by hundreds of feet, but it was covered in dust now, with weeds growing through the cracks.

He dismounted and hobbled his horse. These horses had come all the way from the Argentine, and he didn't want to have to replace them with local stock.

Then they began the climb.

The first few steps were easy enough. The path wound around the hill in a wide arc on a stone base. The important thing was to avoid slipping on the dust that covered everything, which the rain had turned into a slick of slippery mud.

The path, rising slowly, wound almost all the way around the mountain, which had the benefit of interrupting the rain. At the far eastern side of the rocky outcropping, ancient hands had cut stone steps into the hill.

"See," Sundance said. "I told you this was Inca."

"All I see so far," Cassidy replied, "is a long staircase I'm gonna have to climb." As they put one foot in front of the other, he reflected that this was an obvious choice for an Inca site. It was the first of the gray stone mountains that rose above the tree line and the dun-colored hills, but it stood far enough from the bigger mountains behind it to seem like a sentinel. The perfect place to bury your dead—honored but apart.

He shuddered. Cemeteries had always scared him, ever since he shot his first man. Since then, he'd come close to death so many times that he always felt that stepping into a cemetery was to tempt fate. A lot of men never left.

The steps ended at another path, flat and carved out of the rock, which circled the mountain in both directions, more like a platform than a path.

"It must have been hell to build this without explosives," Sundance said. "You ever wonder how the savages did it?"

"I reckon they didn't have much else to do," Cassidy replied.

Following the platform around the mountain took them back into the rain. Cassidy felt his boots slipping on the polished rock as the wind tried to drop him into the valley down below.

He looked out into the rain. You could see for miles from here. The sea was out there somewhere. All this water had come from the ocean.

"Will you look at that," Sundance said.

Cassidy walked up to where the Kid was standing. A cave entrance opened off the platform and dove into the mountain at a slight angle. It was almost impossible to tell how deep the shaft went; however, a lush forest had grown up at the mouth of the cavern.

"I wasn't expecting a jungle up here," Cassidy said.

"Must be all this damned water," Sundance replied, plucking a flower the size of his fist. "These sure don't look like the same plants that live on the plains. The Incas must have brought them in from wherever they came from."

Cassidy wondered about that. Generally, you needed insects for plants to grow this well, but he couldn't detect the telltale buzzing in the cavern.

He pushed past the plants until they thinned out, then turned back. "We're gonna need light in here."

"I've got some flint in my pack," Sundance said. "But I'm not going down to the horses for a lantern."

"No need," Cassidy replied. He dug under the plants and pulled out some thick branches. They lit a branch inside, out of the rain. It burned slowly. "That should work."

They each took a few extra branches and placed them in their belts. Thus armed, they pushed further into the cavern.

"No one has been in here in ages," Cassidy said, pushing aside a wall of cobwebs.

"Good," Sundance replied. "More for us."

The foliage around the cave mouth appeared to serve as a filter that kept the humidity from the inside of the cave. The air against Cassidy's cheeks felt completely dry. Then he stopped, staring at the flame. "You know what?"

"What?"

"The wind is blowing the wrong way."

"How would you know which way the wind should blow in a cave?" the Kid asked.

"It was blowing inward, from the sea, remember? And now it's blowing from inside."

"As long as it's blowing from a big pile of gold, I don't care."

Like the path, the cave floor was well worn, but unlike the path, this one wound its way downward.

Finally, the tunnel opened into a wider cavern, too big for their guttering, makeshift lanterns to illuminate. They saw only large shapes and the impression of a roof high overhead.

"No stalactites," Sundance said.

"I think this is a different kind of cave," Cassidy replied. "More like a crack in the stone than something made by water."

They advanced a few steps deeper into the cave. Something crunched under Cassidy's foot. He brought the torch down for a closer look and saw that he had crushed a skull.

"We're in the right place, at least," he said. "I've already found some of the dead people."

"Good. Now let's find all that gold."

Bones skittered as they kicked them out of the way. A large slab of stone with a flat top blocked their advance. When Cassidy shone his light on it, he saw that the white rock was discolored by dark stains. He shuddered and walked around the stone.

Beyond the altar the cavern continued, still strewn with remains. Sundance walked over to one of the walls. "Look at this."

Cassidy walked over. "What?"

"This wall isn't solid." He moved his torch closer until Cassidy saw long, ruler-straight cracks that ran along the walls, with stone wedges jamming a portion of rock into place. "Help me pull this out. They probably put the gold back here."

They gripped the nearest wedge and, by dint of pushing it one way and the other, managed to pull it out. The stone didn't budge, so they went after the next one.

Four wedges later, the slab crashed to the ground, barely missing their toes as they jumped out of the way.

"Nice," Sundance said as he peered inside the niche in the wall exposed by the missing stone. "Looks like we won't be having any more money trouble with Gómez."

The torchlight reflected off yellow gold: jewelry, tiny figurines, even little disks that looked like coins. There was perhaps a double handful of treasure in the niche, piled neatly at the feet of a desiccated corpse.

Cassidy studied its features. "I've heard of this," he said. "The dry air inside these mountains dries out the bodies and keeps them together. This one looks like it just got really old and never died."

"Who cares?" Sundance said. He scooped the gold into a leather sack and moved to the next set of wedges.

Over a backbreaking few hours, with occasional breaks to get more kindling for their makeshift torches, they pulled down a dozen stone slabs and harvested the treasure within.

"I think we've got enough," Cassidy said, hefting his sack. "We can always come back for more."

"Look," the Kid replied. "Let's just open that one. It looks bigger than the rest, and someone drew a bunch of things on it. It's got to be special."

"I guess," Cassidy replied.

This one wasn't wedged shut but actually mortared, and they spent an hour chipping away the cement with chunks of stone until, with a monumental crash, the big slab, too, fell to the floor.

A cloud of dust obscured the interior of the larger niche, and they waited impatiently for the treasure to be revealed. If the smaller ones had held a fortune, what might be in here?

"Now that's a sight you don't see every day," Sundance said.

"Not unless you're a guard at some museum back East," Cassidy replied.

There were no necklaces or bracelets at the corpse's feet, no shiny disks—just a filigreed gold base with an enormous blood-red ruby at the very top.

As Sundance reached out to take it, Cassidy's eyes were drawn to the stone slab that had covered the larger niche. This one hadn't broken when it fell, and he saw lines, parallel lines, gouged into it.

Four lines, worn through the rock as if by the action, during centuries, of...

"Don't touch that!" Cassidy said.

Sundance turned toward him. "Don't worry, Butch. You know we always share and share alike. I'm not planning on taking it for myself."

With that, his fist closed around the gold base, and he lifted it from the dusty shelf that was the niche.

A keening sound filled the cave—a noise like the screams of a dying horse, except enormous. Loud enough to fill the whole colossal cavern.

Cassidy dropped the bag and put his hands over his ears. Sundance did the same but removed one hand to point at the niche.

The mummified body was sitting up, pushing itself upright with hands that, Cassidy saw, had fingers that were worn down to the knuckle, where white bone could be seen.

That was what had made the marks on the rock slab. That thing was trying to get out.

And now they'd liberated it.

The screaming—Cassidy realized it came from the dead man

climbing down from the niche—died down. He and Sundance stepped back slowly, keeping their eyes on the monster.

As they moved away, the Sundance Kid bent over to pick up the ruby.

"You know it's probably that stone it's coming for," Cassidy said, as he risked a quick glance back to avoid tripping on anything behind them.

"Yeah, well it ain't getting it," the Kid shot back. "Not unless it finds a six-shooter and gets the draw on me."

The cave was suddenly alive with rustling noises. Cassidy tensed involuntarily, because the sound reminded him of bats. Or maybe the other bodies were coming awake. "I don't think a dead thing needs a six shooter," he replied.

"We'll see about that." Sundance lowered his hand to his hip, pulled his gun out of its holster, aimed carefully at the creature shambling toward them, and shot it in the forehead.

A look of utter confusion crossed the mummy's face.

Then it fell into a heap on the ground and once again, the partners were covered with dust as it disintegrated.

"I wouldn't breathe that stuff if I was you," Sundance said.

Cassidy was already moving. He grabbed his bag and the burning stick from the ground and said, "I'm not staying here another minute. I don't know what that thing was, but I'm not looking to find another one."

"I reckon you're right," Sundance said.

They started for the exit but stopped in their tracks. Gigantic red ants poured down the ramp in a living river.

Cassidy tried to stomp through them, but his boot disappeared to the ankle and the ants swarmed up. He jumped away and removed the ants by passing the burning stick along the leather. When it was clear, he realized the boot was gouged and thinned.

"The other way!" he yelled. "They can eat through leather."

They ran back into the large chamber, but the insects didn't follow them inside. Instead, they flowed into the open niches.

Still, more of them poured in.

"Those dead guys aren't going to last them very long," Cassidy said. We need to find another way out.

"I'm right behind you," Sundance said.

They ran into the depths of the cave and burst through an old cloth curtain that dissolved with their passage.

Cassidy tried to stop, but his boot slipped on the polished stone, and he plunged headlong into a black abyss.

For about two feet.

A strong hand grabbed his upper arm and, using his own momentum, swung him back along the ledge and onto the rock.

"Thanks," Cassidy said.

"Now we're even," the Kid replied.

"Even?"

"Yeah, for that time you pulled me onto your horse back in Mercedes."

"What about the time…"

The old argument stopped dead as a roar filled the chamber.

"The hell…" Cassidy said when the echo died down.

"How should I know? But we can't go back."

"We'd better. Look."

Deep in the blackness below, where their light barely reached, shadows folded upon themselves, blackness on deeper black.

"What's that?"

"It's big, that's what it is," Cassidy replied. "And I think it's getting closer."

No sooner had the words left his mouth than a deep whoosh sounded as a cylinder ten feet across shot upward in front of them, occupying most of the shaft.

Then it bent and Cassidy found himself looking into the twin of the ruby the Sundance Kid had pulled from the largest of the tombs.

He stepped away and realized the stone was an eye, set into an elongated head of golden scales. The line of a mouth, with two protruding fangs suddenly gaped open, and an enormous, bifurcated tongue lashed out at him.

A giant snake with a ruby for an eye… and very much alive.

Cassidy stumbled back out of the way and kept going in reverse as fast as he could. He half turned onto his hands and knees and stood, then shouted, "Run!"

"I'm way ahead of you, partner," Sundance said, showing Cassidy a pair of heels as they ran back the way it came. "Did you see the snake's wings?"

"I was too busy avoiding the mouth," Cassidy replied.

They ran back the way they'd come, through the original

enormous cavern.

Suddenly, several bright lanterns illuminated them.

"Hold it right there," a voice said. "Cassidy and Sundance, you'd better put your hands in the air. There's eight of us and we've all got the draw on you."

"Who are you?" Cassidy said, holding his hands above his head and dropping the sack he'd been holding.

"I work for the Pinkerton Detective Agency," the man replied. "And I've been trying to track you boys down for almost a year."

"Gómez sold us out," Cassidy swore.

Sundance, his hands also over his head, spat. "What happened to the ants?" he said.

"What ants?"

"This place was covered with red ants. Big mean things," Cassidy explained.

"They're not here. What are those noises?"

The noise of the colossal snake working its way through the thin chokepoint was getting louder.

"We don't know," Sundance lied.

"And what's that in your hand?" the agent said.

Sundance shrugged. "Some kind of stone. I don't think it's worth much."

"Yeah, right. Toss it over here, real slow," the Pinkerton said.

Cassidy saw Sundance tense. He whispered. "Do it. Trust me on this and do it now."

"They're gonna shoot us," Sundance replied.

Sundance was probably right. Those posters always said "dead or alive," and they meant it. It was much easier to shoot two fugitives than to drag them along alive. It was bad enough when you only had to go as far as the next town, but when you were stuck way down in the wilds of Bolivia, that made it infinitely worse.

Suddenly, a second group of figures appeared behind the Pinkerton and his assistants. In the dim light, these seemed to be animated lumps of clay with skin that moved around.

No, not skin. They were covered with ants... and Cassidy suspected they were the mummies they'd seen earlier.

One of the assistants yelled when he realized what was behind them. At the same time, Cassidy heard a crash from behind and the flutter of enormous wings.

"Throw the rock now!" he yelled at Sundance.

Sundance obeyed, letting the enormous ruby roll toward the Pinkerton. "Thank you," the man said, bending down to pick it up.

That was the signal they needed. Without even having to discuss it, Cassidy dove to his right while Sundance jumped to the left.

Only one of the Pinkerton's helpers let fly, but it was just as well that they'd gotten out of the way because countless tons of winged snake drove through the space they'd just vacated and bowled over men and ant-men indistinctly. Unlike the tight confines of the passageway behind them, here in the cavern, the serpent had room to maneuver.

It coiled back on itself and struck at one of the Pinkerton's helpers. Huge jaws opened and closed like a bear trap, operating so quickly that only the bottom half of the man remained after they snapped shut. The lantern the man had been holding rolled away, miraculously unbroken.

Cassidy stayed behind a solid rock, possibly another altar. The size of the serpent meant that it wouldn't take the mouth to kill you: if the tail happened to slam into you, you would be crushed.

Everyone else—he ant-covered mummies and the detective's posse—forgot about everything except the snake. Shots rang out in the cavern, and one of the mummy men managed to climb onto the snake's neck and was attempting to make its way to the head. The winged reptile thrashed and roared.

"You all right?" Cassidy shouted to the Kid.

The Kid laughed. He always laughed when things got really exciting. "Yeah, I'm good. Watch this."

He stepped into the open and took a bead on one of the Pinkerton's men. The shot flew true, and the guy dropped.

"Stop that. They're fighting our war for us! Let them distract the snake. We need to make a run for it."

"I want to take down that Pinkerton," Sundance retorted. "He's not going to stop."

"You're going to get us killed," Cassidy said. "There's another way out back there. We should go while the going's good."

Screams made it impossible to hear Sundance's reply, but the Kid moved toward the Pinkerton and the serpent instead of the exit.

Cassidy sighed and followed.

Suddenly, Sundance cursed and dropped to the ground, holding his right arm. Cassidy ran over.

"What happened?"

"Someone must have shot a chunk out of a rock and it flew into my arm. Look." He handed Cassidy a shard of stone with a dark edge where it had cut into his skin.

"Don't whine," Cassidy said. "You should have followed me. Besides, I've seen you take a bullet to the leg and not even blink."

"Yeah... well, this one surprised me." He stood, tucking his shirt into his pants, and stared at the fight. "You know... that dragon is going to kill them pretty quick. How about we slow it down?"

"You want to help the Pinkerton?" Cassidy asked.

"Not really. I just want the fight to last long enough to cover our retreat."

Cassidy shrugged and they both emptied their six-shooters into the serpent's back, right where the wings met the scales. The snake, which had been fighting in an upright position, held up by its wings, collapsed onto the ground and attacked from below. The mummy on its head, however, was thrown off and, when it hit the floor, collapsed into a million ants.

They ran back to the rear of the cavern and along the ramp that circumnavigated the huge hole in the ground. The bottom smelled like the vilest sewer they could imagine, but by dint of following the breeze, they found a small crack they could slip though that opened up into a cave and deposited them at the base of the mountain, on the eastern side.

Daybreak was already turning the morning pink when they finally made their way back to their horses, which had been joined by those of the posse. The Indian guard the Pinkerton had left behind was asleep at his post, so they tied and gagged him and took all the horses and supplies back the way they'd come.

The two friends rode into the sunrise and Cassidy said softly, "I reckon we should ride south for a bit. Somewhere the Incas didn't go. Did you manage to bring the bag along?"

"No, I dropped it when that cursed Pinkerton appeared."

Cassidy grunted. "Me, too. But these horses should help us defray some of the cost. So you won't need that ruby."

Sundance rode for a few moments in silence. "You saw that?"

"Of course. That little stone chip didn't drop you. You dove to grab the rock. Then you hid it in your pants."

"It's worth more than all that gold put together," Sundance replied petulantly.

"Yes. But that big snake wants its other eye back. It will chase you all over the world for it, and I reckon now that we broke whatever Inca magic was keeping it controlled, it won't take long to get out of that cave and come after us."

"You're saying I have to give the stone up?"

Cassidy shook his head. "I'd never tell you what to do. I'm just saying that while you've got that rock, I'm not riding with you. So we'll divvy up these here horses and go our separate ways until you cash in that rock. I don't fancy my chances against that flying serpent thing."

Sundance rode in silence for some steps. "You know we'd have a better chance if it was two of us."

"It won't be two of us."

This time, the silence was much longer, and at the end of it, Sundance reached into his pocket and pulled out the stone. He looked at the way the sun glistened redly in its facets, then sighed and threw it out into the scrub, as far as he could.

Cassidy smiled and they rode on.

Hobson's Angel

The rain was little more than a distraction. Carol was not going to let a little water ruin his day. The girl he'd just visited had made his every dream come true and made him feel absolutely alive.

The world was at his feet, and even the weight of being king of Romania could be set aside in favor of the benefits—the feeling of power. His country was at its peak, his people produced more than enough to support the life he wanted to live, and he could afford to simply let the world take care of itself for a few days.

So the fact that he couldn't control the weather was of little import. He could transcend it. The distance to his beautiful, newly completed Royal Palace was short enough that he could luxuriate in the rain.

"Such a day might not be amiss in one of Dante's circles," a man said.

Carol turned to look at him, more curious than alarmed by the appearance of a stranger at his side. Anyone on the palace grounds would have been thoroughly checked before entrance was granted. The man was tall and gaunt, dressed in the dark suit of a clerk and possessed of skin so sallow as to seem gray. He was about sixty years old.

"And yet, here you prance like a carefree child." The voice was mild, unassuming, but with some authority.

Perhaps, Carol thought, *he is an officer among the clerks*. Then he wondered whether there were ranks among the gray men who ordered his food and kept track of the gardeners' salaries. "I would advise you to disappear before you draw the wrong kind of attention to yourself," Carol said, feeling generous. "You come dangerously close to impertinence."

"Truth cannot be impertinent."

"I shall have the first guard we meet put you in irons." Carol was a military man, trained in trench warfare during the days of the Great War, not merely a soft monarch. No elderly clerk was going to worry him overmuch.

He reached the door of the palace, irritated to find that the guard was off on rounds. The impertinent clerk followed him inside. "You understand that you will suffer the hot irons of the torture chamber if you persist in annoying me, do you not?"

"I will burn? Perhaps I will. But that is not the question here." They walked through the echoing corridors, past the formal throne room, and all the way into Carol's private office.

Carol's secretary was out for lunch. He sighed. "You have gone well past the point of mere incarceration and torture. I suppose there is something you want."

"I want nothing for myself. I am only here to open your eyes."

At this, Carol II, King of Romania, laughed. "And what is it you see from your desk in my cellars that I cannot see from the pinnacle of our society?"

"I can see the signs in the clouds. The darkness of the clouds of war that will engulf Romania while you flitter from one puerile pleasure to another. I can see them; many can see them. But you are blind."

"Romania is not involved in the war. Let the French and the Germans keep their little spat to themselves."

"And the Soviets? Do you think that Hitler will tolerate Stalin on his borders? Or that Stalin doesn't know that he can't survive having the Fascists on his?"

"That is of no concern to me. Romania has nothing to do with the conflict."

"For a king, you seem to have little grasp of geography. Where, exactly, do you think this war will be fought? And which convenient, nearby oil-rich nation do you think will fuel it?"

Carol lifted his arm to pick up his phone, to order the man publicly hanged. The only thing that stopped him was the fact that the man's words echoed the fears that he himself harbored. The voice that kept him awake at three in the morning, long after his mistress of the night had drifted into the peaceful sleep of the peasantry. "We are neutral," he insisted. "The British and the French guarantee our territorial rights."

"The French are as good as defeated, and I imagine the British will soon have bigger problems to worry about."

Carol just stared at him, arm outstretched.

"Perhaps it is something you should consider, instead of thinking about which girl you will bed next."

"What do you mean?"

"You need to choose. You need to take a side because a war is coming that will tear Romania apart."

"We are neutral."

"That means less than nothing." For the first time, a hint of emotion entered the man's voice. "Two madmen, madmen at the helms of two of the greatest armies the world will ever see, are about to fight to the death. They define the reality in which they function, and their troops enforce that definition for everyone else. Do you really think they care about your blessed neutrality?"

Carol said nothing.

"You will die against a wall of this palace, shot like a dog. And so will many, many other Romanians. The difference is that you have the chance to decide your fate. They will not. You must choose."

"But... But who? Who should I choose?"

A dry chuckle. "That is your burden, not mine. But you must choose wisely." The man took one last look at Carol and stood, nodded once, and walked out the door.

Carol sat for an eternity, head in hands. And then he stood up and walked into the parade ground, in an attempt to clear his head. The rain beat down on his shoulders like molten lead.

He knew it would be too heavy a burden to bear, and an image of himself, alone and far from home, came unbidden into his mind. But it was still better than standing against the wall blindfolded. It was still better than having to choose.

Frozen Meat

"I don't care about any of that. All I want to know is whether we can land," Hermes said between clenched teeth.

The pilot looked unhappy but nodded. "It will be risky, the wind..." That was as much as the Belgian heard. He was already heading back to speak to his team, shouting, "Do it," back at the flight crew.

Six men and two women were huddled in the inadequate seats of the borrowed Antonov AN-12, shivering in the cavernous cargo area. "We'll be on the ground in a few minutes," he told them. "And it's going to be cold as my ex-wife's heart."

"You've never been married," a woman's voice, laconic but hard-edged, emerged from under a parka's hood.

"Of course not. With my luck, she would probably have looked like you."

That got a chuckle from the rest of the team, not because Karla De Jong was ugly, but because she'd been riding them all hard about preparation for the conditions ever since the project had started. Even though she certainly had the credentials, being the only team member to have wintered in Antarctica, everyone wanted to see her drop a couple of notches.

"Then you should play the lottery. Sounds like you have all the luck you need." She looked up at him, green eyes blazing. "Not much for brains, though. You act as if cold in Antarctica is something special. What temperature should we be prepared for?"

"Fifteen degrees below zero, Celsius."

"Wind?"

"Twenty-five miles per hour."

"Pfft. Cakewalk."

Hermes smiled. "For all our sakes, I hope so." He looked over the rest of his team.

The triplets sat on a bench, together as always. Edward, Robert, and George had grown up on a farm near Stellenbosch before their father had decided to sell the land to the South African government's redistribution program. Dark-haired, beefy, and ruddy-skinned, they were there to do the heavy lifting.

Gael Benoist was a former Lieutenant in the French Foreign Legion, Hal Cleveland an American who'd been in South Africa to study languages and had met Hermes in a bar.

Hiro Suzuki was the money man. He was there to make certain that the interests he represented received their share of the profits. Only his face was visible under the winter clothing, but that was heavily tattooed. Hermes imagined the rest of him was equally inked.

The final member of the team had been added at the last moment, at the request of Suzuki's employers. The pretense was that she was an American there to help them identify which equipment would be most valuable—but she had hair so pale as to be nearly white, with skin to match, and an accent that said Moscow more than Washington. She didn't even make much of an effort to hid it; she'd introduced herself as Irina.

Hermes kept his suspicions to himself. He was being paid to lead the team in, run a quick salvage operation of questionable legality, and get them out again. He'd already earned most of his fee by bringing the crew together and temporarily liberating a Congolese airplane and the DRC's best pilot and co-pilot. Fitting out landing gear that could deal with both snow and the grass field they'd had to take off from had been the hardest part. The on-the-ground work, on the other hand, promised to be easy—more monotonous than anything else. The trick would be to find the good stuff and load the plane as quickly as possible. It should be child's play to clear a few million.

The plane shuddered a bit on final approach, bounced once, and then landed without further ado.

Hermes was the first out the door, bracing himself for the freezing air.

"Well, that's disappointing," he said. "I've skied the Swiss Alps on colder days than this."

"It's only April," Karla said. "And we're too close to the sea for the temperature to really get nippy. You should walk inland a few hundred kilometers. Besides, it's not the temperature that gets you. It's the wind chill."

"Seems all right."

"So far," she said. "Let's go see the base."

Belgrano II was the southernmost of Argentina's Antarctic stations, the only one on Antarctica proper and not on the Peninsula. It had briefly been in the news in February when it had gone offline and the icebreaker *Almirante Irizar* had been sent in to relieve it.

Then... nothing. No reports about rescued scientists and military personnel, no reports about their tragic demise. No news at all.

Most of the world, of course, hadn't even noticed. The loss of twenty scientists and a minor research installation from a politically negligible nation wouldn't have made a blip on a global media stream obsessed with Northern Hemisphere happenings. But there should have been something other than radio silence about the outpost's fate.

Hermes had paid it no attention until Suzuki had shown up with an idea for a black salvage op. Apparently, abandoned property in Antarctica was pretty much up for grabs, and the base had some decent equipment.

It sounded silly to Hermes, but when the initial fifty percent of his fee had landed in his Swiss account, he'd asked no further questions. A job was a job, whether in Angola or in Venezuela. The nice thing about Antarctica is that the likelihood of people shooting at him was only just slightly less than the likelihood of lawyers popping up to ask what they were doing.

If more of his jobs were like this one, he'd need fewer antacids.

The base consisted of a cluster of red buildings on a slight rise a half-klick distant. Keeping the sea to their left, they trudged over, progress slowed by the calf-deep snow.

"What the hell?" George said.

The place looked like it had been shelled. Every window was shattered, at least one wall broken through, and the corrugated semi-cylindrical hangar that Hermes's map of the installation said was used to store food looked like it had been attacked with a giant can opener.

"Any comments?" Hermes asked Suzuki.

The Japanese man shrugged. "We expected to find the base out of commission. Well, it's out of commission. Let's see if there's anything of use here."

"You sound pretty relaxed for a man who invested a lot of someone else's money to get here. What if we don't find anything in the base?"

"Anything we find here is a bonus. The real money should be on the ship."

"What ship?"

"That one."

He pointed to the left, out over the frozen plain that, come high summer, would be ice-covered sea as opposed to a solid shelf.

"I don't... oh, crap."

A snow-covered hillock maybe a klick out resolved itself, when you stared at it long enough, into the shape of a fo'c'sle and bow of a ship tilted slightly to one side. The nearly cubical central section was immediately identifiable as the *Almirante Irizar*. So that was why they'd included so many pictures of the vessel in the briefing docs.

He swallowed. Like the hangar, the ship also looked like it had been ravaged by a giant kitchen implement.

***

"Countries like Argentina don't just abandon expensive helicopters," Karla said as they passed an apparently undamaged Sea King half-covered in snow.

Suzuki beamed at it. "Better for us. The parts will pay for a good chunk of the costs of coming here." He pointed at the cockpit, from which a seat and a good portion of the dash had been torn out. "That's why they left it here. Can't do much without the avionics. You and you," he pointed to Robert and Edward. "Could you get to work on dismantling this? Concentrate on electronics and engine parts, and check if any of the weapons are in place. That should make us a bundle."

"Sure," Robert replied with a grin. "It certainly beats walking out across the open ice."

"Oh, you'll get to do that, too," the Japanese man replied.

They walked on, leaving the groaning duo behind.

Hermes walked ahead to where Karla headed the group. "Did

you see the frozen liquid on the floor of the helicopter?"

"Hydraulic fluid. Dark red and viscous."

They walked in silence for a few steps. "Do you really think that?"

"I don't get paid to think. I'm here to keep you guys alive in a climate I know well and you don't. If you want speculation talk to Irina. She looks like your type."

"She would be anyone's type, or at least anyone with a pulse."

Karla snorted.

Then she recoiled. "What's that smell?"

They were passing a broken area of ice ridges that formed crevasses and caves. Hermes sniffed the air. "Smells like rotten meat. Some of the base supplies must have been dumped here. Maybe their trash."

"Trash doesn't smell in Antarctica. Not in April. Hell, not even in high summer. Frozen biological waste just freezes. Bacterial growth is negligible."

Hermes shrugged and moved on. It smelled like rotting meat to him, but long experience had taught him never to argue with Karla. She was always right, even when she was wrong. If she hadn't been the best option available to lead a questionably legal operation in Antarctica, he would have hired anyone else. But she was just too good to pass up.

They trudged the rest of the way in silence, seven dashes of color in the endless white.

"What the..." her voice trailed off. "Hermes, what have you gotten us into?"

He didn't reply, just stared at the ship.

The ship's bridge was dented, a can kicked once too often by a schoolboy. The steel bulkheads had been torn asunder to expose the interior of the accommodation. Every railing on the ship appeared to have been torn off. It listed at a rather extreme angle.

Hermes could tell that the thing would have sunk long ago if it hadn't been gripped solidly by endless ice.

Suzuki was exultant. "It's here; it's really here! I can't believe it." Hermes could almost see the dollar signs flashing in the man's eyes. And something more, perhaps. The cold glint of ambition, advance in the Yakuza, or whatever criminal enterprise he belonged to.

"Long way to come on a hunch."

"One can't win if one is unwilling to take risks. I thought you knew that."

"Looks like you won this time. What are we looking for?"

"The infirmary. The ship had just been refitted when it moved out in February, and there's some high-tech equipment in there."

Karla broke in. "I hope it's above sea level. That ship looks like it took on a metric crap-ton of water. And if it was water in February, it's ice now. Anything below the waterline is going to take pickaxes to reach. And a few months, too."

Suzuki smiled and pointed to the second floor of the bridge structure. "It's right there."

They found a gangplank half-buried in the ice, still connected to the prow of the *Irizar*. The bow was low enough at this point that they could have climbed on deck without it, but Suzuki led them up the wooden passageway, sliding his hand along the railing to displace the accumulated snow.

Moments later, they entered the torn central castle. The ship looked like something from a bad movie: broken glass clouded by frost, ice in the rigging, the wind whistling around the jagged edges. The only off note was that, other than the steel being broken and bent, everything was too clean and bright. Where was the rust?

The light was strange. It wasn't bright enough for noon, even with the snow acting as a giant reflector. Hermes knew that night wouldn't fall until May, but it was still almost like being in twilight. The sun seemed farther away than the warm, friendly globe of his beloved Africa. He shuddered.

They climbed a couple of sets of stairs, and the impression that a battle had taken place inside the ship grew stronger. This time, there was no mistaking the blood on the floor. Drops on the white steps, frozen there almost as soon as they'd landed, were easy to identify.

"This is the recovery room," Suzuki told them.

It was a bright, cheerful room with rubberized floors and four beds—modern, fully automated, and white. It would have been a beautiful place to rest from a broken arm or something and watch the sea slide past from the panoramic window.

Except the window was broken, with a snowbank piled up beside it, and one of the beds was overturned and broken in half.

"Irina," Suzuki said, "help me look at these beds. You know more about hospital equipment than I do, and I want to check if they're worth our time. The rest of you can go into the operating room, that door over there, and let's start piling the equipment on the deck so the triplets can haul it off on the snowmobile sled."

Hermes nodded and tried the handle.

Jammed.

He put his shoulder to it. "I felt it give a little. Hal, give me a hand."

Together, they inched the door open. Darkness met them—the room beyond had no windows.

"Who's got a flashlight?" Hermes reached back to grasp the proffered cylinder that Karla was handing to him.

Hal, not waiting, pressed ahead.

A clatter sounded, as if Hal had run into an instrument tray in the darkness and knocked it onto the ground. It was hard to tell with just the light from the door, and Hermes looked down at the flashlight, trying to see which way he needed to push the big yellow switch. He fumbled with it a couple of times and then cursed and removed a glove with his teeth. He'd never be able to work the switch using the mittens they were wearing. The things were warm, but useless for any kind of fine manipulation.

Hal screamed.

Hermes jumped, but the yell lasted only for a moment. It died into a gurgle and more clattering.

"Hal, you all right in there?"

Nothing.

He finally got the light on and shone it into the room. It was a big space, probably eight meters deep and five wide. Big enough that the beam couldn't illuminate all the corners. Two operating tables complete with an impressive array of overhead light fixtures held center stage, while supply cabinets and a lab bench surrounded them, not against the walls, but close enough that people standing at one of the tables could reach anything they needed with a minimum of fuss. A passageway wide enough for a stretcher led between the furniture to an elevator on the far wall.

There was no sign of Hal.

Hermes held up a hand to keep the rest of the group out and stepped into the darkness, flashlight forward. He took a cautious step into the dim room, his right hand automatically sliding into his jacket to retrieve the Glock 17 that lived in his shoulder holster.

That was when he remembered that both pistol and holster were in the gun case he'd brought with him. On the plane.

After all, other than his companions, who was he going to shoot in Antarctica? And he wasn't being paid to shoot his companions; shooting people for free was bad business.

He stopped, then shrugged and began to walk. There was no movement in the room, no sound of breathing. Hal had probably fallen down a hole into the floor below. Hermes had a sixth sense about rooms occupied by another living being... and this one didn't feel that way.

The edge of one of the cabinets was coming up to his right. If anyone was hiding in the operating room, that was where he'd be.

Hermes decided to round the corner fast. He was sure there was nothing, but he wasn't going to start taking chances at this late stage. He'd survived a career as a private contractor in the hottest of African hotspots, and this was the job that was going to allow him to retire somewhere sunny without any insurgents. Getting killed on this ice cube of an excuse for a continent wasn't in his plans.

He jumped out from behind his cover, his flashlight pointed in just the right direction.

A face lunged at him.

Only his momentum, the fact that he was moving quickly, saved him. Claw-like hands tore through the fabric of his jacket, but that was all they got. He rolled aside and the flashlight clattered away to shine ineffectually at a wall, illuminating nothing.

The light from the doorway disappeared and the room went nearly completely dark. Hermes flinched, anticipating the killing blow.

It never landed. One second a shadow blocked the threshold, the next it was gone.

"Hermes," George's voice called. "Are you all right?"

"Yeah, I'm fine. Is he gone?"

"I'm not sure it was human... but yeah, whatever that was is gone. You can come out."

Hermes got himself back together and emerged, never turning his back on the darkened room. "Where's Hal?"

"That thing was carrying him," Karla replied grimly.

"We need to go get him. Why are we just standing here?"

"We can't help him. His head was hanging by a thread. He's dead, Hermes."

Hermes felt sick. He'd lost men before, but never because he'd led them into an obvious ambush. "I don't care. I'm getting him back."

Suzuki stepped up without a word. Everyone looked at him. "We don't have time for heroics. Mr. Cleveland was aware of the risks."

"He was aware that there would be something deadly out here in the middle of nowhere, waiting in an abandoned ship?"

"He knew this wasn't a holiday trip. All of us do."

Hermes gave the man a hard look. His employer, he was sure, knew more than he let on. "Now, tell me—"

The radio on his belt blasted static and the pilot's voice filled the recovery room. "Hermes, Suzuki, anyone, can you hear me? Anyone?"

"Yeah. Calm down. We can hear you."

"There's some guys trying to get in here. We shut the plane up."

"Guys? What kind of guys? In uniform?"

"Maybe they once had uniforms. Not anymore. They're dressed in broken stuff. Rags."

"Okay, don't let anyone in."

"They're banging on the doors, Hermes."

"Sit tight."

"This isn't a bunker, man. It's an airplane. Made of aluminum, not steel. You best done hurry, you understand?"

"Yeah, we're on our way." Hermes headed toward the stairs.

"Wait." It was Irina's voice.

"What? I need to talk to those guys are before they break the only way we've got to get off this refrigerator." He gave them a steady look. "And I want to get my gun."

"You'll never make it. The people at the plane are the same as the thing we found in here."

He wanted to ask her how she knew, but the time to recriminate her, and Suzuki, would come later. And so would retribution, if he decided they deserved it. "And what, exactly would that be?"

"Zombies."

She said it in a toneless voice, with no trace of a smile, no indication that she was kidding.

"Don't give me that," Hermes said.

"It's true. I studied it in a man who came back from Antarctica in February. He died of the wounds he had sustained here... but he didn't stay dead."

"And you brought us here anyway?" Hermes didn't believe a word of what she was saying, but he knew what the guy in the infirmary had looked like. Not dead, but very, very sick. Irina was using irrational fears to keep them away from the real truth: someone had been very naughty with biological weapons in Antarctica—and he really didn't think it was the Argentines.

"We didn't think there would be any here. I only came to try to find out what caused it."

"Whatever." He thought furiously for a moment. One decision, at least, was taken. Irina and Suzuki weren't going back to Africa with them. Their bodies would remain here in the frozen wastes, after dying slow, painful, traitors' deaths.

Unfortunately, there were more pressing matters to deal with.

"Guns," Hermes said. "We need weapons."

"I have this," Suzuki said. He pulled a long-barreled revolver that looked like a joke, something from Dirty Harry's wet dreams.

"You go ahead and hold on to that," Hermes replied. "This ship belonged to the Argentine Coast Guard, right?"

"Yeah," Karla said. "They came to our bases a few times. Always full of soldiers."

"Good. Then there has to be a gun locker somewhere, either near the bridge or the captain's cabin. Maybe even inside the captain's cabin."

"You're selling it short. This was a major military vessel. They had a complement of three hundred men. You would need an armory."

"Yeah, but I'm assuming that ended up under the water line. Ice central."

They headed toward the bridge. Four flights of dark, slightly leaning stairs brought them to the wreckage of what had once been a modern ship's control center. There was very little of it left—the bottom half of a sailor lay in a corner, looking for all the world like the rest of him had been bitten off by something with big teeth.

"Who says the Argentines have bad taste?" Hermes said, smiling. He'd found the weapons storage—a row of guns that had once been locked together by a metal bar. But the bar was nowhere to be seen.

Clearly, a crewmember or two had gotten there and armed themselves, not bothering to lock up afterward. What Hermes saw made him happy. FAL rifles, four of them.

He pulled a gun off the rack and handed it to Karla. Another went to Gael and a third to George. "You know how to use these?"

The men nodded.

"Wonderful guns. Belgian. Like me." They looked slightly different than the ones he was used to. The standard stocks had been replaced with telescoping items and the top cover was ridged, but the bones could be seen. These were the rifles he'd cut his teeth on, a staple of NATO for ages.... The older Argentine-produced versions had also popped up everywhere. They were the guns the CIA had supplied the Contras in the early eighties and, in most African conflicts, both sides had at least a few of them. Only the AK-47 was more ubiquitous between Jo'Burg and Tripoli.

Spare clips lined the bottom of the shelf, and behind these were boxes of 7.62 ammo. Hermes filled his pockets with bullets.

"Let's get back there." He turned to Suzuki, who hadn't protested not getting a rifle. "You coming?"

Suzuki shook his head. "We need to keep working on the medical center. Otherwise, we came all this way for nothing. Go out there and clear those things out."

"Are you kidding me?"

"No. If you must, take Gael with you, but the rest of us are going to work on getting our money." Seeing that Hermes was about to protest hard, the Japanese man went on. "How long do you think the Congolese will be after you if you don't pay them for the use of their plane? General Mbuyi isn't renowned for his forbearance."

"Dammit," Hermes said. But Suzuki was right. If they didn't pay, Africa would be off-limits to him for a long time. Mbuyi liked to send messages to people who were thinking of annoying him. "I'd rather take Karla," he said between gritted teeth.

"I'm touched, but no can do," the woman replied. "I think I remember that there's something very valuable on the bow deck."

He scowled at her but left.

They trudged across the ice plain, Gael continuously moaning that he'd been trained for desert duty and that someone else should be freezing their butt off in the snow.

"Shut up. We should be reaching the helicopter soon."

"I see it. It's right over there. Looks fine to me," Gael replied.

"Yeah? So where are Robert and Edward?"

"Oh."

Footprints surrounded the aircraft, but the snow had been packed down so hard that it was impossible to tell if there had been a fight. There was no sign of the farmboys.

"Maybe they heard the pilot's call and went off to help?"

"Maybe." Hermes doubted it. He'd been involved in military campaigns for too long to believe in best-case scenarios. When an operation went wrong, old Murphy brought his law to bear with full force, except that it became past tense. Hermes's version would be once it hits the fan, everything that could go wrong has already gone wrong... it's your job to either deal with the fallout or become part of the fallout. Under that motto, he had to assume they were both dead. "Let's get to the plane."

Sometimes Hermes hated being right all the time.

The plane was a shambles. The lateral passenger door on the starboard side hung from a single hinge and the loading ramp was halfway open. But what made Hermes's blood freeze was the guy who'd poked his head through one of the cockpit windows, forcing out a square of glass. He'd once been a dark-haired fellow, with the Mediterranean skin coloring to match, but now... now the skin had a grayish-green tone, and his purple lips appeared to be frozen in a rictus of pain around bloody teeth.

"Crap. If they've been in the cockpit..."

"The flight crew."

"Screw the flight crew," Hermes said. Like most infantrymen in Africa—you couldn't really call for an air strike in a bush war—he often thought pilots were worthless freeloaders who had things just a little too easy. "I'm worried about the instruments. If that thing trashes the cockpit, we're swimming back."

Rifles in hand, they ran towards the plane as fast as the snow permitted.

"Cover me from the ramp," Hermes said when they reached the door. He peered inside, planning to get to the cockpit to dispatch the—crap, he might as well call them zombies until someone told him what was really going on here—and secure the plane. "No, no! Get back, get back!"

Gael watched in stunned silence as Hermes pulled his head away from the opening and ran away from the plane.

Moments later, the crowd of grayskins he'd seen inside the fuselage boiled out of every opening. Some fell from the ramp, others followed Hermes out the door. The guy in the cockpit window was pushed out by someone behind him and fell to the snow headfirst with a thump that should have left him out of action. He got up and shuffled after his peers.

Enough was enough. Hermes opened fire on the crowd and Gael followed suit.

"Don't hold the trigger down," Hermes shouted over the infernal din. The FAL was a wonderful gun, but the automatic setting was nearly useless because of violent recoil. FN, the Belgian manufacturer, had eliminated the option on NATO-issue guns, but the Argentines had left it in.

Hermes showed him how it was done, shooting controlled chest bursts of three individual shots on semi-auto. He chose a big guy at the front of the back advancing on them.

Nothing happened. The big guy kept coming.

"Fall back," he shouted.

"Way ahead of you," Gael replied. "Where are we going?"

"Back to the ship."

Maybe the steel bulkheads would hold them off while he asked Irina how to kill the things.

Fortunately, the zombies didn't move quickly. They advanced in a ragged pack, torn clothing fluttering around awful, gaping wounds. They looked like a pack of shark attack victims, and they definitely had no right to be ambulatory. Many of them were covered with bright, fresh blood. Clearly, going back for the pilots would be an exercise in futility.

They turned their backs and ran, even though every nerve in Hermes's body protested against leaving an enemy behind him. But what choice did they have? A slow, orderly retreat would only eat time they needed once they reached the ship.

As they passed over the broken terrain, up one ridge and down another, gaining ground in the pursuit, the stench, the one he'd smelled before, hit him again. Clearly, it was coming from the undead monstrosities—or whatever the hell they were—behind them.

He realized too late that the wind was blowing in the wrong

direction for that.

Gael disappeared from the path ahead of him. One second, he was there, the next, he simply wasn't.

Hermes's reflexes kicked in and he fell behind the nearest cover, a large chunk of ice in the broken terrain. He hadn't seen where the strike originated, and had no clue, at least on an intellectual level, if he was moving in the right direction. Nevertheless, instincts bred in the jungle must have worked in his favor; his subconscious must have realized that the attack came from upwind, even if his waking mind didn't. Hell, he couldn't have told you which way the wind was blowing right then.

Still, he made it back to his feet without getting grabbed and even without having to turn to find his assailants. They were right in front of him, just three meters away.

There was nothing else to do. Hermes opened fire, an unthinking stream of bullets emerging from the rifle in fully automatic mode.

What happened next was exactly what the textbooks said would happen.

The FAL rifle has very little kickback in single-shot situations, but the recoil on automatic is brutal, and this one was no exception. The rifle pulled up. His bullets drew a nearly vertical line along the nearest zombie, cutting bloodlessly into the gray flesh from crotch to forehead.

And when the thing's head exploded, something wonderful happened.

The zombie fell over. It twitched once and lay still.

Hermes didn't need to be told twice. Regaining control, he began to shoot like the professional soldier he was. But this time, instead of aiming for the heart, he took head shots.

Less than a minute later, the creatures coming toward him were all dead.

The final one was otherwise occupied; it was bent over Gael's prone form and appeared to be...

Hermes retched, but he'd eaten nothing, so there was nothing to throw up.

...eating Gael's face.

"Die, you ugly bastard."

A single round beside the ear ended that particular meal with a bang.

Hermes leaned over Gael. The man was quite clearly dead, most of his face gone and a ragged hunk of gore where his neck should have been. Just in case, though, he put another slug into the dead Frenchman's forehead.

He studied the bodies. Men and women who had apparently been in their twenties, thirties and forties before whatever happened to them happened. Mostly men. Mostly in good shape. The age, general health, and remains of uniforms of the dead indicated that they were probably from the Antarctic base and the icebreaker. Military people.

Each showed large areas of scarred flesh—bite marks? But how did dying of a large bite turn you into a zombie? Or was whatever biological agent had turned them into the walking dead responsible for the marks?

He didn't know. But other pieces fell into place. The base must have had an outbreak of some sort and went offline, and then the *Irizar*, thinking that it was just a communications glitch like so many others—after all, a base hardened against the Antarctic winter was unlikely to suffer a catastrophic demise in the middle of summer—sailed straight into the disaster.

Among the dead, Hermes searched for the big guy who'd led the charge from the disabled plane.

There was no sign of him.

Also, there were too few bodies in the pile. This was a different group.

And that meant that the others were likely still following.

He climbed the nearest ridge and realized that his worst fears had come to pass. The zombies, shambling randomly, had managed to cut off his retreat toward the icebreaker. In fact, he appeared to be completely surrounded.

Hermes shrugged. Could be worse.

He took aim and dropped the dead thing directly between his position and the icebreaker, then he shot a couple more that stood a little too close to his intended route, clearing the path. Watching the crystallized chunks of brain matter explode from their heads as the bullets tore through them at close range was immensely satisfying. Better still, it didn't feel like he was killing people. Even if they weren't really the living dead—and he had his doubts: why would a reanimated corpse need to eat Gael's face?—something about the poor, sick bastards made them less than human.

Hermes ran for it. Once out of the encirclement, he was confident that he could outpace the zombies and make it to the *Irizar* long before they did. Long enough to warn the others.

Then, when the horde arrived, it would be a skeet shoot until the continent ran out of zombies... that would happen long before the weapons' locker ran out of bullets.

He crossed over one ridge—were they carved by the wind?—and through the resulting canyon. The zombies around him weren't moving fast enough to cut him off. He should be able to make it. Just.

Breath came hard. The deep snow, especially in the lower areas made the going tortuous, but he'd done long marches before, usually with a pack, through sub-Saharan mud. This was a walk in the park in comparison.

The last rise crested, and he started to run for the icebreaker.

His foot caught on a loose chunk of ice, and he landed flat on his face in one of the valleys. The FAL flew three meters further away, shoulder strap flailing uselessly behind.

He scrambled for the gun, but movement out of the corner of his eye caused him to change direction at the last moment.

The big guy, the zombie who'd led the charge out of the plane, stood on the ridge above him. The painful grimace seemed to grow wider as the thing looked down on him. One step. Another. Arms stretched forward like claws to tear him to pieces, and all Hermes could do was stare dumbly at the bullet holes in the thing's tattered shirtfront. It would be cold comfort to die knowing he'd shot true, but better than no comfort at all.

Now, he had to wait for death.

The thing exploded in a shower of frozen mist and the foulest stench. Bits of foul ice stung his cheek.

It took him a moment to process what had happened, and another to believe it.

As impossible as it was, the creature that had been just about to devour him had suddenly... burst. There was no other way to describe it. Its torso had flown apart, throwing its legs to one side and the shoulders, the right arm and head to another. The left arm had disintegrated.

Hermes stood. Miraculous delivery aside, he still had to run from the rest of the pack, and they did say that God helped those who helped themselves. He ran, gathering up the FAL as he went.

Only when he was a good twenty meters ahead of the nearest zombie did he turn back, and he regretted it immediately.

The one that had exploded was also after him, its remaining arm dragging the disembodied head and shoulders along the snow.

***

A few meters before the gangplank, Hermes heard the unmistakable sound of a gun and turned back. The nearest zombie had suddenly collapsed, most of its torso gone.

Another one exploded behind that one, then a third.

He didn't need any more prompting. Using the FAL, he assisted his unseen rescuer by taking headshots at any creatures the unseen gunner missed.

Eventually, the zombies kept coming, even though he was pretty sure there were more of them. Finally, he headed back to the ship.

***

"It's a Bofors 40-millimeter gun," Karla said, eyes bright. "I think I'm in love."

She patted the weapon, which was set up on a raised platform on the bow deck. It had a long, wide single barrel with a conical end and a seat at the back where the operator could sit, and it was still hot from having cleared the ice of everything that moved. If any zombies had survived, they'd made themselves scarce.

Hermes raised his eyebrows. "It looks like an antiaircraft gun from World War II," he replied. "An antique."

"Don't knock it. You'd be dead if it wasn't for this baby. Besides, classics are classic for a reason. Don't tell me you've never used one of these."

He looked at it critically. "I've never served on a ship."

"These aren't ship guns. Most of them are land-mounted. And not just AA weaponry. You can use them against infantry, especially mechanized infantry, just as well. You should see them blow away a pickup truck."

"Yeah, but you'd need a flatbed to pull that thing around unless there's a wheeled version. And the tow rig would be too slow to use in small-scale operations in Africa. You'd get cut up by the guys with the pickups you're trying to kill before you could bring it to bear."

"Well, we've got one and the Argentines have apparently maintained it well. If I had to guess, I'd say someone's been firing it recently."

"How come I didn't see it on the way in?"

"Karla pointed at a sheet of deck steel. "That chunk of bulkhead was lying on top of it. Took an age to pull it off." She looked around at the ravaged icebreaker. "I wonder what happened here."

"Just off the top of my head, I'd say zombies happened."

Karla shook her head. "I don't know. This ship's been smashed to pieces. Do you really think zombies could do that to a steel superstructure?"

Hermes thought back to the airplane. Even though it was packed with the things, dozens of them, little damage had been visible from outside. "I'm not sure. But I think I know who will."

He headed back to the infirmary. The team had set up a bunch of battery-operated lights, and an impressive pile of electronics and assorted medical equipment was stacked in the recovery room. Suzuki looked up from inspecting the loot as Hermes entered.

"Where's Gael?" he said.

Hermes just shook his head.

"Damn."

"You said it, brother. We ran into a whole bunch of your girl's zombies out there."

George rushed in. "What about my brothers?"

"I honestly don't know. They weren't at the helicopter, but I didn't see any sign that anything had happened to them. My guess is they spotted the baddies and are laying low."

Hermes didn't want to tell him that he had several other guesses as well, most of them more plausible than the one he'd confessed. It wouldn't have served any purpose.

He turned back to Suzuki. "I want some answers."

The Japanese man gazed back impassively. "You're not paid to need answers. You're paid to do a job."

"This isn't the job I signed up for."

"I define the job, not you."

Hermes resisted the urge to cut him in half with a short burst from the FAL. There would be time for that later. "Well, if the job you defined included getting back on the Antonov, you'd better start redefining it."

"Demolished?"

"Oh, yeah. Big time." Hermes didn't know that for a fact, but he wanted to see what the Yakuza goon—he was sure the guy was Yakuza now—would do if he thought they were stranded. Hell, they probably *were* stranded.

The man didn't bat an eye. "Then we'll need to ensure we have the merchandise my employers want. Otherwise, it will be a long walk."

"This junk?" Hermes kicked at the pile on the floor. "We might as well get going. Also, it's a swim, not a walk."

"No, not this junk." Hermes had to resist the urge to lean over and take Suzuki's pulse. At least the dead guys looked like they were grinning in a sick way. "Irina, could you join us?"

He didn't raise his voice, didn't change his intonation, but even though she was in the next room, Irina appeared as if by magic.

"Yes?"

"We've just moved the timetable up. You're on."

She nodded. "I'll need someone to come with me. Someone good with guns."

"Hermes will accompany you. Is it far?"

"The scanner says only a few hundred meters."

"All right. You can go now. We'll finish up here. Hermes, please go with her."

She nodded and took a gun and a couple of clips from the rack. Karla must have brought hers back. Hermes followed her lead—he suspected he would need the ammo. They filed out.

"Are we actually going to go out onto the ice again?" he asked.

"Yes."

"That's stupid."

"It's the only way we're getting back to civilization." She looked back at him. "And if you're so worried, why don't you stay behind?"

"Suzuki's orders."

This time the ice-blue eyes burned through him. "You don't look like the kind to follow orders you don't agree with."

"And you don't look the kind to make character assessments."

"Fair enough." Irina turned and walked down the gangplank.

Hermes followed. "All right. I came because I want some answers, and Suzuki isn't going to give them to me."

"And what makes you think I will?"

"Well, at the very least I'll be able to see what was important enough to send you out into the zombies' domain."

"So now you believe me about the zombies?"

"I believe there are people out there who… aren't right."

"They're zombies, I tell you."

"Why should I believe you?"

"I already told you. I studied one."

"Who?"

She shut up, clearly realizing she'd already said too much. Hermes smiled to himself and followed her through the snow.

Irina followed a beacon on a screen, a piece of equipment that had to be looped directly into a satellite, probably military—and most likely Russian.

She stopped in front of a pile of snow. Just another hillock in the middle of nowhere.

"Damn," she said.

"Missing something?"

"No. But this is the part where I remember that I should have brought a shovel."

Hermes groaned. "I suppose that means I'll have to dig?"

"Are you kidding? You keep watch for zombies. I'll dig."

And she did, surprisingly effectively. Armfuls of snow were dumped to either side as the girl dug in.

"Of course," she said after a while.

"What?"

"I got the wrong end."

Hermes stepped closer. Under the snow, a gray, mottled surface could be seen. "Congratulations," he said. "You found a rock."

"It's not a rock," Irina replied, moving around the mound to the far side. She started digging again.

He kept one eye on her and one on the ice. The missing zombies hadn't appeared since Karla's massacre at the *Irizar*. The Bofors might be a museum piece, but it was still good enough to tear apart a few human bodies. Were they smart enough to recognize the threat? Or had they simply been distracted by something else?

His eye drifted skyward. It felt like twilight had lasted forever.

"There!" Irina's voice sounded excited, so Hermes bent to look over her shoulder. A yellow eye the size of his fist looked back at him balefully.

"What the hell..."

"A nothosaur," Irina said.

"A dinosaur? You expect me to believe it's a dinosaur?"

"Not a dinosaur, a prehistoric reptile. Cold-blooded."

"And that makes it better?"

"It makes you less ignorant." Irina kept digging as she spoke, pushing snow aside to reveal an elongated snout and a mouth. "Thank God, the mouth is open."

"What difference does that make?"

"Saves ammo. I would have had to shoot holes in it to take the samples. Hold this." She handed him her rifle and pulled a Ziploc containing small empty vials out of her pocket. Then she produced a miniature chisel.

Irina reached deep into the reptile's mouth with both hands and chipped at something with the chisel. "A saliva sample. My boss insisted," she said. Somehow, Hermes got the distinct impression that she wasn't referring to Suzuki. There were more players involved, guys that Hermes was pretty sure he didn't want to tangle with. "But I don't think the answer lies in the saliva. Hand me my gun again."

She studied the telescoping butt of the rifle for a few moments and shrugged. "I guess it will have to do." Locking it in the shortest position, Irina grasped the rifle by the stock with both hands and pounded downwards with the butt. Once, twice, again. She put all her weight behind each blow.

"What are you trying to do?"

"I'm trying to dislodge a tooth."

Hermes knew better than to ask why. None of the answers he'd gotten so far had made him happy. He couldn't see this one being any different. "Here, I'm bigger than you. Watch for zombies."

It took him four blows, but finally, one of the three-inch-long daggers this thing had called teeth came loose. He fished around for it in the darkened, frozen maw and finally presented it to her.

Irina grabbed it like a kid with a candy bar. She studied the back end. And whooped.

Hermes couldn't believe his eyes. This one had seemed such a cold fish, a murderess well matched to Suzuki and his ilk, and here she was celebrating like she'd scored a goal in the World Cup final.

"Are you going to tell me what you found?"

Irina didn't seem to have heard. "Yes! I was right! I told them all along that the saliva wasn't the clue. They condescended to me, saying that the bites were like Komodo Dragon bites, that the saliva was a biological agent. But I knew the bite pattern was more consistent with venom."

He was amazed at the sudden change that came over her, but something she said made him stop and pay attention. "Venom? That thing is poisonous?"

If the rest of the body, still covered by the mound of snow, was proportional to the head, the creature they were looking at was the size of a small bus. Why would something like that need poison, too?

"From what I know, it isn't actually venomous. Oh, they must have been at some time, a few million years ago. Or they descended from something venomous. But now—they kill you with their jaws, and the venom tracts inject... something else."

He saw it now. "Something that brings you back as a zombie?"

She nodded.

"But why?" Hermes said.

"We have no clue. There's no evolutionary advantage. We think a nothosaur nest got dosed with weaponized anthrax... and we're still trying to understand the consequences."

"How... No. Don't tell me. I really, really don't want to know. If you've got what you need, let's get back to the *Irizar.*" He stopped. "Wait. Are there more of those things out there?"

"Zombies? I don't know. Nothosaurs? From what I read, they're all dead."

"Yeah. I thought all the dinosaurs were dead, too. But that was a totally different kind of dead—not the kind that lets you go around biting people and turning them into zombies."

"They're all dead. This place was a battlefield in February, and an observer on the ground reported that all the nothosaurs were killed."

Hermes knew just how much you could trust that kind of assessment, a report from the heat of battle. No one had done a census of nothosaurs, and even if they had, there was no reason more of the things couldn't hatch or whatever.

The walk back was tense. Just when he thought that nothing could be worse than the victims of some bioweapon, the universe had to throw poisonous dinosaurs into the mix.

But they made it back to the ship without incident, just as twilight darkened to nearly full night. George had relieved Karla at the Bofors, but other than that, there was no change in the situation.

"Do you have the samples?" Suzuki asked.

Irina nodded. "Teeth and saliva."

The Yakuza man shrugged as if to say that the composition of the merchandise made no difference to him, as long as they were getting paid for it. "Good. I'll call for pickup." He disappeared into the infirmary room.

"Well, we might as well make ourselves comfortable," Irina said. The ice-cold quality had left her, as if being right about the nothosaurs had brought her out from under a cloud. Hermes began to wonder how much choice the woman had had in being there. He would have to find out before he killed her. If she wasn't a willing participant in Suzuki's plan, he might let her live. Or maybe he would give her a quick, clean death.

"You must be joking," Hermes said. "We need to fortify this place. Those things are still out there."

"Not the ones I saw," Karla said with a grin. She was munching on a sandwich… where the hell had she gotten a sandwich?

"Well, I know how many came out of that plane, and I saw the ones you shot. The numbers don't add up. There have to be at least fifty of them still out there."

"I'm not so sure," Karla said. "From what you told me, it sounded like they'd come after us if they were out there."

"Why don't we ask our expert?" Hermes said, nodding in Irina's direction.

"I… the one I studied was mindlessly aggressive. It certainly wouldn't have rested while there was a living person nearby."

Hermes laughed. "So you've only ever seen one?"

"These things don't exactly grow on trees. You have to come to Antarctica to get them."

George walked in. "No use my freezing my ass off anymore. It's too dark to see them more than three meters away."

Hermes sighed. "All right, then. Can we at least set sentries at the windows so we can see them coming before they eat us?"

They grumbled, but they agreed to take positions, one looking out from each side of the rectangular bridge structure. Suzuki's pickup team was still more than four hours away.

Hermes looked out over the ice. The moon was out, a crescent on its way to becoming a quarter moon, down near the horizon. The cloudless sky plus the reflection from the white surface gave the night an eerie, almost ghostly light. Wind whistled past the ship and blew loose snow around on the frozen wasteland, making it look like the ground itself was crawling toward him.

The ship creaked as the ice inside contracted in the night chill. Fortunately, the weak sun hadn't really warmed the air outside, so night was just a few degrees colder than day. Hermes tried to keep his face outside the open window as much as possible. The cold was preferable to the groaning of the dying ship. Dead ship, more likely. With the damage it had taken, it was unlikely that it would ever sail again, and, despite Suzuki's optimistic project, Hermes doubted anyone else would consider it a profitable salvage candidate.

Another loud crack echoed through the ship, amplified by the metallic structure. Hermes shuddered. It was the sound of a haunted house settling on its foundations.

The next sound froze his blood. A scream, unmistakably human, came from just a few meters away: George's position.

Hermes lowered his rifle and charged to where the man was posted.

He never made it. For the second time in six hours, he was forced to run in the opposite direction from the one he wanted. Zombies were crushed in the stairwell, falling over each other in their desperate struggle to get through the hatch and get to Hermes. He fired a quick burst, head-high, and backpedaled through the door that led into the recovery room.

Then he slammed it behind him, delighted to see that it was a solid wooden number with a locking hasp.

Suzuki, Irina, and Karla joined him in the room, Suzuki with his ridiculous artillery piece out and cocked.

"Is there a way out through the infirmary?" Hermes asked.

"No."

"Damn."

Karla leaned over the window ledge. "We can probably go that way," she said.

"We'll be killed."

The door to the room thumped. It thumped again.

The third thump splintered it, but it held.

"Damn!" Hermes shouted. He swung one leg over the sill and looked for the series of handholds and footholds that would let him down. A meter away, Karla was doing the same.

The wall below them would have represented an impossible climb in normal circumstances, but the damage to the ship had left it pockmarked and torn—badly enough that it could be scaled with very little difficulty. The inclination was enough to keep it from being a sheer drop. Just enough to turn it from impossible to merely stupid.

"Where did they come from?"

"George's side, I guess," Hermes replied.

"Impossible," Irina said from above them. "I was with him until a few minutes ago. Nothing came from that side."

They reached the deck, none the worse for wear.

The crunch of the door finally breaking reached them from above… and almost immediately it began raining zombies. They hit the deck with a sick thud and immediately stood up and came after the four living people.

"Follow me!" Karla said.

At a run, she led them around the central structure toward the bow and sat down at the Bofors. Her white teeth could be seen in the dim light. "Just keep them off me. I'll send all of them back to hell."

"Fire at their heads!" Hermes shouted. He and the others fired their FALs into the encroaching undead. Even in the dim light, the spray of frozen, crystallized brain matter could be seen.

Hermes expected them to react the way a human crowd would have under withering fire from two automatic rifles and that overgrown handgun Suzuki carried… but instead of retreating, or at least dispersing, the zombies behind simply pushed aside the latest casualty and kept coming.

The darkness made it difficult to aim. Suzuki and Irina seemed to be doing more damage to the superstructure and the bridge than to the zombies. Even Hermes himself was missing the occasional shot, despite the short range.

"Get out of here," Karla yelled.

The barrel of the 40-millimeter Bofors swung around and boomed once, leaving Hermes's ears ringing. The four zombies nearest the gun simply disappeared, and a round hole was punched into the bulkhead behind them.

"I mean it, get the hell out of here!" Karla repeated. Her voice sounded far away, distant through the buzzing.

"What about when you need to reload?"

"I've got twenty shells in the autoloader," she nodded toward a crescent-shaped metal rail with slim projectiles hanging from it. "That should do the trick—but I'd feel better if I didn't have to worry about you, too."

Hermes held her gaze. "Whoever gave you a dishonorable discharge was a complete moron."

Tears welled in Karla's eyes, but she didn't look away. "Nah," she said. "He was right. I was a disgrace to the uniform. Now get out of here."

Hermes nodded once and ran. Behind him, the Bofors began to fire.

Thud.

He reached the prow.

Thud.

He looked quickly over the side and saw that Suzuki and Irina had already jumped down and landed in the snow. He went over the edge.

Thud.

He ran through the snow, trying to follow the other two's footsteps.

Thud.

He smiled. Those zombies were being taught a lesson. If they had a choice, he suspected they wouldn't mess with the South African Army again. He caught up with Irina and Suzuki and motioned them behind a snowy hillock to wait for the next shot.

But it never came.

Instead, a scream. Thin and long and... gone.

"Dammit," Hermes said, bitterly.

They climbed the hillock and waited, but the zombie horde didn't come until an hour later. When they came, they were all covered in blood. Apparently, it had been lunch hour.

Less than twenty of them remained. Hermes used them for target practice; ignoring Suzuki's useless flailing with the hand cannon, he took his time and picked them off one by one, at long range. One bullet, one zombie. Replace magazine and keep going. One bullet, one zombie.

The zombies were all down before they could get within fifty yards.

Hermes turned to the Yakuza goon. "When are your friends coming for us?"

"Oh, no one's coming for us. I just told you that so you wouldn't freak. We needed to hold it together. Now, we should get back to the plane to see if we can—"

Hermes shot him in the stomach. Then he took two steps forward and kicked away the giant Magnum. Finally, he searched the writhing man's coat, removed the satellite phone, and pocketed it.

Irina stared at him wide-eyed, her gun up. It was shaking so hard that she would probably sign her name on him if she decided to fire. Or she could miss altogether.

"Don't worry," he said. "I've decided not to kill you."

"Why?"

"Because I think you had no choice in coming here and had no choice in telling the rest of us."

"And if I did?"

"I don't know. Did you?"

"No."

"I thought so." He turned away from her. She could shoot him if she wanted.

Irina lowered the gun. "So, what now?"

"This way."

He began to walk, ignoring the shouted swearing coming from Suzuki. Threats, insults, and promises of dire retribution—much of it anatomically questionable—weren't pressing when the man screaming them would bleed out within the next few hours unless someone took him to a hospital.

And Hermes wasn't in the mood for ambulance work.

"Well, we could try to call for help using this thing." He held up the phone. "But it might lead to some awkward questions... and I don't feel like spending the rest of my life in jail or running from the Yakuza."

"He wasn't Yakuza. He was working for Russia."

"And how is that better?"

"Point taken," she conceded. "And what other options do we have?"

"Only one, and that's if you're willing to risk something insane."

"How insane?"

"A three-hundred-kilometer walk along this coast to the Halley Station."

"You know how to get there?"

"I have the coordinates, and your boss' phone is hooked to a GPS system. We should be able to get food from the plane and tents from the ship." He looked at her earnestly. "But I'm going to be honest with you. We're probably not going to make it. Even with all the cold weather gear we brought with us, Antarctica is way too cold for human life. It's a six-day march, and God knows what the weather is going to do to us."

Irina held his gaze but then broke it abruptly. She chuckled. "You're so cute," she said.

"What?"

She laughed a bit more and then asked, "Have you ever heard of Yakutsk?"

"No."

"It's the coldest city in the world."

Comprehension dawned. "Let me guess. You're from Yakutsk."

Irina laughed harder. "I wish I was from Yakutsk. I'm from a little town called Eldikan a couple of hundred kilometers away. Our winters make Yakutsk look like the Caribbean."

"So I guess this will be a walk in the park for you."

"Yes. But don't worry. I'll take care of you." She smiled. "And I know a few ways to keep warm if the weather actually gets cold."

Redemption

"Damn, Neill, I don't think that there's the sheriff."

I had known for quite a while that it wasn't. The sheriff was a tough old codger, hard as nails if you tried to keep him from getting his cut, but he was no driver. It had to be Bert doing the driving, and that was bad news. He might only have gotten the deputy's job and the easy life that came with the badge because he was the sheriff's favorite nephew, but there was no question that he *could* drive.

Of course, if I'd mentioned that to Jed, he would have fidgeted. Besides, I could outrun anyone in this valley, even if the local cops had wised up and gotten flatheads under their hoods to chase us with.

At least that's what I thought. But the headlights on the brown car behind me were doing a pretty good job of keeping up. Were they actually getting closer?

"Don't worry 'bout it," I replied, slotting the box into third. I needed Jed to stay calm. "Just remember that this is a trick car. As soon as the road straightens a little, we'll leave him in the dust."

He sat back and shut up. He knew I was right. A four on the floor and the special camshaft would more than make up for the extra weight of the moonshine in the trunk, especially once the road ran straight. Just a few more curves and we'd make the highway—this section of the road was already out of the mountains and in the woods around the old dairy farm. We'd be out of here and on our way to Bristol in no time.

I checked the mirror, and damned if the thing wasn't right on my bumper. Well, the last couple of curves were a sharp right and a doozy of a left. I'd show ole Bert a thing or two.

I gunned the engine and felt the Ford leap under me. The dirt was loose here, but I could hold it, tail out, on the throttle. It was a fine line, of course, but I'd done it more than once, without even a scratched fender to show for it.

My lights, illegally bright, showed me the position of the curve by where the road twisted between the trees. I turned in, balanced the car in a slide and felt it take the perfect pitch.

Then I saw the water reflecting on the road. I tried to correct for the lack of grip, but it was already much too late for that. A tree appeared right ahead, moving at incredible speed, and the sound of breaking glass exploded around me for a tiny fraction of an instant.

***

Where was I?

I shook my head to clear it and found that it wouldn't quite move the way I wanted it to. At least nothing hurt.

There was something wrong with my eyesight, though. It was like looking through a tunnel. The crash must have scrambled my eyes. And it was daytime. It had been three in the morning just before I hit the tree. Had I been out? Maybe I was still trapped in the car, only dreaming I was awake.

But no, I was definitely awake. I was sitting in some kind of seat and, though it took me a moment, I quickly realized that what looked like hundreds of tubes around me were actually the inside of a car. I could hear a V-8, muffled by whatever they'd wrapped my head in, coming from in front of me, and the sound of quite a few more coming from all around.

I might not have a clue as to where I was, but my foot had no such problems; it moved of its own accord, blipping the throttle and pushing me forward, almost into the car ahead of mine.

I looked some more. The car in front was like nothing I'd ever seen before, squared off and low, like one of those fancy imports or something on the cover of a magazine about the future. Men from Mars might use something like that to cross through space. And the pink paint hurt just to look at it. Maybe I was in a circus?

No. Not a circus. A racetrack. The car ahead of me turned into the curve, and I saw that, apart from the garish paint, there was a huge number on the side. To my right, what I'd thought were painted walls were actually grandstands, filled with what must have been thousands—*tens* of thousands—of spectators.

I realized that I was at the back of a long row of cars—no, two rows, I realized as the nose of another vehicle appeared at my left—and we were in some deep-dished oval. It was as though the dirt track we'd hang out in on Saturday nights had grown into a monster.

The car in front accelerated and my foot moved again, rocketing me forward. The old moonshine jalopies never had this kind of horsepower.

But I couldn't enjoy the sense of speed. Why was my body moving on its own? Why were my hands controlling the wheel without my help? And why on Earth were they doing it so badly? Some of the lines the car took would have shamed even the old sheriff. No wonder cars passed on all sides.

When I tried to improve things, my body resisted. It wanted to do things its own way, while I wanted to pass the red car that had just gone by. I moved one way, my body moved the other, and my ride would probably have ended in disaster if the pink thing I'd seen earlier hadn't spun lazily into the infield coming out of one of the turns and tapped an inside wall.

Everyone slowed like they did in midgets after a wreck. I tried to move the steering wheel from one side to the other, to keep heat in the tires, when I heard a voice crackling in my ear.

"Pit in," it said. "Four and fuel."

I tried to look around and see who'd been talking, but my head didn't want to obey orders any more than my arms and feet, and besides, I was tied in too firmly. My mouth, of its own accord, replied, "All right, and gimme a half-turn of rear bar, it's pushing in three and four."

I had no idea what I'd just said and could do nothing but watch as the car came to a stop in a huge pit lane, where a bunch of big guys in black armed with tires, a jack, and a big fuel can attacked it. Hard as it was to believe, twenty seconds later they'd gotten the tires changed and the car sped back out onto the track.

Soon enough, the green came out—I saw it this time—and I found myself sawing at the wheel ineffectively as other drivers went by. Why had I suddenly forgotten everything I'd ever known about driving a car? After ten minutes, I wanted to take over and do it right so badly that it hurt.

Around one curve, the line the car was taking was so awful that I couldn't resist and put my entire strength of will into pushing it back online. My body resisted for a second, but then gave way, and we went through the corner at a decent speed.

What's going on? Who are you?

I jerked suddenly and almost put it into the wall. That voice had been *inside* my head. Not scratchy, like the radio—I wondered if it actually was a radio—but scared. One scared southern boy talking at me in my own mind.

Had I finally lost it? How did one answer to a voice in his mind? I thought at it: *I'm driving this thing. Unless you wanna be dead last before the next five laps are up, let me take over.*

What? How?

The voice shut up, but I found that my body gradually stopped resisting when I sent the car through the curves. Whatever, whoever, was in my head seemed to understand that we were going much faster this way, and as he stopped resisting, he began cheering every time we'd pass some other driver.

I fell into a groove and relaxed, and I had time to notice what the writing on the outside wall said: BRISTOL MOTOR SPEEDWAY. At least I was still in good old Tennessee. I wondered if any of the boys—especially Jed—were up there in the stands. Swell track like this one, I'd bet anything they wouldn't miss it. But when had they built the thing? Certainly hadn't been there this morning.

I had the ugly feeling that this might be the same Bristol, Tennessee I'd known back when I was running moonshine, but it wasn't the same day. There was something strange going on.

But there was also a race on, and that was something I couldn't ignore—partly because that was the way I was and partly because of something I couldn't define, pushing me on. Some of these guys were pretty good, but I could see that none of them had grown up on the dirt roads around this valley. There was nothing like driving on loose earth at eighty miles an hour in a heavy pig of a sedan to give you a feel for where the weight of the car was taking you. And this one might be powerful, but I could tell in every curve that it weighed as much as—if not more than—my old jalopy.

We—my partner, whoever he was, and I—clawed our way through the field. There was one driver left to pass as we entered the last five laps, and I could tell that this guy knew his way around the circuit. He skidded just the right amount of time and then caught it, pulling through the curves faster than anyone else except for me.

All of a sudden, he seemed to slide a bit more than normal and left the door open for me to pass him on the inside. I floored it and was through before he could react. I wondered what had happened; I'd been watching this guy drive for the last thirty laps, and this just wasn't like him.

But I wasn't going to worry about that right now. I had one lap to go, and the fellows on the radio were going wild, screaming their heads off at me through the link.

Three corners.

Two.

"Inside!" a voice called out over the link.

Coming out of the final curve, I suddenly saw a flash of blue half on the track and half on the grass, and then the world went around in circles. I think we hit the wall first, and then the rest of the field collected us. I found out then why I was so well tied in, and what the bars were for, because after getting smacked around for what seemed like forever, my body, with no help from me, began unbuckling the straps that held it in, and I couldn't feel any pain.

I was already fading. A feeling of anger swept through me, but it seemed to come from the very earth the track was built on—it certainly wasn't mine. All I knew was that my job was done and that I'd failed. For the second time in what seemed like a few hours, the world went dark.

***

But I learned from it. I learned that things weren't quite as gentlemanly in the new world as they'd been in mine. Even the old sheriff wouldn't have bumped me off like that. But I could give as well as take, and in the time since my first race, I've won more than I've lost.

I also learned that the track pulls me out of the ground—yes, I must have died against the tree that day—whenever there's a risk that some Yankee or some Californian is going to win the big race. This track owns me, or maybe it was built on my grave and I'm a part of it, but anyway, it can't bear the thought of an outsider, someone whose blood hasn't done its time in these mountains, winning on its surface. I've run more laps on this track than any man, alive or dead.

It always puts me inside a car on the back rows. A driver on a small team or a youngster doing his first race. Always someone that no one expects to win. And always a nice mountain boy from Georgia or Virginia or Tennessee.

And, like I said, we win more often than we lose.

So, listen to me, rookie. If you want to be anything in this sport, stop fighting the wheel and let me do the driving. We don't have a lot of time before the pace car pulls off, so make your decision quickly.

If we win, I won't ask for much. Take some of your winnings and buy a wreath. Find the access road to the circuit, the one that comes down from the mountain and cuts into the highway. They've paved it now, but those two nasty curves are still there, one left, one right.

Just leave the flowers under the big bent tree.

Aulus Fabius Ambustus

Leinth watched the sun, swollen and red, set behind the long-shadowed trees while polished ebony statues with jeweled eyes guarded the entrance to the temple at her back. Her temple.

While the temples of Uni faced east to greet the rising sun, and those of Tin were open on all four sides with a hole in the center of the roof to welcome the noonday sun, hers faced west. Hers was a temple of sunset.

The people feared her, making superstitious and useless signs against the furies of the underworld as she passed. The city of Tarchna itself had refused to allow the temple to be built inside the city limits; in exchange for the use of their workforce and their military protection, the elders had demanded that the temple be built in a woodland a day's ride northwest of the city. And it was the only temple to Mania and Mantus that the Rasna had allowed to be built.

All that had been four hundred years ago. Now, the Etruscan League of Twelve needed her. While they privately felt that the powers her order wielded were unholy and obscene, at least they were wise enough to understand that her gods, unlike those others who were so fond of the sun, actually *listened* to her. And they would, if it was within their sphere of influence, do her bidding. Only her gods could save the Etruscan people.

For a price, of course.

The League had come crawling to her. Or, more precisely, to Mania. They had come bearing sacrifices and praising the Lady's power. And the goddess, as was her habit for those willing to pay the bloody price, had responded.

Twelve dead nobles, young and firstborn all, lay in the cool damp catacombs of the temple, killed without ritual, simply put to the sword. The goddess of the underworld wasn't interested in showmanship. She was interested in numbers.

In exchange, Leinth had been instructed to aid the League in its scheme and had been granted the power to do so. Enormous power. Godly power. She hoped she would be able to face the price that she, also, would pay for this privilege.

But for now, all she could do was wait, impatient but powerless to make things happen faster. She was not waiting for the gods now, but for a man—a soldier. A noble of the lowest level but one without whom she could do nothing. And while he had the ability to feel the presence of a human spirit, she wasn't certain that he was gifted enough to do what was necessary.

So it could take months, months the League didn't think it had; the Romans could be ready to move at any time.

Sadly, there was no choice. All any of them could do was rely on the goddess and hope that her wisdom was not misguided. She continued to wait uneasily for any sign of his coming.

Near midnight, her patience was rewarded. Coming up the road from the city, she could clearly hear the jingling sound of a team of oxen drawing a cart, accompanied by the echoing clop of a horse's hooves. Thon was on his way.

Time passed with infuriating slowness as the cart made its way up the slight incline to the temple, but eventually, it arrived. Thon descended from his horse and bowed deeply, while the driver of the cart only stared at her sullenly, fingers obviously itching to perform some kind of warding gesture but too afraid to do it openly. It was one thing to defy the minions of Mania in broad daylight surrounded by townsfolk, and quite another to do so in the depth of night on the unholy doorstep of her temple.

"I'm not going in there," he told Thon, who glared at him.

"Fair enough. But help me unload."

The driver shrugged and hopped down off the cart, moving to the back and pulling the coarse covering sheet off the cargo bed. He climbed inside and pushed a sack-covered bulk onto the ground, where it fell with a dull thud. In the gloom, it wasn't possible to tell the color of the stains on the sack, but the shape and size of the contents would have identified it as a human body even if Leinth hadn't been expecting it. Another two sacks joined the first on the ground, and the driver grunted and drove off.

"That was the best driver you could get?" she asked him mockingly. "I hope your merchandise is better."

Her sarcasm was rewarded with a sour look.

"The only reason he came at all was that I got him to accept the job in front of ten witnesses after paying for his wine all night to get him drunk enough to accept. Everyone else simply stopped talking to me when I told them what was required."

"So, what have you got for me?" she asked him.

"A Roman patrol. One officer and a couple of foot soldiers. The enlisted men's spirits feel about how you expect from young men cut down in their prime, but I think there's something really special about the officer, something major keeping his soul from moving peacefully to the afterlife. He'll probably still be around in four or five days, but if you're planning on using one of the others, you'd better hurry," Thon said.

"Open them up."

He used his sword, a short infantryman's weapon, to open the nearest bag. Leinth observed the contents: a short, unshaven man with two broken-off arrows protruding from his chest. The remaining spirit-force was weak but usable, the body itself fresh. She gestured to the other two bags.

Thon opened the second, and Leinth knew immediately that the third would be unnecessary. A battered breastplate indicated that this man, darker-skinned and also unshaven, was the officer. But what truly took her breath away was the feeling that his soul was still strongly present. Not inside the body perhaps, but certainly not far away. Nowhere near crossing into the underworld, in any case.

Now she had to choose. While the officer would certainly be better for her plan, it could be dangerous to interfere in something as powerful as that which was holding his spirit on this plane. Such a force could make the undead *willful*.

On the other hand, only a strong sense of unfinished business could hold the spirit in this way. If she could identify the cause, it would give her leverage—a carrot. Willing undead were always more effective than unwilling ones. And, she thought, shrugging to herself, if that didn't work, the stick was always effective.

"This one," she told Thon, prodding the dead officer with her toe.

"Are you certain?"

"It will be easier with him." It was a lie, but he would accept it, believing that the goddess would exact a smaller price from the priestess. He wasn't aware that, to the goddess of the underworld, the distance of the spirit from the body is of no consequence. The price was the same for all spirits save those who had crossed the dark river. Those could never be called back.

She would bear the price. The Etruscan people and gods demanded it of her. Could she be less than the nobles who had sacrificed their firstborn? Never.

But her price, like her power, would be greater.

***

Despite the grandeur of the temple, the deepest recesses of which, in the flickering torchlight, looked haunted by myriad evil spirits, the ceremony itself was simple.

The soldier's lifeless body had been laid on the slab, and the arrow removed from its neck. There could be no metal in contact with the body, so, for safety, all his clothing had been removed. He looked gray even in the ruddy torchlight, prompting Leinth to think that, while he might be an effective tool, he would never be a pretty one.

The rest of the ceremony depended on her. As Thon and her acolytes watched silently from the shadows, she removed her robe and mounted the corpse on the slab, her pelvis above the shriveled, dead genitalia. Invoking Mania, she told the goddess what was needed.

The answer came from Mantus, Mania's husband and god of the underworld. The dead flesh beneath her became hard and virile. This revival lasted only for an instant, but went deep inside her, with a sharp but blessedly short stab of pain.

She climbed from the Roman officer and recovered her robe, fighting to keep her composure. This was her price. The seed of the dead body was even now racing towards its destination, guided and sped by a god's power. It would fertilize her, and, as soon as it did, two things would happen. The first was that the baby inside her would grow and develop, perfectly healthy, allowing her to feel the life blossoming inside her. But that same healthy baby would be stillborn.

The second was that the Roman soldier on the altar would, in a way, regain his life. Not a full life, of course. He would have the life of the undead: cold, painful, unsatisfying. But the gods would be unable to reap his spirit.

A soul for a soul. That was her bargain.

The gathered Etruscans waited in silence, but this lasted only a few moments. Then the carcass on the slab tried to move its arm, and Leinth knew that she was pregnant.

***

Thon Velathri had marched with men from many stations in life. During campaigns against the northern barbarians, he had fought alongside farmers and blacksmiths, sharing their food and wine, sometimes even sharing his own fur-lined cloak with a less fortunate comrade-at-arms whose clothing was insufficient protection against the cold mountain air even in spring. But he had always drawn the line at marching alongside the dead.

He wasn't stupid. As a military man, he could easily appreciate the value of a wall of shock troops that were nearly unstoppable, and who advanced until their physical bodies had been hacked so badly to pieces as to prevent movement of any kind. It was, after all, better to waste soldiers who were already dead, while keeping the regular troops behind. If they were slow, they made up for it by being implacable.

But it had always seemed wrong to him, somehow. Dirty. Unholy. And now that he knew the price that was paid by Mania's witches, he had to suppress a shudder each time he looked at the Roman soldier lurching beside his horse.

He had to remind himself that he was doing this for the Rasna, the Etruscan people. But in his mind, he did it for his twelve dead cousins and friends, which only luck, skill in Latin, and the fact that the Romans knew his face had prevented him from joining them in death. He knew that otherwise, he would have been the ideal sacrifice.

So he had no choice, other than to stay upwind of the undead and watch him. The monster was not able to talk, and his walk was still jerky, but, slowly, the imprisoned spirit was learning to control once again the body it had inhabited.

The witch had informed Thon that the undead would be in constant pain at first because the only way she could make it move and keep it under control in the initial stages of reanimation was what Leinth called "the stick." She had explained that the pain was inflicted directly on the soldier's spirit, causing an agony more acute than mere mortals could imagine.

The monster moaned as it walked. Leinth rode up beside it.

"If you understand me, lift one arm," she said. The undead soldier started but just kept walking forward.

"Roman," said Leinth, "I can make the pain stop. But you must do as I say. Lift an arm."

The soldier advanced toward her horse. It had come to within an arm's length when it emitted a louder, agonized moan and stopped suddenly.

"Or I can make the pain much, much worse. Now lift an arm."

The dead man obeyed and was immediately rewarded. The moaning quieted and the corpse looked at the witch in wonder, the expression eloquent despite the difficulty it was obviously having in controlling its facial movements.

And then the moaning resumed.

Leinth spoke to him. "When you can talk, inform me. Maybe we can come to an agreement, and you won't have to suffer constantly. Now walk." She rode forward again.

***

By nightfall, the Roman had already started to form words. It was simply amazing. Leinth had never seen a spirit so closely linked to its body, with such determination to live. A young officer, probably of the low nobility, could have many reasons for wanting to live, even in this diminished state, but the strength of the spirit made Leinth suspect that a young woman would be involved in this particular case. That was good; she should be able to easily use it to her advantage.

She signaled a stop for the night, and Thon began setting up camp. The Roman, as she knew he would, walked up to her. He stood there for some moments moaning unintelligibly before finally managing to master his vocal chords and slur a single word.

"Aulus," he said.

She waited, saying nothing, knowing that this would be a painstaking process, but a crucial one. The undead Roman, however, seemed to draw strength from that single word. Spurred on by his success, he beat his chest.

"Aulus," he repeated, this time beating his chest.

"Your name is Aulus," said Leinth, receiving a triumphant nod from the Roman in agreement.

"Aulus Fabius Ambustus."

She nodded and began the negotiations. She asked him about his childhood, his military service, his life in general. This was partly to learn more about him—he might be dead, but his personality and values remained in his spirit—but mainly to give him time to learn to control his vocal cords. The wight was having to relearn movements that it had taken for granted all its life, and it was crucially important to her that he be perfectly intelligible when she started asking questions that really mattered. That was the only way to ensure that she would not miss any signs that might allow her to control this monster without resorting to punishment. The willing tool was always the finer instrument.

Soon, incredibly soon, the conversation was flowing, almost normal. Only a slight rasping hoarseness indicated that her companion was in any way dead. The gloom hid the pallor of his face.

Thon, however, wanted no part of this exchange. Ostensibly checking the horses and establishing a defensive perimeter, she noted that he stayed upwind of them at all times. She sighed. It was ridiculous of him. The undead weren't truly dead, and the body, including its defenses, was functioning, in a way. Aulus wouldn't start to smell for ten or twelve days, and visible decay would take nearly four moons.

She finally felt that the conversation could be steered to truly important issues.

"A young, dashing soldier like yourself surely has a woman back home?" she asked him.

The effect on Aulus was immediate and violent. He groaned loudly, a truly sepulchral sound, and writhed. Only the iron hold that Leinth established on his spirit kept him from thrashing uncontrollably.

Interesting, she thought, *there is unfinished business here.*

"You love her." It wasn't a question.

"I loved her." How quickly the dead learned to think in the past tense.

"It is within my power to return her to you. You can be together always."

He thought about this for a few moments.

"I can never be with her now, and we have never been together. We were married, but that is all."

So, a typical story. A soldier marries the girl he loves, but then, on his very next posting, he's killed, having never enjoyed the life of a husband. Sad, but typical.

"I can give you back the time that was taken from you," she said, but Aulus indicated his reluctance to continue the conversation by moving off into the woods.

He was soon replaced by Thon.

"Can you trust it to go off by itself?" he asked.

"Him. His name is Aulus. And yes, I have him firmly under my control. He just needs time to wrap his imagination around an offer I just made him."

"I still don't understand why you had me kill him just to bring him back to life. There are plenty of Roman raiders and scouts on our land these days. Surely one of them would have taken a bribe. We don't need this ghoul." He didn't mention the price that had been paid, knowing that it would never be far from her thoughts.

"For what we are going to do, we need complete control. And we need someone who will not be stopped easily by arrow or sword unless the number set against him is huge," she said.

"There are assassins who could do it."

"It's too late for assassins. The Romans are certain of their civilization, even though they control only a section south of their city. They have grown arrogant since they overthrew the Tarchinian kings. In order to crush their spirit, we must divide them. As many tribunes as possible must be killed in cold blood by another Roman. A Roman who will be carrying a very political letter explaining his actions. Only that will divide them sufficiently to allow Etruria and the Rasna to retake a city that, by rights, custom, and tradition, is ours." Leinth felt herself growing passionate. Yes, she remembered the terrible price, but she would pay that and more to ensure the survival of her people, her temple, her city, and, above all, her goddess.

So, keeping the Roman far from them through the iron application of her will, she began to dictate Aulus's letter to the Roman people, which Thon dutifully translated and wrote down.

"I, Aulus Fabius Ambustus, citizen and soldier of Rome,

denounce..."

***

They walked their horses for two days after that, Thon staying out ahead, Aulus walking beside Leinth's horse and occasionally talking to her. Little by little, Leinth felt that she was managing to convince him to accept her offer. Though she was surprised at how skeptical and sometimes even violent he became when she mentioned his wife, she refused to back down and had gotten to the point where at least she could talk without sending him into a paroxysm of incoherent, animal groaning.

She supposed this reaction was natural enough. How would she feel, she wondered, if she received a similar offer? Would she allow a practitioner of the dark arts to do their work on someone she loved? Or would she, too, scream in rage?

But it still presented her with a problem. The assassination would be realized with a lot less risk if she could only get Aulus to cooperate. Otherwise, she would have to fight him all the way. There was no doubt that she would win since the power she had over him was irresistible to any soul, but a hesitation at the wrong moment could ruin everything. And the price had already been paid.

A shout from Thon caused her to look up. Five horses blocked the road fifty paces ahead, their riders beside them, reins in hand.

"Brigands," spat Thon. The uneasy political situation between Rome and the Etruscan league of twelve cities ever since the Romans had overthrown the Tarchinian kings had caused the Etruscan armies to be moved south, near the border, leaving much of the countryside unpatrolled.

Seeing that Thon was about to draw his sword for a mad charge at the men, she placed a hand on his arm.

"Wait," she said. Then, turning to Aulus, "Kill them."

Aulus advanced slowly. To the brigands he must hardly have seemed a threatening figure; his cloak hid his pallor, and his movements were nearly normal.

When he reached the nearest man, the rest of them came in all at once, surrounding the undead Roman with murderous intent. One pulled a short sword similar to Thon's, but by then, it was too late. Aulus reached out with both hands and took a surprised outlaw by the neck in each. Even from fifty paces away, Leinth heard a snap and a crunch, and both men collapsed.

The rest renewed their attack, shouting angrily and swarming over the undead Roman. The man with the sword thrust, driving the steel deep into Aulus's abdomen—deep enough that it caught on bone, and he was unable to pull it out. Aulus turned on him, releasing his grip on another man who was no longer struggling, calmly gripped the swordman's arm and pulled him toward his body. The cloak slipped off Aulus's head, revealing the dead features beneath, and the man screamed, struggling to get free, beating his free hand into Aulus's face.

The wight simply pulled him even closer and bit into his neck. The screams and struggle continued, and then only the struggle, and then limpness.

The final would-be thief had long since mounted a horse and ridden off.

Leinth spurred her mount into a gallop, arriving at the Roman's side in seconds.

"Spit it out!" she screamed. Aulus looked at her in confusion and convulsed suddenly as she sent all the pain at her command into him. "Spit!"

A gob of bloody flesh fell from the wight's mouth, dribbling down the front of his robe.

"Good. Now wash out your mouth with this." She handed him a wineskin and turned to Thon. "Once they feed on human flesh, they are impossible to control. If you ever see him feeding, you must immediately cut off his head. It won't kill him, but it will confuse him enough that you can hack him to pieces at your leisure. Now pull that sword out of his body."

When the task was done, she walked to the Roman.

"Aulus, you did well. Any woman would want to stand by someone as powerful as you are now. I can make her love you."

"Quinta loves only beautiful things, and I am not beautiful now," said Aulus, and then, under his breath, "I was never beautiful."

Leinth only heard him because she was attuned to his spirit, but her hopes sank with that declaration.

And then he surprised her.

"I know what you want, and I will do it, on one condition: you must allow me to say farewell to my beloved, and to my blood brother, Lucius Cassius Sula."

"Done," said Leinth.

***

Rome.

The upstart city. Founded and peopled by Latins, it was an Etruscan city in all but race. Yet they had rebelled against their mentors and thrown off their rightful vassalage. Leinth could see the fruit of that rebellion even in their architecture. Traditional wooden or light brick construction was beginning to give way to stone structures along many of Rome's boulevards. A confident, vibrant pulse could be felt as she walked those streets. Here was a people who believed that their greatness lay ahead.

But they were not there yet. How many city-states had believed themselves destined to become the next imperial power, only to topple in the course of two or three battles? The Romans might be a strong military and political force, but they controlled only the center of the peninsula, surrounded by Greek cities to the south and the Etruscan League to the north.

Rome was at a balance point. Greatness and oblivion were both equally possible; a single nudge could determine their future.

Leinth had come to ensure that the nudge went in the direction most beneficial to Etruria.

A little bit of powder on Aulus's face had disguised his condition sufficiently to pass casual scrutiny, and the fact that he was once more dressed in his uniform and breastplate did the rest. The frequent patrols simply let them through, sometimes saluting the Roman officer in their midst.

Thon had secured quarters in the merchant's sector, near the marketplace: a low, squat building in baked brick with a small courtyard containing a pool in its center. Now, all they had to do was get close enough to members of the plebian tribunes to kill as many as possible. They often passed through the marketplace on tours of inspection, so that part, at least, should be simple enough. There would be guards, but not expecting trouble, and Aulus could easily deal with a few guards.

The wight, however, had become difficult. Despite renewing his pledge to her that he would do as she wished, he was often up in the middle of the night, roaming the dark streets. Through her bond to his spirit, she could feel what he was doing—just walking around and speaking to no one—and it represented a risk. Should he be discovered, all would be lost. But as long as he did nothing more than walk, she decided not to stop him. Their agreement was too valuable for her to risk.

What she did do, however, was to place Thon at the door to Quinta's house. Aulus's lady love would have to be carefully watched if they were to be reunited for his farewell. She also wanted Thon to make certain that Aulus did not approach the house, an added measure of security despite her certainty that the undead could be controlled, because that could *really* ruin everything.

This routine went on night after night, save one. On that night, Leinth woke in a cold sweat. *Something's wrong.* In her just-woken state, it took her a moment to realize what it was.

She couldn't feel Aulus. The bond that connected her to his spirit was absent; she didn't know where he was, what he was doing.

Icy terror gripped her. If the Romans had destroyed the wight, it wouldn't take them long to find the Etruscan priestess who had created it. Their own priests were not without skills, for all that their gods were still trying to consolidate their earthly power. She would be found before dawn and killed before sunset. If she was lucky.

Quickly, she began to put a small bundle of clothes together. Flight would probably be useless, the brigand-infested roads suicide—or worse—for a lone woman, but she had to try.

As she was reaching the door, however, her execution was deferred. The bond to Aulus suddenly reestablished itself. She could feel him walking slowly and peacefully back to the merchant quarter.

What had happened? She was too far from her temple to consult her goddess, and she was certain that Aulus would not be able to tell her. Had he gone too far afield? She didn't know the answer, but it seemed that everything would be all right, after all.

She collapsed on her bed, drained by the ordeal. Only by the strongest control did she manage to avoid shredding Aulus's soul with one savage burst of power.

Unable to sleep for the rest of the night, she paced, and accosted Thon when he arrived.

"Did you see Aulus near Quinta's house tonight?" The woman

lived far from where the undead had reappeared to her senses, but she had to ask.

"No," he replied. "Nobody went near the house save for our monster's blood brother, Cassius. He went in after sundown and was just leaving as I started back." He leered. "Strange customs these Romans have, taking care of their blood brothers' wives for them. I don't think the messengers should have arrived with news of his death yet, do you?"

Leinth considered this development and decided it didn't matter. In fact, it would make finding Cassius so that Aulus could say farewell much easier, as long as the wight didn't find out. But on no account would she allow Aulus out the next night, since that would, if everything went according to plan, be the last night before the assassination.

She went off to explain this to Aulus.

***

The marketplace was wide but crowded with stalls, smells, and bustling merchants. The tribunals would not be arriving for a few hours more to inspect incoming Greek merchandise and measure the mood of the people. So Leinth waited with Aulus for the arrival of Quinta and Cassius who were being brought by Thon under the pretense of selling a shipment of Etruscan wine for her cellars. Having Thon and his Roman connections along was finally proving to be worth the aggravation.

Aulus seemed unusually animated that morning. He paced, he moaned softly. Eventually, Leinth was forced to exercise her control, lest he attract unwanted attention, even hooded as he was.

Nevertheless, she could still feel the agitation in his soul. Everything he was still capable of desiring was coming to him. In a few minutes, his spirit would be at peace. He would not be able to rest, of course, not for a long, long time. But at least his existence would be somewhat easier.

Thon arrived leading a man and a woman, presumably Quinta and Cassius.

Quinta was young, younger than Leinth had expected, dark-haired and ordinary looking, although her large, expressive brown eyes made her face almost pretty. Cassius, on the other hand, was beautiful. Not in a muscular, rugged, manly way, but a delicate, almost girl-like beauty. Shoulder-length light brown hair framed a face that would have been angelic were it not for the slightly cruel shape of the mouth.

Both of them looked suspicious as Thon led them to Leinth, immediately recognizing that she wasn't a wine merchant. Furthermore, they didn't seem happy about the cloaked figure beside her.

Leinth smiled at them, trying to put them at their ease. One thing she couldn't afford was for them to make a scene, especially considering that two priests of Jupiter, easily identified by the medallions worn over their brown robes, were wandering the marketplace nearby. They seemed to be minding their own business, but if Aulus was revealed, he would instantly *become* their business.

"Greetings," said Leinth, "I have come to bring you peace, news of a loved one."

"What is the meaning of this?" asked Cassius, suspicion turning to anger, making him rather less pretty in her eyes.

"This is," spoke Aulus. He removed his hood before Leinth could react, revealing his face in all its horror—pale, bloodless, and unmistakably dead. Only the fact that they were in a passageway between stalls and that Quinta and Cassius stood directly in front of him kept the crowd in the marketplace from seeing the wight.

Cassius paled, his already creamy features turning an almost unnatural white. Quinta gasped.

"But... You're dead!" she cried, reeling. Cassius had to steady her.

"Yes," said Aulus. "But what surprises me is that you knew of it so quickly. Or perhaps it shouldn't surprise me. Was it not your father who sent me on that suicide mission into the heart of Etruria? Was it not because you begged him to do so? All so that you could continue to bed my blood brother?"

"No, it wasn't like that..." Quinta tried to back away, but Aulus was quicker. He grabbed her arm with a lightning motion and pulled her close, ignoring her protests.

"Wasn't it, my dear? Did you not slip off with him the very night of our wedding? At the very feast in our honor? Did you think I was too drunk to notice? Or were you too drunk to care, knowing that I would be sent off to my death in a few days anyway? I followed, and I watched, and from that moment, I lived only for revenge. As you can see, death hasn't stopped me."

Acting too quickly for an astonished Leinth to react, he pulled her even closer, kissed her lips, and bit down hard. Blood poured from her mouth, and she screamed. Then, moving his mouth down to her neck, he bit down once more and pulled, tearing free an enormous chunk of her flesh. He chewed and swallowed as he watched her sink to her knees, uselessly trying to staunch the pulsing, squirting blood with her fingers. A look of stupid incomprehension marred her features, and she finally fell, slowly, forward into the packed dirt floor.

Cassius reacted, pulled out a dagger and attacked the wight with a cry, ramming it through his torso and out the back of his tunic.

But Aulus, ignoring the blade, simply took hold of Cassius's arm and bent it back at the elbow until it broke with a sickening snap. He grasped Cassius's head and looked him in the wide, panicked eyes.

"I loved you both," he said, "but you were my blood brother. From you, I expected more. The gods will not be merciful." So saying, he twisted Cassius's head until the pretty face was looking straight backward, and then dropped the body to the floor.

The violence was over a few moments after it had begun, and Leinth had been powerless to stop it. Something had interfered with her control of the wight. Now it was too late. Aulus had fed on human flesh, and that would be its only driving force from now on. It was now truly an uncontrollable monster, the hunger stronger than any pain she could inflict.

She turned to run and immediately knew that all was lost. Thon lay in a crumpled heap some distance down the corridor, a spear buried in his side. He was alive but badly hurt. The two priests of Jupiter blocked her way, ten Roman soldiers behind them.

"Hello, witch," one of them said to her in Rasna, the language of the Etruscans.

Leinth was about to protest that she wasn't a witch, that the undead monstrosity had been keeping her hostage, but knew it would be useless. They knew.

She turned to Aulus.

"The night before last, when I lost the link with your spirit, you were in the temple of Jupiter. That's why I couldn't feel anything. It was you. You betrayed us. You're no better than they are." She kicked Cassius's body.

"Oh, but I am much better. I took an oath to serve Rome, and I did so to my dying day and beyond. The opportunity to kill these two was simply the gods' way of repaying my faithful service."

"Be that as it may, your punishment will be much worse. You will inhabit that body even after it is dust. Forever. Until the gods of Etruria lose all their power," she told him, sending as much pain into his spirit as she could. Tearing, twisting, *torturing*.

"Once more, it is you who is mistaken. My pain will only last until your gods realize that the promised price will not be paid after all. It is you who will continue to inhabit that body until the gods of Rome are dust. And I think that will be a long time in coming."

Tearing open her robe, he punched her naked stomach, very, very hard. And as she doubled over from the blow, she felt him open his hand and *push* his fingers into her abdomen, felt the skin sinking, sinking, and finally tearing. Felt the agony of his fingers in her womb, fist closing about the embryonic child, and the hand pulling back, taking pieces of her insides with it.

On her side on the floor, she heard only the priests invoking Jupiter, trapping her spirit with their power. She saw only her blood, turning the floor into black mud. She thought only that her life was flowing onto the floor, and she knew that she would be dead in moments.

But the reason she screamed, through the pain and the ever-growing weakness, was that she also knew that she would be awake again a few hours later.

Awake, but not alive.

Shadow of the Ape

For a moment, Verstappen found himself believing that, just maybe, Conrad had been right about the place. Night seemed darker here than anywhere the Belgian freighter captain had ever been, despite the life he could feel buzzing and flittering just beyond the reach of the electric lights. The illumination was weak, as if it knew it didn't belong.

The *Étoile Ostend* didn't belong there either. If it had been entirely up to its captain, the ship would have left Verstappen and his men to fend for themselves in the jungles of the Congo—or was that Zaire now? Mugabe's soldiers would have little doubt about what to do with a group of white men unaligned with any of the major power blocs.

The captain's attitude was understandable. The cargo hold was almost completely laden with copper from the inland mines—the supposed reason for their trip—and a container full of chemical drums lifted out of South Africa just before a UN inspection, which were to be dumped in the middle of the ocean for a tidy profit. But the money would only be paid if they managed the operation unobserved. If they left now, all of them could retire wealthy men, but if the American or Belgian special force troops that seemed to be so prevalent since about 1965 or so spotted them, they would likely spend the rest of their penniless lives in prison.

What the captain didn't know was that the final piece of cargo had a price tag that made the South African money seem like pocket change. If he'd known that, he wouldn't have been so anxious to leave—but he would certainly have demanded a cut.

Finally, the truck, a twenty-year-old Saab, turned onto the potholed loading dock, right under the only functioning crane in the entire port of Matadi. Thierry, the driver, climbed out of the cab and made a beeline for Verstappen.

"I swear, if we hadn't been through three wars together, I'd beat you to a pulp."

Verstappen grinned. "Tough trip?"

"I can't believe they call these things roads. Even the paved parts look like they've been bombed."

A shrug. "They probably have. How is the cargo?"

"It woke up a few hours ago. Dented the container." Thierry pointed to a massive bulge on the side of the ribbed box. "We just opened a hatch and hit it with elephant tranquilizers until it shut up. If it's dead, it's dead."

"Unlikely."

"Yeah, I heard. The chief made me pay a huge blood price. He says he lost half his village squeezing that thing into the container."

"It's peanuts, Thierry. We'll be rich men when we get back to Brussels. But I'm still amazed that they managed to get it in at all."

"It's a pretty tough squeeze, but anything much bigger than a forty-foot container was going to look suspicious when we unloaded. We made it a little wider and a little longer. Let's just hope no one measures the thing."

"We'll worry about that when we get there. Just get it loaded. The sooner I get out of the Congo, the happier I'll be."

***

Carolina checked her phone and smiled: a dancing iguana figure with tropical music blaring told her who the message was from with no room for doubt. Felipe might be unreliable and capricious, but she was totally worth it, especially in bed. And the fact that he'd actually come all the way down to Tapera to see her—a bit of a hitchhike from the center of Florianopolis—meant that she'd actually managed to get far enough through his armor to avoid becoming the latest in his series of one-night tourist girls.

She walked across the road, removed her sandals, and felt the sand on her feet. The guy at the caipi bar smiled at her hopefully. "Later," she told him in Spanish—he was actually from Uruguay, she'd learned—and kept walking. A single dark-skinned man was sunning himself, clad only in a *zunga*, about fifty meters down the beach. She knew that body.

"Hi."

He smiled up at her, dazzling white teeth nearly blinding in the sunlight. “Hello, there *garotinha*. I didn’t think you’d be here so quickly.”

They both knew that was a lie, but Carolina ignored it and sat down beside him, enjoying the caress of the warm sand on her buttocks. “And I didn’t think you’d be up so early. When I left, I wasn’t sure whether you were alive or dead.”

He shrugged, barely moving on the sand. “I’m used to not getting much sleep. It’s kind of par for the course.”

“What’s that?”

“Can I look later?”

“No, look now!”

He grumbled a bit but moved. “I have no idea.” He made to lie down again, but she stopped him.

“Is it a tsunami?”

“We don’t get tsunamis in Brazil,” he replied laconically. “Wrong sort of climate for it.”

She counted to three, reminding herself that, if she wanted intelligent conversation, she shouldn’t look for it from surf bums. “Look, there’s a huge lump of something dark over there. It might be a wave.” Ever since the southeast Asian tsunami, she’d been anxious about giant swells.

“Not a wave. A wave would take up the whole horizon. Looks more like some kind of tall boar.”

She stared out onto the bay, trying to make out further details. “Gray and green? And shaped like that?”

He shrugged. “If it’s coming this way, we’ll find out what it is. Relax a little.” He reached out a hand and caressed the inside of her thigh.

She decided that the ship, or whatever it was wasn’t so important after all and bent over, pretending to kiss Felipe’s forehead with a move that pushed his hand into a more favorable position.

***

Verstappen wasn’t happy with the delay. They could have dumped the South African chemicals the day before, but the captain hadn’t wanted to do it. He’d said that the only other craft on the water, a fishing boat under Angolan registration, was probably a

Soviet spy boat in disguise.

Verstappen had responded that the Soviets couldn't care less if a Belgian ship dumped a load of South African chemicals, but the man had refused to see reason and had sailed deeper into international waters. It hadn't made anyone happy, especially since the most precious container on board was perched precariously on top of two others, right at the summit of the pile of metal shipping boxes.

When the storm hit, the Belgian went below in disgust, while the captain began the procedure to unload and sink thousands of yellow drums, some marked with biohazard warnings, others with radioactivity labels, and all with large, stenciled DANGER signs. And though it wasn't the first operation of this kind they'd put together for some government or other, it was always nice when the evidence was safely at the bottom of the sea. It made for much more relaxed cruising.

He'd just closed the door that separated his smallish cabin from the rest of the ship when he heard a clatter from above, as if some of the drums had gotten away from the crane operator. Verstappen smiled. If the pompous bastard of a captain had splattered his ship with radioactive tailings, it was going to be fun watching him try to get through a Geiger check on his next port of call. The Cold War seemed to be making everyone paranoid—and the seventies were probably going to be the worst decade yet. They'd certainly started off badly enough.

Footsteps on metal alerted him to someone's approach, and Thierry poked his head in without bothering to knock. "You need to come quickly, boss," the soldier-*cum*-driver said. Another crash sounded overhead.

Verstappen didn't waste time arguing. He'd chosen his men well, trained them better. If they said he had to come, then he had to come. They ran along the passage and up to the deck.

The expected scene—drums of chemicals rolling over the container deck—was absent. Instead, Verstappen found the crew desperately trying to curb the movement of a single oversized container: the container holding the ape.

The enormous gorilla-like creature they'd tracked and captured had somehow managed to push a leg through the corrugated steel of the container, forcing one of the door hinges—hinges that were as thick as a man's leg—to break free. The creature's free leg was pushing the container across the planking on the deck, straight toward the crane. More ominous, though, was the fact that the movements weren't designed to move the container; the ape was trying to get its arms free. That was unacceptable.

"Quick, bring the tranquilizers!" Verstappen shouted. Thierry ran off to get the gun crew, and Verstappen joined the captain, watching helplessly as a team armed with poles tried to immobilize the container. They seemed like flies trying to maneuver an elephant. Every once in a while they spilled across the deck as an unexpected lurch threw them off their feet.

A single fist, almost as tall as a man, suddenly shot out of the box and flattened a pole-bearer against a bulkhead with a sickening crunch. As the man—instantly turned to jelly—slid slowly down the wall, the rest of the sailors fled.

It was just as well that they did. With a deafening roar, the fifty-foot ape inside the container flexed its muscles and tore the container to shreds like a horrendous black chicken hatching from a rectangular egg. A scrap of discarded metal flew over the captain's head and broke the forward window on the bridge tower.

"Where's that gun?" Verstappen screamed.

Small arms fire erupted from the deck—someone, it seemed, had managed to locate a gun or two. Verstappen wanted to tell them to stop, that they would only succeed in enraging the beast, but remained silent. Their gnat stings would serve to distract the thing, and it would concentrate on the immediate irritants while his own team prepped the tranquilizer gun. And who knew, maybe they would get lucky and hit something vital.

Thierry arrived with Jan, the chemist. "What dose do we need?"

Verstappen sneered. "What do you think?"

"I'll give it everything we have." Jan set to work on loading the glass cartridge, full of a viscous yellowish liquid, into the wide barrel of the modified elephant gun.

Some reflection must have given them away, because suddenly, the huge ape turned toward them. It took less than two huge strides—maybe three seconds—for the creature to reach them.

"Shoot it! Shoot it!" Verstappen cried as a huge hand descended onto them from high above. Jan fumbled once, twice with the unwieldy firearm before managing to press the trigger. It was the second fumble that killed them all since that was the one that ensured they were flattened before the dart left the muzzle. It was a pity, actually, since Jan made a beautiful shot, managing to embed the dart in a blood vessel just outside the ape's right eye socket.

But, though he was dead, Verstappen missed little that would have interested him. The captain watched with satisfaction as the drugged ape fell overboard, to sink to the bottom of the cold, dark sea. He ordered the crew to keep dumping barrels into the ocean, few knowing that the barrels were landing on the unconscious ape, soon to be drowned. Then he had the bodies thrown off the ship.

Then the *Étoile Ostend* sailed off to disappear into the murk of Cold War recordkeeping, never to be heard from again. The barrels, meanwhile, were breaking under the pressure of the fathoms.

***

"No, no!" Felipe shouted. "This way!"

Again, Carolina shook her head. The guy was trying to lead her into a structure that seemed to be made of straw and thin sticks. That... thing... would tear it away like so much paper. She ran into the cylindrical concrete structure in front of them. Felipe, cursing, followed her through the dark opening.

The first thing that hit her was the smell, as though a mammoth had died in an open sewer. "What is this place?" she whispered.

Felipe looked around, illuminated by the sunlight from the outside, and shrugged. "Utility of some kind. Probably a pumping station."

"So that's why it smells? This is connected to the sewer?"

Felipe, despite his obvious fear, laughed. "No, that is the smell of the *Sem Terras*. They sleep in here."

The *Sem Terras*. As far as she knew, they were a political movement, but most Brazilians seemed to hold them in contempt, as though they were leeches on an otherwise productive social system. Carolina had her doubts—but this certainly wasn't the time or place to express them. "What is that thing?"

He shrugged again, making her remember again that she'd selected him more for the shape of his pecs and the washboard beneath them than for his mind. "Some kind of sea monster. First time I've seen it."

"It didn't look like a sea monster. It looked like something from land, something that shouldn't have been in the water at all. And it looked like it had pieces falling off."

He shrugged and said nothing.

"I'm going to have a look." Carolina walked toward the rectangle of blinding light that marked the entrance, blinked a couple of times, and then stared. The thing approaching had to be fifteen meters high, vaguely humanoid, with slimy greenish-gray skin on which small, matted clumps of fur seemed to be barely hanging on.

Felipe had come up behind her. "It's a gigantic monkey," he said. "And it smells terrible!"

The creature was tearing up the beach bar that Felipe had wanted to hide inside. The screams that had been coming from that direction died down after one of its blows landed with a particularly sickening crunch.

"That's the smell from the sewage," Carolina said.

"No way. Look, we're downwind from the thing. It's the monster's smell."

Trust a surf bum to know precisely where the wind is coming from, she thought. But the guy was right. The smell—worse than the stink from inside the concrete bunker—was definitely coming from... well, from whatever it was. The stench was completely out of place on that beach, which should have smelled of cool breezes and coconut-scented tanning lotion.

"It sees us!" Felipe ran back into the darkness of the cylindrical building.

Carolina hesitated for a second, thinking that she had plenty of time, and also that a round structure with no back door might not be the best place to avoid a charging monster.

The hesitation almost cost her life.

Moving amazingly quickly for something so big, the creature took two strides and, in the same motion, drove its gigantic fist toward the doorway. Carolina jumped back just far enough to avoid being crushed, but not quite far enough to avoid the spray of noxious slime that sluiced out of one of the fingers. She ran back toward the opposite end of the building and, forgetting for a second that Felipe was nothing but a bit of fluff, she grabbed hold of him for dear life.

The monster, the giant, the monkey, whatever it was that pursued them, began to attack the small utility building. The walls shook and dust fell in clouds from the ceiling, but the builders of the building had apparently decided that the integrity of the sewage inside was paramount and had designed the bunker to be able to withstand anything thrown at it. A mere overgrown monster wouldn't faze it.

"You need to go out there!" Felipe shouted.

She pushed him away. "What? Are you out of your fucking mind?"

"No, really. You know how it is! These huge monsters are always weak where women are concerned. Especially beautiful women. As soon as he sees you, he'll become as tame as a puppy."

His charm was nearly enough to make Carolina smile, but he was as dumb as a brick. He probably didn't have much experience with puppies, either. "He already saw me. Don't you remember? It was just before he tried to flatten me."

"Maybe he didn't see you well. You were standing in the shadows."

"I'm not going out there, and that's final."

The building had stopped shaking, but they could still see the monster's shadow cutting off the bright light from outside. A huge eye, bloodshot and gray, suddenly filled the hole, followed almost instantly by a huge hand that squeezed through the opening and groped around, trying to catch them, to squeeze the life out of them. Carolina screamed, knowing it was a stupid thing to do, and still completely unable to make herself stop. At least she could take some comfort in the fact that, right beside her, Felipe was screaming in counterpoint.

They'd pressed themselves back as far as they could go, unconcerned about what the pool of foul-smelling liquid they were lying in might be. Despite cramming themselves into the deepest corner, it seemed that the fist would inevitably turn them to jelly. The monster was pushing it further and further into the opening. It was three meters away. Two.

Less than an arm's length out, it stopped. The twists of the bunker's interior had finally thwarted any further attempt to thrust the arm inside. They could hear the creature's enraged grunts, feel the building shaking all around them as the monster raged.

And though she hated herself for it, Carolina buried her face in Felipe's chest. She knew it was pathetic, but there was no helping it. She heard him chuckle. "I can't believe you brought your purse," he said, his typical male obliviousness not allowing him to spot the difference between a purse and a beach bag.

A pause ensued, as if the creature was distracted by something. The giant hand menacing them stayed suspended in midair, quivering slightly, smelling like rotten fish.

Suddenly, without warning, it retreated, leaving the opening free. As sunlight poured in, they could feel the building vibrating—not violently, but as though giant footsteps were moving away. A bellow of absolute rage reached them from what was unquestionably a good distance.

"It's gone," Felipe said. "Let's go!"

"Go? Where?" But it was too late. Felipe had already sprinted for the door. Carolina followed a bit more cautiously, popping only her head out of the bunker in order to look around. There seemed to be no sign or threat of the creature, so she stepped all the way out to try to see where it had gone.

Its path wasn't difficult to deduce. A line of palm trees had been pushed aside like matchwood directly behind the little building, and the destruction led all the way to the two-lane road that ran parallel to the beach. The monster could be seen sitting directly in the center of the tarmac, tearing apart a container that had been on a truck. The truck itself was lying on its side on one shoulder, looking like a discarded plaything. It raged at the container itself, as if blaming it for some terminal misfortune. Scraps of steel painted hull-red flew until there was nothing left.

A small figure caught her eye then. Felipe had instinctively run for the road, but on finding his path blocked, had stopped like a rabbit in headlights. He stared at the creature in his path, as if wondering what sauce would go best with it. Carolina reasoned that that probably wasn't the best way of dealing with it, but she didn't want to call out in case the ape—it looked more and more like an ape the more she looked at it—heard her.

In the end, it made no difference. Finding that the last pieces of the container had disappeared, the monster looked up to see Felipe standing motionless as if in challenge. It bellowed again and Felipe ran. Carolina was relieved to see that the creature was far enough that Felipe would make it to the bunker long before the ape would.

But Felipe panicked. Instead of running toward the safety of the concrete box, he headed for the sea, perhaps in some instinctive "back to the womb" reaction. What he hoped to achieve by this was unclear, but he never made it. The ape, eating ground efficiently with its enormous legs, caught him just as he was about to reach the edge. A single swipe of an enormous hand lifted Felipe high into the air. Carolina could hear his screams as he reached the apex of his parabola and braced herself for the bone-crunching impact that would come when he hit the sand.

But Felipe never made it to the ground. A huge mouth intercepted his descent, and the jaws closed on him. Even from that distance, Carolina could see the spray of blood as his body burst.

The enormous eyes fastened onto her, and a second later they were back to their original position; she was huddled in the corner while a huge fist groped blindly for her in the dark. Now that she was alone, she found her urge to scream had gone. She cried to herself in the semi-darkness, going over Felipe's last seconds again and again.

After what seemed like an eternity, the ape tired. The hand retreated, but instead of bright daylight shining through, there was little change in the quality of light. Carolina understood that she'd spent the entire afternoon stuck in a round concrete building—and had it not been there, her day would have ended badly indeed.

Where is the army? she wondered. *The cops? Someone must have been told about this by now.* But that, like the origin of the creature, seemed to be just another mystery. And she really, really had to pee.

That last was easily solved, at least. A few seconds after removing its hand, the creature once more obstructed the entry, but this time, it was neither its hand nor its face in the opening. It was just a big bit of rotting fur with some kind of huge warts. Thus unobserved, Carolina allowed herself to crouch in one of the smellier corners and relieve herself.

Spurred on by this act of bravery, she walked toward the door, her eyes able to make out some kind of pattern on the fur, roundish, elongated and…

She screamed and skittered back into the far corner.

Fused to the skin of the ape, melted and deformed, but easily recognizable, was a human face. No, there were *two* human faces, melted together at the chin like monstrous Siamese twins. And the other mounds, the bigger ones, could only be their bodies.

She could probably have taken that, she felt, had it not been for the fact that on one of the horribly grimacing figures, she could clearly make out a single eye, staring at her with a madness she'd never imagined possible.

But what could she do? She moved forward, slowly, afraid that the human figures would jump off the creature and kill her—or worse. They stayed where they were, however, with that shingle baleful eye the only sign of movement. But what movement it was: the eye followed her around like a spotlight, pained and malevolent at the same time.

The face the eye belonged to contorted, grimaced, pulled, and finally, with a gush of foul-smelling black bile, opened. The only sounds that emerged were gurgles and clacks.

She stared, and then, impulsively, touched the cheek of the other face, the one without eyes. There was no human suppleness to the skin, just hard, cold and dry parchment. Like fish scales left out in the sun. The rotting fur that framed it didn't help, either.

The eye followed her hand, rolling unnaturally around as it did so, and widening in obvious fear as she reached toward the face. She could see muscles working in the jaw, trying to free the mouth from some other obstacle that she couldn't see. They stood out like thick cords. With an audible snap, something let go, and the face emitted its first sound, a tortured keening unlike anything a human being should be capable of creating. There were no teeth in the mouth.

The sound made Carolina step back, her motion followed by the eye. She hoped, now that it had managed to break through its chains, that the face would be satisfied, stop contorting, and fall back into its previous torpor.

But she had no such luck. Its mouth continued working, its eye kept revolving, and sound kept pouring forth. She imagined it was trying to speak, but all that emerged were moans and sobs, punctuated by an occasional screech of superhuman pain.

Night fell. The ape's shadow had been replaced by the true darkness of tropical night. Stars gave no illumination, and the new moon never would.

But the sound didn't cease. Eventually, by dint of what sounded like supremely painful efforts, the face began to gain coherence, or at least the semblance thereof. Now, instead of sounding like the grunting of some big cat, the noise was that of a foreign language being spoken in slow motion. Moans echoed around the bunker, making the warm tropical blackness feel like a lonely Scottish moor in the dead of winter, complete with howling wind sound effects. She huddled in her corner, afraid to move lest that single, mad eye should report her presence to the monster above. Sleep was fitful, but, surprisingly, not inexistent.

She woke with a start. In a groggy state, she thought the sharp pain in her side, a consequence of the position she'd been reclined in, was the culprit, but then she realized that the voice had become almost recognizably human and that was what must have woken her up. It seemed to be a stream of some kind of Germanic gibberish whose meaning she could almost make out—some of it seemed similar to the English she'd learned in school.

"Hallo."

This was sudden, unexpected, out of the blue. For a second, Carolina thought that the Brazilians must have finally gotten their act together, that the army had been mobilized and the threat removed. People must be combing the beaches for missing tourists. But then, she heard the same voice, this time spouting the gibberish from before.

"Wait, hello," she whispered without thinking.

The voice stopped. Silence echoed through the bunker more powerfully than the earlier sound. "Hallo… English?"

Should she respond to this? Should she interact with the monster? "Yes, some English," she said.

"I… need… help…"

The first thought that crossed her mind was that whatever else might be happening, the owner of that face, that voice, was beyond all human help. "How can I help you?"

There was a pause, long enough to make her wonder whether she'd dreamed the whole thing.

"Kill me…" Another pause ensued as Carolina processed this. "Please…

"Please…"

Still, she said nothing.

"Please…"

"But how? You're a part of this huge thing. How can I kill something like that? How?" Desperation lent her a fluency that she could never recall having had when taking her lessons.

The voice gurgled. With one final wet sound, it seemed to disappear. And then, with a final effort, more of a series of coughs than real words, it said: "Fire… the chemicals… use fire…"

"But how? I don't have any fire! I don't even smoke."

But all she got from the face was a series of gulps and wheezes.

More snaps and pops showed that the figure it was attached to was still moving, but its capacity to speak seemed to have disappeared.

At dawn, it was no longer creaking and popping. But it wasn't dead: that single, insane eye revolved in its socket and reminded her of her promise to help—a promise she'd never made, but one that the revolving orb seemed determined to hold her to.

I don't even smoke, she thought, but the eye didn't seem to care.

With the rising sun, her giant adversary stirred. The ape stood, letting the blinding morning light reflect off the white sand into the bunker like a searing flame. The very same flame that she didn't have. Her heart thumped as the beast took three steps away—could it be leaving? Would she be able to escape none the worse for wear?

No such luck was forthcoming. After its short walk, the rank-smelling creature returned to the utility structure, and the tiny, rolling eye of the thing fused to its back was replaced by the enormous, evil orb of the creature itself, followed in short order by the grasping hand. Carolina, seated in her corner with the bag that had caused Felipe so much amusement, barely even flinched. The growling in her stomach seemed louder and more threatening than the giant ape she'd already grown accustomed to.

She opened the bag, hoping against hope that she'd remembered to pack some cookies, a cereal bar, something, but no such luck. All she had was a thermos full of now cold water and the implements to make and clean the maté—her single concession to infusion addiction—she went nowhere without, some money, and her cell phone. That last was useless there in Brazil, but she lugged it around anyway, feeling naked without it.

No lighter, no flare gun. No hope.

She tried to get into a more comfortable position. Maybe if she ignored it, the thing would go away.

But it didn't, and after hours, there were no comfortable positions left, and no question of moving into a different spot to pee. All she could do was to try to stay as far from the small puddle beside her as possible.

If only I had a box of matches, she thought. And that thought brought back a memory. A cold spring night camping in Patagonia, and the discovery that the lighter they'd been relying on to light their nightly fires had somehow broken. One of the guys in the group had managed to get a fire lit using only a cell phone and something in her maté kit. The *virulana*, the steel wool. And she'd brought that very same chunk with her—it was still inside the bag.

But how had he done it? She recalled that he'd taken the phone apart, so she did. Then she stopped to remember the guy himself. As far as she could tell, just another Felipe: good looking, hair too long, and better in bed than in the daytime. She clearly had to change the kind of guy she fell for—but, to be fair, he'd known the cell phone trick, and she didn't. Even with the cell phone battery and the steel wool in front of her, she had no clue as to how it would work.

The battery was a featureless flat rectangle as long as her thumb, and the only thing about it that didn't look completely inert were a few tiny strips of copper on one edge, with the positive and negative signs beside them. She pressed the steel wool to the edges and nearly dropped the battery into a pool of her own urine when a small spark flew inside the black piece of *virulana*. She did drop the steel wool, but luckily, it landed on her foot.

Carolina studied the steel wool. Tiny singe marks scarred it, barely visible in the dim light of the utility bunker. But the verdict was clear: the wool had burnt, and it was time for her to make a decision.

Should she attack the monster and try to set it alight? Would that even work? It seemed much too large to be flammable. Maybe her best bet was to sit tight and wait for the authorities to do something about it.

But that could take days. There was no question that the government knew about the creature, but they were probably waiting to see what happened. Without thinking about it, she pressed the steel wool into the battery again, this time making sure she kept it there even after smoke began to pour from it. *Didn't these batteries have acid in them?* She just hoped it would hold out long enough to get a decent fire.

A tiny dot of light appeared on the *virulana*, and she moved without thinking toward the gigantic hand resting on the floor. She reached out and tried to press the smoldering steel wool onto a finger.

Carolina realized almost immediately that this was a big mistake, that she'd stepped well inside the beast's reach. But almost immediately wasn't good enough. Moving with lightning speed, a huge fist wrapped around her legs and pulled her out of the building. Only quick reflexes allowed her to duck in time to avoid leaving her brains splattered all over the top of the concrete doorway.

The ape moved its fist right in front of its face and studied her for a second. She thought she could see malicious gloating in its eyes, but soon the stench overpowered her other faculties—it made the putrid interior of the bunker seem like a flowery meadow.

A second later, panic kicked in. This monster wasn't going to keep contemplating her forever, and soon, she would follow Felipe's lead and become a shower of blood and bone, to be washed off the beach by the next high tide. She frantically pressed the steel wool to the battery, pressing the smoking concoction against the fist with trembling hands.

A small patch of flaking, rotting material came alight, and she had hope for a second, but it was too little, too late. She was already being conveyed to the giant maw, and the monster wouldn't even notice a flame that size.

But in the instant before she was consumed, the flame suddenly spread as if the creature had been made of gasoline. The hairs on her arm were singed with heat, and the beast screamed like a banshee with a bad headache. Before she had time to react, Carolina was falling to the floor from thirty feet up. Only a glancing blow against one of the ape's knees slowed her descent and saved her from being killed by the impact with the sand. It didn't save her from hearing several bones break.

She lay there, determined to watch until the beast was gone. It took a surprisingly short time to be consumed, but that time was employed in running to and fro—nearly crushing her with a giant foot in the process—and screaming. When it finally fell into a smoking, ruined heap, she allowed the darkness to overcome her.

***

She woke to screams in Portuguese. Hands placing her on a stretcher, lifting her over the sand at a run to a running helicopter. A doctor telling her that she was going to be all right, a guy in a uniform apologizing, saying that they'd had no idea that anyone was left alive, that they were observing the creature to decide what to do with it. Another asking if she knew any of the victims.

The doctor told her not to answer any questions.

But what could she have said? She really hadn't known Felipe—

or at least not anything about him that was anyone's business. But as she drifted into the fog of painkillers, she knew this particular version of the dumb guy would be her last—but it would also be the only one she remembered.

Christopher's Retreat

On a bright, sunny summer day in 1788, Christopher put down his hammer, removed his apron, and walked out of the foundry. He ignored Mr. Bristle's shouted demands that he return to work. After all, the shouting of his former employer was just another loud noise in a city that was full of them.

The city seemed to have become full of sound. The hammering in the foundry was just a small part of it. There was a new mill across the road whose hundreds of identical machines produced the unholy screeching of banshee legions. And the workers who tended the machines would all pour out of the building at the same time and fill the street with their coarse language, expressing their blasphemy at the very top of their lungs. Even the usual cacophony of schoolboys and livestock and policemen's whistles was defeated by that infernal barrage.

For a single second, he faltered, fearing that he was overreacting, but in each sound he heard the echo of Mary's screams—the screams that had shaken his world, that took him back to the moment when the light of his life disappeared and took his not-quite-born son with it. It was not a moment he could bear to repeat, even if he could only hear its echoes in the clashing sounds.

The hesitation passed.

The air was so full of noise that Christopher was convinced that there could be no room for him, so he left his tools off to one side and walked out, to find a place he could fit.

He walked up the street to where the mills and their legions gave way to the stately houses of the owners. But here, too, the sound of carriages and horses and—again—the infernal whistles of the law informed him that it was time to move on.

The street turned into a dirt road, and the post jangled past him every few hours, keeping him from the silence he craved. Birds tweeted annoyingly in trees. Once, a whole regiment went by, surely with no other purpose than to stomp its boots on the packed earth.

The road went up, and his spirits rose with it. Up into the mountains, above the lakes and tree line. The birds had gone and there seemed to be a still calm upon the land. Perhaps there was room for him there. But, upon turning a corner of the path, a herd of cattle blocked his way, and upon the lead cow… a bell.

He walked off the path, along the rougher, rock-strewn spines of the mounts until he came across a small ridge overlooking a tiny lagoon. It was a secluded place surrounded by mountains that blocked off the wind, and it seemed completely silent.

There, Christopher rested. And there, with no echoes to remind him, Christopher forgot.

As he rested, he listened. Without the constant noise of life and bustle filling the air and the inside of his head, he could hear the words that could only be said in silence.

He listened to the Earth and to the stars. He listened to the distant oceans and to ghosts of fallen soldiers. The voices in the silence taught him the ancient secrets of the Titans and the hidden shame of the gods. They taught him to live forever and to gain nutrition from the very air. They taught him to control the fabric of reality and to see beyond the veil of death.

Christopher sat and listened to the voices and grew fat on the thin mountain air. He listened for days, years, decades. He listened for centuries and was at peace.

One day, however, the shout of a hiker broke through the silence. It was miles distant, and only reached the ridge on which Christopher was seated because of a fortuitous gust of wind. Its power when it reached him was akin to the sound made by the flapping of a butterfly's wing.

The thunderous noise nearly killed him. He felt a searing pain in the very atoms of his body, and he was sure that he would never recover.

But the sound didn't repeat itself. The wind was still, and no further interruption was carried up to his retreat. Over the next few weeks, the atoms of his body healed, and the pain receded.

But Christopher remembered that day.

He could not bear to remember that day.

On a bright, sunny summer day in 2012, Christopher wrapped

himself in a shield of silence and walked away from his ridge. He retraced his steps across the tortuous hillsides and came to the small mountain path he'd walked before.

There stood not a herd of cows, but a flock of sheep and a shepherd. He saw that one of the lambs had a bell.

Christopher gave a silent command and the shield around him expanded to give them the gift of silence. As he left them behind, he saw that they were cold, immobile, and blessedly quiet.

He walked on. Birds fell from the trees as he passed but hit the ground with no sound. The rustling of the leaves ceased to be, forever. A row of army trucks on the paved two-lane that had replaced the dirt track of yore suddenly stopped. No men descended, and no men ever would.

The city had grown, and the mills had spawned countless progeny. But he pushed back the noise, filling the previously cramped air with the power of eternal peace. As he walked across each intersection, the city behind him went cold and lifeless—glorious in its lack of noise.

Christopher kept walking. He walked until he'd given his gift to all the living creatures of the land and the seas and had brought absolute peace to the world. But the perfect stillness was incomplete.

He listened to the voice of silence to discover what was amiss. And then Christopher, understanding, smiled.

He banished the winds.

And he was content.

Borrowed Gods

"I didn't hear no one building this. Didn't see them, either," Old Carl said for the hundredth time. "Saw it when I woke up."

Quigley had arrived just after dawn, when Carl had raised the alarm, but he'd stayed in the background as the man told each townsperson who showed up the story of what he'd discovered. It wasn't often that people listened to Carl, and he was milking it for all it was worth.

Two parallel lines originated in the middle of the road and stretched off into the distance. They traversed the dirt main street until the road turned left toward Denver and the mountains. At that point, they went into the scrub, straight as a gunshot. Quigley imagined they would cut through anything that might be in the way.

"What are they?" Anna asked. It was mighty unusual to see her out and about that early, but it would have been more unusual for her to miss anything important in town. She made it her business to know what was what.

"Ain't it obvious? Those are train tracks," a cowboy, one of the Lorraine boys, said.

Carl scratched his head. "They ain't got no sleepers. What's to hold 'em together?"

Men kicked at the metal lines embedded in the ground. One dusty traveler pulled a sledge out of a wagon and gave them a good whack. "Them's more solid than any train lines I ever seen. Shinier, too. And if you go back along them, you'll find that there's no joins. I looked especially. Them's just straight metal lines all the way across the desert. And they're so solid I bet they reach down into the center of the earth."

"Into hell itself, I reckon," Carl said.

Everyone started talking at once then, everyone except Quigley. He listened.

And then he heard another sound. Not a loud sound… but dark.

"Listen," Quigley said. "Can you hear that?"

Everyone stopped talking. They always did when Quigley spoke. Even as a child, they'd listened to him.

"It's like a humming," Anna said.

"Yeah. Fills you, like. Makes your bones shake."

The guy with the sledge leaned down over the rails and screwed his eyes shut. Then he straightened and walked to his wagon. "I'll be on my way to Denver," he said. "I don't want to be here later." He nodded to where the tracks disappeared into the distance. "Those tracks, they're humming. This is the end of the line… and a train's coming."

They watched him leave with a creak of wheels and tack. Finally, Anna said in a voice completely unlike the hoarse whisper of her coquettish nights, "Shouldn't someone go get Cooper?"

***

The town marshal placed his fingers on the vibrating tracks and then stood, glaring into the distance. "We need to get to the Parker place," he said. "Who's comin'?"

Quigley stepped forward. "I reckon I will."

Cooper didn't look happy, but he nodded. They'd butted heads but tolerated each other because they both wanted what was best for the town. The disagreement was how to go about getting it. "Who else?"

Two of the Lorraine boys volunteered, which was no surprise, and then Anna stepped forward, which was. With a stare that dared the men to argue, she said, "Tara Parker was one of mine. If there's going to be business with the old man, I'm going to be there to make sure it's fair business."

"For all we know, the old man was the one who scared Tara out of town," Carl said. "And killed all those people." He didn't glance at Quigley.

"And for all we know, he wasn't. I'm coming with you."

Cooper shrugged, and since no one else volunteered, he led them toward town.

Most of the buildings fronted Main Street, but others, places that needed a little room, were outside the town on the grassy hills that commanded a view of the eternal plains to the east. The church was on those hills, and so was the Parker House, the last remnants of one family's glory.

The house had been built with the proceeds of cotton farming in Georgia, which had allowed Zacharias Parker to move west with his family and household staff. The man's vision was to establish a model community where people of all creeds and colors—white settlers, freed slaves, and Indians from the surrounding hills—could live in harmony, learning from one another, in a territory far removed from the arguments about free states and slave states.

But Zacharias had died within a year, and his wife weeks later, leaving his two young children to be raised in the thirty-room house by their colored servants.

Whispers about what had happened in those years had sprung up around the Parker Trading Post: witchcraft, communing with spirits, forbidden liaisons, death cults.

But the children had grown. Zebadiah Parker became, as a young man, the head of the community. Any darkness he might have been subjected to didn't make itself known. He was a good man, solid.

Until,twenty years before, on the day his sister and her husband disappeared. On that day, he locked himself in the mansion, never to emerge again, and expelled his niece, fifteen-year-old Tara, who everyone believed would be the next town beauty. Homeless and penniless, with no way to contact relatives back east, she'd had only one option, and only Anna's patronage had kept her from becoming the woman of some blacksmith's apprentice or stagecoach driver.

Some said she might have been more respectable if she had.

Cooper knocked on the dry wooden door, causing flakes of ancient paint to float to the porch floor.

Footsteps within told them that their call had been heard, but it was an eternity before the door creaked ajar to reveal the deeply creased mahogany features of a man in a dark suit holding a threadbare feather duster.

"The mastah does not receive visitors," the man said in an eternal drawl that made the speech of passing Texans seem clipped and rushed by comparison.

He tried to close the door, but Cooper's foot barred the way. "I'm the law around here, and we need to speak to him."

"Town law don't apply to the mastah. That's for town folk."

"The law applies to everyone, high and low," Cooper replied.

Quigley had to smile at that. He suspected that the marshal wasn't talking about whatever was coming on that train, but it certainly fit. A train from nowhere, carrying God-knew-what, would make few distinctions of class.

"I'll tell the mastah." The old retainer attempted to close the door, but the marshal hadn't moved his foot and if it came to a physical altercation, the enormous lawman would not find much of a challenge in the old servant. The retainer shrugged and disappeared into the gloom of the house.

Not waiting for him to return, Cooper swung the door fully open and invited himself inside. The others followed.

Quigley brought up the rear and studied the entrance hall. A chandelier, dark and covered in cobwebs, hung from the ceiling, and a two-armed staircase at the back of the room led upstairs. Wooden paneling gleamed darkly in the reflected sunlight, and the room smelled of wax. No lights burned.

The servant returned, and if he disapproved of their presence inside the sanctum, it didn't show on his impassive features. "This way, please."

They followed in silence, through a doorway, a long dark dining room with sheets over the chairs, and into a sitting room where a single candle threw flickering shadows over every wall but gave very little light.

"A delegation, no less," a strong, masculine voice said from the shadows. "To what do I owe this pleasure?"

Quigley tried to find the source of the voice, but he could barely make out the shape of a man seated in a tall armchair in the deepest of the room's gloom.

"It's a time of reckoning," Cooper replied.

"All times are times of reckoning," the man responded. "Won't you sit and tell me about it? I suspect there must be some wine somewhere."

"We don't have time for wine," Cooper replied curtly. "The time has come for you to face your sins."

"All of them?" the voice sounded amused. "I'm not certain even a true reckoning could do that. Or perhaps you're trying to assign me sins that aren't on my soul."

"I assign nothing. It's the train that will do the assigning."

"A train, you say?" Now the voice sounded more interested. "Is the railroad finally coming to our little corner of the world?"

"This is no human train. And it's coming for you."

"Ah. I see."

"Your black magic has run its course," Cooper said. "It's time for you to face the consequences so we can go on with our lives."

The figure in the corner stood with a rustling sound and Quigley gaped as the candlelight revealed the owner of the house. He'd never seen Old Man Parker before… and this was anything but what he'd expected. The man was in his early fifties, slightly going to fat but still sporting powerful shoulders. His beard, though graying, was cut short and dark eyes peered out at them. "I admit I'm curious to see what you describe," he said. "I will go with you."

"You're already dressed," Anna noted.

He cocked his head as if noticing her for the first time. "Anna," he said. "I never thanked you for saving Tara, did I?"

Anna turned away. "Tara would never have needed saving if you hadn't forbidden her this house."

"In that," he responded softly, "you are wrong. If she'd stayed here, she would be as dead as her mother. Dead like so many others. And yes, I'm already dressed. I felt it coming."

Quigley stared hard at the man, trying to see if his words were an admission of guilt, but found no clues in the impassive features.

They walked out of the house. Out in the sunlight, a sense of oppression, of being constantly watched and judged, disappeared. Quigley breathed easy again.

Parker peered around the members of the group. His eyes lingered on the Lorraine boys, young, sullen, and menacing. "You didn't think I'd come quietly?"

"I didn't know what we'd find in there."

"And if I didn't want to come, you would have tried to take me by force? Inside my house?"

Cooper shrugged. "I would have tried to do my job."

"You would have failed," Parker replied.

"Maybe. But then there would be no more doubts about where the evil that weighs us down is located. The town would have been free to act."

"The town is always free to act. There's no one around to keep you from lynching a lonely old man or burning his wooden house around his ears." He held each of their gazes in turn. "It's your own doubts that are holding you back."

"I don't have any doubts."

"No. You wouldn't. They say my father was like that, and look where it got him... dead, a world away from his family."

"If that were true, his family wouldn't still be here tormenting our town."

Quigley stepped between them. Parker was shorter than the marshal, but broader across the shoulders, which would only matter if the fight remained on the physical plane. If the rumors were true... "This isn't the time to argue. There's something coming," Quigley said quietly.

"Very well," Parker replied. The marshal just nodded. Both stepped away and the group resumed its walk.

Moments later they approached the crowd standing beside the tracks, which ended abruptly in the center of Main Street.

"It would seem to me that if a train's coming, it's not coming to my house," Parker said. "Maybe you should ask the bank if they've been playing with dark forces they don't understand." He nodded towards the nearest building and seemed to be smiling under the beard.

"Humming is getting louder, Cooper," Carl said.

Cooper bent over the metal and stood, nodding. "Comin' closer."

"What are we going to do?" Carl said.

"We're going to meet them. Go get the pastor."

"I don't want to be here when..."

"I said, get the pastor," Cooper said.

Carl ran off toward the church.

They waited tensely until Reverend Jameson arrived, flanked by his wife. He was tall and sallow, all fire and brimstone... but the town feared Mrs. Jameson above him, and it wasn't even a contest. She ruled the congregation with an iron fist concealed behind raised eyebrows or pressed lips.

But even as they joined, the crowd thinned. Carl only returned as far as the corner, and others who'd been inspecting the tracks drifted out to watch the proceedings from windows or down the street a ways. Pretty soon, only Cooper's little group, the preacher, and his wife remained. Quigley was surprised that the Lorraine boys hadn't run for the hills. But it made a certain amount of sense: if they ran, they would lose what all respect anyone had for them, and they were too young to be able to survive that kind of humiliation. The oldest must have been twenty-one. The other, probably seventeen.

"Look," Anna whispered, pointing down the tracks.

Smoke floated in the distance. Black smoke, the darkest shade of night.

Quigley waited for the wind to dissipate the dark cloud, to turn it light and insubstantial, but that never happened. The smoke remained dark and evil even as it floated into the cloudless sky. "Should be here in a few minutes," he said.

The marshal put his hand on his six-shooter. One of the Lorraine boys walked over to his horse tied in front of the bank to retrieve a Winchester from the saddle. The wind kicked up dust and scraps of grass from the floor, a cold wind more suited to February than to May.

Then the sound arrived. Quigley had heard trains before, and this roar wasn't like those. This one was angry, a screech more than a roar, the sound of metal grating against metal, of souls being torn from unwilling bodies. His stomach turned to water, and his body wanted to run, but he stayed. This was his town, it was the town where his family had grown, and the town where his youngest daughter had disappeared one morning on her way to church, never to be seen again. One of several women and children to have vanished in the past twenty-five years.

If he ran now, he suspected he'd never learn what had happened to all of them. He wouldn't be able to live with himself.

The preacher broke their silence. Ignoring the growing screech, he began to pray in a loud voice, his prayer book open in the palms of his hands. Quigley had noticed his wife speaking to him only moments before, probably commanding him to banish the beast.

Quigley suspected that that wouldn't work.

Now they could see the train, a black dot beneath the black cloud. Every eye was glued to it as it approached, every ear filled with its unholy sound roaring in counterpoint to the preacher's booming prayer.

"That don't look like any train I ever saw," the elder of the Lorraine boys said.

"Hell-trains aren't regular trains," Cooper replied grimly.

It consisted of a single black carriage, twice as long as a steam locomotive, but shaped like a bullet. The black shone in the sun and the smoke emerged from both sides of the train. It had no windows.

"Watch out," Cooper said. "Ain't no bump stops here. Not sure if the train will stop at all."

If it didn't, it would slam straight into the buildings behind them. They moved to a side and watched.

It was moving faster than any train Quigley had ever seen, even that time when he'd traveled to Chicago to buy supplies for his store.

The group moved to one side, out of the way of the rails.

A higher-pitched screech added its unpleasant sound to the train's roar, and it began to scrub off speed. As they watched—fascinated and aghast—the black bullet stopped right at the end of the tracks.

"Pray for it to leave!" the preacher's wife shouted. "We can defeat these minions of the devil."

Quigley studied the machine in front of them. While he didn't think it was of human construction, something about it told him that the devil wasn't involved, either. This seemed like something outside of the Christian faith, something like the stories they told of African religions. Parker would know, he suspected; everyone knew his servants were more than just servants.

Then he moved back. Heat rolled off the train in waves.

With a crack that hurt the ears, the front of the train opened like the mouth of some obscene serpent and three figures emerged.

A man with skin so dark as to be nearly blue and his face painted white, taller than everyone in the road, a woman whose brown skin was creole-light, and another man, a muscular figure with skin so white as to glow in the sun, with pale gray eyes and curly white hair. All three of them wore nothing but loincloths and bead necklaces. The tall man held a staff in the form of a snake.

"Pray!" the preacher's wife shouted. "These are the servants of the dark one."

Parker fell to his knees. "Sacred loas!" he whispered hoarsely. "I repent my errors."

The tall man stared at him and nodded. "It is good that you do so. You have much to repent. A true man would have protected his niece under his own roof." The man's voice was so deep that it made the ground shake.

"Have you come for me?"

"Not unless you desire it. Your life has been blameless, albeit weak. You should have led this town. You had the knowledge to stop the darkness, and you chose to hide from it. Knowing that you could have acted is enough punishment." He looked around. "But this town must be cleansed. It has fallen afoul of dark things."

Cooper had his gun out and pointed it, trembling, at the tall man. "The only dark things here are you. Foul creatures from hell."

The black man gazed impassively at the marshal and gave a rumbling chuckle. "We can be dark, that is true. But there are rules about the darkness. Innocent blood, though valuable, is also sacred. It is not to be taken lightly, never to be spilled without cause. It brings power, but also responsibility."

Quigly felt anger growing in him. "Innocent blood?" he asked, stepping forward. "Like my daughter's? Little Mary is dead?"

"She is."

"All to give this—" he spat toward Parker— "this monster power to do evil."

"To give a monster power, but that man isn't a monster; he is just weak."

He took a step toward the place where the Lorraine boys stood beside the preacher and his wife.

"Stop right there," Cooper commanded. "Not another step."

The trio ignored him and kept going.

A gunshot brought everyone back to their senses, breaking the mesmerizing spell of the three figures. Cooper had fired, and now he fired again. Two bullets aimed at the man's head.

Cooper never missed.

But the tall man simply smiled a broader grin and kept going, completely unmarked, completely unaffected. Three steps sufficed for him to stand facing the quartet. The younger Lorraine boy broke and ran, but the preacher stepped forward.

"I'm not afraid. I'm a man of God. I've lived a life of virtue and have nothing to fear from the denizens of Hell."

The big smile broadened even further. "You are right. We have no issue with you... but mostly because we are not from your Hell. Step aside."

The preacher did so, unthinkingly. He either didn't realize he'd left his wife alone to face the loas or had fallen under some spell.

The severe, black-clad woman, so feared by the town, stepped forward. Her hair had somehow escaped from the tight bun she always wore it in and framed her eyes, wild with rage. A large wooden cross appeared in her hand, and she brandished it like a shield.

"Begone, foul creatures! I command it of you in the name of God!"

The tall man raised an eyebrow. "That is not my god. That is not your god."

"I am a woman of the church!" she screamed.

"You are a woman of the spirits, but not the ones from that cross. You know the lore, taught by one of this one's—" he nodded toward the kneeling Parker— "former servants. You were given the power, but you never showed the respect and never gave as much as you were given. You killed without giving thanks, without sharing the glory. That is why the town sank into evil. And it would have sunk even further had there not been someone stout of heart here to stop you from turning this into a witch's mire, a den of darkness."

The tall man turned from the voiceless wife of the pale, silent preacher and walked to Anna.

She stood her ground, defiant to the last, as if facing a drunk in her house of ill repute.

The tall man put a hand on her. "You are the spirit of light in this town and, though you are not of our spirits, you have our blessing."

As Quigley watched, years seemed to evaporate from Anna's face. Lines she'd earned through long nights, the bags under her eyes from lack of sleep—even her corset seemed to fit more comfortably, suddenly compressing less of her sagging flesh.

The preacher's wife broke the moment. "You honor the whore?"

"We honor the woman whose bravery and kindheartedness saved the town and kept the niece from joining the sister who was her mother. Had you been able to partake of that blood, you would have been too powerful to stop." He paused and grinned, impossibly, even wider, showing more teeth than humans should have in their heads. "And you would have been strong enough to resist us. But thanks to her, you aren't."

The preacher's wife screeched and ran toward the big man.

His grin nearly split his head in half.

An explosion rocked the street, sound and black smoke filling the empty space.

When the smoke cleared, the preacher had joined Parker on his knees, the prayer book forgotten in the dirt beside him. The rest stood dazed and pale, all except Anna who glowed with health and radiance.

The train was disappearing into the distance, the track disappearing in its wake. Where the tracks had ended stood a grotesque statue of the preacher's wife. It was the same woman, but her face was contorted in a rictus of hate, her formerly smooth features lined and wrinkled. It showed the preacher's wife as a hag. She stood on a cylindrical base, on which were inscribed several words:

This monument marks the place where Francine Jameson, witch and blasphemer, was taken by her gods to account for her actions. She was the murderer of...

A list followed, headed by the name of Renée Parker.

Quigley walked up to the base and, ignoring the statue and the rest of the lettering, ran his hands over the shape of one name: Mary Quigley.

He felt the tears run down his cheeks and felt thankful. Thankful that he knew, now. He was free to mourn.

And when he felt a hand on his shoulder, he knew without turning that it was Anna's. The gods, the loas, whatever they were, were right. This woman—a woman he'd barely acknowledged as a neighbor and had often pointedly ignored when they passed on the street—was the soul of the town, the light against the darkness. She should be the town's leading citizen, not him.

Quigley cried into the dirt of Main Street.

***

It was late afternoon, and Quigley was tired and very old. But he wouldn't let that stop him from taking the pilgrimage he'd taken every day for the past forty-five years.

The statue was exactly where the strange visitors had left it. The street was now cobbled, and the horses were slowly being replaced by the new-fangled horseless carriages that were sweeping the nation. A Ford, one of those Ts everyone was buying cheap, narrowly missed him as he tried to cross into the middle of the street.

It wasn't Main Street anymore. Since they couldn't remove the statue or dig it up—not even with dynamite—they'd simply moved Main Street one block over and renamed this one Second Street.

Quigley didn't care. The statue was as crisp and fresh as when it had been erected. No bird ever perched on it; the rain was as powerless to erode it as the dynamite had been in removing it.

No one else remembered when it came. Anna had left a few weeks after the black train, and the people—fathers, siblings, husbands—who'd once come to run their fingers over the names of lost loved ones had stopped coming. Some had died, some had left town, and some had simply moved on with their lives.

But Quigley would come every day for as long as he lived. He'd sold the store to Sears years ago, and his children had left town, but he never would—not as long as Mary's name was on the statue. No matter how the town changed, how the world changed, it was his comfort to know that, when he and all his other children were forgotten, Mary's name would live on as long as the statue remained in place.

From what he'd seen, that would be forever.

This time, his tears fell on the cobbles of Second Street.

What i Never Told Them

"I once wrote a story about sentient seaweed," I said.

The other panelists laughed. The audience laughed. It was probably the most successful panel I'd ever been on. There were actually humans in the audience.

The next day, people would tell me that they enjoyed the panel, buy one of my books in the dealer room, and ask me to sign it.

All was well until someone asked me to send them the story about the sentient seaweed. That's when I realized I'd screwed up.

I mumbled something about sending it over and planned to forget. But one of the other panelists chose that moment to drop by and say, "Oh, that's right. I want to read that one as well."

It got worse. Unlike the editors I'd tried to sell that story to, everyone wanted to read about sentient seaweed.

The story had appeared in an antho that paid very little and sold even fewer copies. At the time, having gotten the thing out of my system, I was relieved that not many had read it. Exorcised at little cost to myself or others.

Five years later, the debt was coming due because I couldn't keep my mouth shut.

***

After the con, everyone went their different ways. I flew back to my new home, where I'd moved after it all happened. I changed planes in Rabat and mounted an ancient propeller-driven craft that deposited me in Timbuktu, where the customs people already knew me and gladly accepted a pair of bottles of duty-free whisky in lieu of a resident's visa. I had a visa, but playing the game turned the officers into coconspirators.

The final leg of the journey took me to the village of Aguelhok, where I was considered the crazy stranger, and inevitably asked to assist any foreign tourists who happened to be passing through.

I'd chosen the village because it was as far into the Sahara Desert as I was willing to go.

But the internet reached me, and I scanned the obituaries of the writing associations for the inevitable.

They trickled in. A rash of science fiction writers and fans—missing. Some were tracked as far as a plane to Southeast Asia... and then disappeared.

No one knew where they'd gone. After a while, the genre world went on with its life, more amused by the string of coincidences than saddened by the losses.

But I knew what had happened and I mourned each loss.

***

The well water was always crisp, cool, and perfect. But that evening, as I approached the little circle of dusty gray stones that surrounded the village's only source of water, little Youssouf, the ten-year-old son of the owner of the general store, stopped me.

"Water's green," he said in French, the language we had in common. His was bad. Mine was worse. "Don't drink it."

"No," I breathed.

I stared into the depths, dropped the bucket into the darkness, and pulled it up hurriedly.

Whether the water was green or not, I couldn't tell, but I could smell the earthy smell of algae inside.

My heart sank.

I left the bucket on the edge of the well and walked home.

Darkness fell and I covered my head with my pillow, but to no avail.

I heard the sibilants first, like static from a mistuned radio in my head, but then I felt the peace overcome me, and the words formed.

You sent supplicants, the voices said.

Many supplicants.

But they don't last very long.

Your teachings are good, in that they come, but you do not teach them to last.

How can they attain a true state of peace in such a short amount of time?

"Humans can't survive underwater," I screamed.

Then I ran into the night, heading north, deeper into the desert. It wasn't a place of dunes but a place of rock and dirt, but I'd felt safe there.

No longer. I'd been found. I needed to run to drier ground.

***

A drop of water hit my parched lips. Warm but pure. No algae lived in the well from which that had come. A little more, and the tang of a metal cup.

"I didn't want to die," I told the man who'd found me out on the dry, rocky plain and who'd propped me against the side of an ancient Toyota Land Cruiser. "That's why I did it."

He looked at me, not understanding, not judging. Patient.

"I told them I'd write their holy book. I'd seen them all drown, you understand. Elena. Diana. Ricardo. So peaceful when we pulled them out of the water."

I coughed, my throat too dry to pull up anything.

"I resisted the pull as long as I could. And when I couldn't resist any longer, I made a deal with them."

He looked at me impassively.

"Do you understand? I made a deal. I told those telepathic plants that I would only achieve peace if I could do their work, send them acolytes. I explained about holy writing, and how it moved us." I laughed. "You don't believe me. You don't believe that there is a shallow pool beside an artificial island in the sea near Borneo where sentient seaweed can make you feel at peace with everything. So at peace, in fact, that you'll drown there with a smile. And you can't resist it." I tried to give him a smile. "Of course you don't. It's stupid."

He returned my smile. His was sad, gentle. He had graying hair cut near the scalp and a graying beard.

"I didn't want to be a prophet," I said. "I just had no other choice. Do you understand?"

He murmured something. It sounded like a prayer.

He was right to pray, because I felt life leaving me as darkness overcame everything.

With my last strength I rubbed my hands against the dry, lovely dust.

Dry dust.

I smiled.

The Smoke, and Mirrors

"Dead?" Erik said with a chuckle. "I think not. Which is, unfortunately, more than I can say for you."

Before Hilaire could react, Erik threw the noose around his neck and shoved him in the chest.

The man screamed and clutched at air as he stepped off the plank high above the stage floor. Erik watched, fascinated, as his victim's eyes grew wide with the knowledge that he was going to die. Then the man was gone.

The rope taughtened, then it snapped with a sound like a gunshot. Hilaire fell, still screaming, onto a pile of sandbags. They broke his fall and saved his life.

Erik smiled. He'd cut the rope himself, just enough that it would break when tensed. He'd also placed the sandbags there when no one was watching. That Hilaire was dazed and terrified—albeit breathing—was according to plan.

But there was still an act of this performance to be played out, and Erik held the leading role. He descended the stairs and stood menacingly, as if about to charge at the wounded Hilaire and finish him off. He left his face uncovered to ensure that the French actor couldn't fail to recognize him.

In response, Hilaire struggled to his knees and shouted. "Fiend!" at Erik, but then, seeming to remember that he was in mortal danger, the actor raised his well-trained voice and yelled: "Help! Murder! I'm being attacked! Help! It's the Opera Ghost. He's here!"

Now Erik smiled. It was his cue for a grand exit. Covering his face with his cape, he dashed for the door that opened onto the stairs. Before heading down, he looked back to see two stagehands helping Hilaire to his feet. As they started after him, he dashed down the steps into the darkened storage sector beneath the stairs.

Again, he was forced to wait for the men to catch up. He didn't want them to lose the trail. Not yet anyway.

When the telltale signs of a sputtering lamp finally illuminated the area, Erik opened a door in the far wall and slammed it behind him with a crash. Another flight of stairs led deep into the ground.

He felt no fear of capture; even lightless, he could outpace the men, a legacy of his years in the damp and dark below the Paris Opera House. He waited until he heard the door open.

Then, making enough noise so they could follow, he ran into the maze of old sewers and tunnels beneath Terry's Theater. There was no lake under this playhouse, which meant that if they brought dogs, they could follow his trail. He was, in fact, counting on that; the British loved their hunting dogs.

Even without a lake, the tunnels were humid. The Thames was less than a hundred paces away, and the dirt of the floor was saturated almost to the point of becoming mud.

It felt like home.

Erik turned at an intersection, then turned again and again, following a roundabout path to his final destination, a path calculated to leave a good set of tracks—a nice scent for the dogs to follow.

Then he stopped and reached out a hand in the pitch blackness.

He gripped a rope, exactly where he knew it would be. Even after a decade of living aboveground, hiding among the throngs of unsuspecting Europeans, he was still the master of darkness.

Somewhere in the distance, a clumsy group of men followed, crashing about like elephants.

He sang to them, the first few lines of "Avant de quitter ces lieux" from *Faust*, letting the deep notes echo through the tunnels, folding back on themselves and becoming ever more ghostly as they went. A sound that would haunt all who heard it.

Erik didn't plan to let them see him leave. He needed the mystery to be complete. Grasping the rope in hands that, despite his deformities, were strong and capable, he climbed three floors up an air shaft until he reached a grate in a cupboard on the ground floor. He pushed it aside, pulled the rope up after him, and pausing only to don a workman's cloak and pick up a toolbox he'd left there earlier, he slipped out the tradesman's entrance.

The grizzled man at the door, his youth likely eaten up by the

Crimean War, showed no interest in the nonentity passing his post. In honesty, he would have shown no interest in a carnival troupe at that point. The bottle of gin Erik had unobtrusively forgotten beside the door had taken care of that.

Avoiding the crowds around the Savoy, he crossed the Strand and lost himself in what seemed to be the beginnings of a really good London fog.

While others might have been thankful for its concealing presence, Erik ignored the fog. He didn't need it. Fog was for uncivilized criminals, brutes like the Ripper of a few years earlier. Erik was an artist, not a savage, and the fog was almost a professional insult. What he did was finely tuned, precise and considered. It could have been done in daylight as easily as it was in the evening.

Minutes later, he reached his home, a typical townhouse, the abode of a well-to-do family. He placed the key in the lock and entered.

Bess approached, holding a lamp. It was for his benefit, not hers. She never believed him when he told her he was perfectly comfortable in the dark and insisted on protecting him against his natural element. "Is that you, my dear?"

"Yes," Erik replied, his heart racing at the beauty of her voice, a deep, rich contralto that shook him to the core. Even her delicate, innocent face paled beside the velvet tones. "I was held up at the station."

"How was Manchester?" she asked him.

"The same as always. Satanic mills, and even more satanic hearts in the chests of the owners."

She smiled sadly. "You always say the same. You're too tenderhearted to deal with such men."

"We must eat," he replied. "And pay the servants. For that, I must work."

"I suppose we must." She put a hand on his face, unflinchingly. He'd told her that he was awful, deformed, twisted. She had replied that it made no difference to her, as long as she could hear his beautiful voice filled with love for her.

She handed him the candle and called the housemaid, who brought her own lamp. "Mary, please light up the house and warm the roast. The master is back."

"Yes, marm," the young woman replied, and went about the sitting room, lighting the lamps.

Bess never wasted oil when she was alone, and only permitted the maid and the manservant a small lamp for their own chambers.

She didn't need light for herself.

She was blind.

***

Erik stayed at home the next two days, avidly reading the newspapers and smoking his pipe while Bess kept him company and filled the days with pleasant conversation. Had he not known firsthand how well one could function without being able to see, he would have been fascinated with the way she managed the house. She could even knit, and the *click-clack* of her needles sounded through the afternoon.

The papers he read were not of the sort one would have expected in a house such as his. *The Times* would never deign to print scandals among theater people, so he also received the *Telegraph* and several other penny papers. He didn't want to miss his chance.

He needn't have worried. On the morning of the second day, the item he wanted was printed on the front page of no fewer than three of the lesser rags, and even the *Telegraph* had a piece, albeit buried among the police items.

Bold, blocky letters announced several variations on the theme of *Directors call in Police to search theater catacombs for Paris Ghost.*

He scoffed. Those weren't catacombs. They were mere basements, mostly made of brick and likely used to store barrels from ships along the rivers in some past age. Just like the theater itself was a mere pimple compared to the grand opera house he'd become famous in, the underlying levels were nothing compared to the glorious expanse he'd roamed under that building.

But they would serve his purpose well enough.

The articles all agreed on one thing: the operation was to begin at eight o'clock in the evening. All exits from the theater and along the waterfront would be covered and the building would be searched with a fine-toothed comb, from the top of the roof to the lowest of the catacombs. Sources expected the activities to take all night.

Which was exactly what Erik wanted. If things went well, he might even join the inevitable crowd of gawkers the following morning, to snicker at the frustrated face of officialdom, which was a traditional Londoner's pastime.

At ten o'clock on the button, he donned his cloak, kissed Bess on the cheek, and explained he would be late in returning. Outside, he hailed a hansom and asked to be driven to Covent Garden. It was a short distance, and he would normally have walked it, but it would behoove him later to have an easy way to prove his movements.

Then, he donned an old cloak and retraced most of his steps until he arrived at the door of a townhouse much larger than his own, fronted by an impressive iron fence. As the hour was getting late, he hid himself in the shadow of a nearby staircase and waited for the lights in the house to extinguish themselves.

By midnight, all was dark except for a single gas lamp a few paces off. He briefly toyed with the idea of extinguishing it to hide his activities but thought better of it. He hadn't brought the right equipment to douse a lamp, and he would be doing enough climbing without adding more to the bill.

So, with one last careful look along the road, Erik crossed the street and soundlessly climbed the iron gate. Once on the other side, he took hold of a rain pipe and went all the way up to the wrought-iron balcony on the third floor.

It took less than a minute, and he waited another two or three in case the slight scuffling sounds he'd inevitably made drew any attention.

Nothing stirred inside, so he got to work on the window.

For a moment, he suspected he might have to choose a different form of ingress; the window that opened onto the balcony was covered in thick paint, but once he ran the blade of his chisel along the paint holding the two panes together, the door sprang open with a groan before he could stop it.

Again, he stayed perfectly still, holding his breath.

He heard nothing, so he opened the window far enough to enter.

An empty room greeted him, the smell of dust bearing witness that it had been empty for quite some time. Scattered furniture covered in white sheets gave the nearly dark room an aspect of ghostly habitation.

He slipped to the door and opened it. Another creak, again unavoidable.

Erik cursed John Riley, the house's owner, for a skinflint. A man of his eminence, worth a million pounds if he was worth a penny, a director of the company that owned half the theaters in the West End, should maintain his house.

He crept down the hall.

"Who's there?" a voice asked.

Erik soundlessly returned through the doorway and crouched down. Experience had taught him that people seldom looked for threats at ankle level.

The next door opened, and light spilled into the passage. A candle entered the hall, followed by a plump, gray-haired woman in the gray clothing of a housemaid.

As Erik watched her from below, she turned towards the stairs, her back to him.

It was the maid's last mistake. He sprang from hiding, placed one hand over her mouth, and slid a stiletto between her ribs from behind, straight into her heart. She died without a sound.

He was about to lay her on the bed of the room she'd emerged from but then had a better idea. He manhandled the body to the last door in the hall.

That opened into a study with a strongbox inside, and Erik smiled when he saw it. He closed the door behind him, sat the corpse on the chair in front of the desk with a book open on her lap—he chuckled to see it was one of Dumas's silly romances—and turned his attention to the box.

It would not be child's play, but then, he wasn't a child. He was a man who'd learned, in the blackness away from the stage in Paris, to use his other senses. He could pick locks in the dark just by the sound and the feel of the tumblers and picks.

He let the woman's candle burn, however. The light wasn't unwelcome and might tell any of the other inhabitants of the house that the room was occupied by a friendly presence, someone not inclined to hide his activities. Anyone standing at the door would see only the old lady slumped with her book.

But he wasn't too concerned. Riley wouldn't be in the house. He was aiming to be recognized on the New Year's Honours List... which meant that he wouldn't return until the Theater had been well and truly searched. There were too many newspapermen present for Riley to retire early.

He hummed softly as he worked the door, only stopping because he recognized one of the execrable tunes from the play—not an opera, a musical *play* of all things—that Hilaire's troupe had been rehearsing.

The door finally gave way. No screeches or groans came with these hinges, but a sound more akin to a satisfied sigh. Riley might house his person and his servants in an ill-maintained abode, but his wealth was well cared for.

And what wonderful wealth it was. The first thing to disappear into Erik's sack were the bank notes. Several hundred pounds—theater payroll, surely—were quickly absorbed.

Next, he took the gold coins and small jewels. A beautiful velvet bag held diamonds. He left the larger jewelry. He was not going to sully himself with pawn shops and fences. He was above all that.

Erik hesitated over the stock certificates. Some of them were tradable, even if stolen. There were men who could tell him which, and even make an offer for some, but those men represented a risk. Erik's was not an easily forgettable face, and if the men were caught… he could be traced.

The stock stayed where it was. He had quite enough to eat and maintain his household for some months.

With another satisfied sigh, he closed and locked the strongbox and, leaving the unfortunate housemaid in her candle-lit perch, left the house the same way he'd entered, even managing to jam the window shut so no one would understand how he'd made it in.

Let them wonder about a strange, silent murder in a locked house. Let the household accuse each other. It would simply delay the discovery of the true crime and muddy the waters of the investigation.

***

A week had passed since the robbery and Erik watched the theater's carpenters putting the finishing touches on the mobile scenery for the first scene of the second act. They looked like ants all the way down there.

The little curtained-off platform high in the rafters was often used by the actors for their trysts and today was to have been no different except that, when the young chorus girl arrived, panting from the climb, expecting Hilaire, she'd found instead the tip of Erik's stiletto.

He contemplated the woman's still form, the crimson rose blooming on the front of her gown and lamented the waste of a beautiful young woman.

But he didn't lament it too strongly. He'd heard them sing, each and every one of them, and this one... this one was not in the cast because of her voice. So it was an acceptable loss, and more importantly, a necessary one.

Footsteps on the plank announced his real visitor, so he moved aside, stood by the door, and let Hilaire enter.

The actor stood for a moment, staring at the girl on the floor. He was expecting a quick romp with his little mistress, and it took his mind a few moments to change tracks and understand what he was looking at.

Erik placed the knife on Hilaire's kidney. "Such a sweet thing. She even made it look like she enjoyed it. Although with you, none would." He wanted the actor to know that nothing was secret from the Ghost.

To his credit, Hilaire didn't splutter, he didn't scream, he didn't beg. He merely said, "We searched for you. You weren't there. I never expected you to run."

Erik chuckled softly. "You were fools to hope to catch sight of a Phantom."

"Perhaps. But I've seen you. And you are just a man." He nodded toward the dead girl. "A cruel man."

Erik chuckled softly. "I am no crueler than many, more merciful than most. You, who have always walked to applause, holding your head up proudly in public, will never know how cruel men can be."

Hilaire turned to face him. Erik allowed it, keeping the knife in full view.

"You are a murderer."

Erik shrugged. "Society's definitions mean little to one such as me."

"Then what would you call yourself?"

"An artist."

Again, Erik moved too quickly for the other man, looping the noose around his neck with a practiced gesture. Then he pushed Hilaire in the chest and watched him teeter at the edge of the platform before finally overbalancing and falling. The symmetry of the end of this chapter being exactly like its opening pleased him.

Erik turned away, heading for the escape route he'd planned beforehand. As he walked, the sound of the rope tautening reached his ears.

This time, the rope held.

He smiled; it was over.

Comrade at Arms

He collapsed into the drift but felt no cold. Prumathe longed for the bite of the snow to wake him from the numbness, but that sensation would never be his again. The man who'd hit him had walked on, ignoring him. It was a logical enough attitude; after all, the Eluveitie tribesman knew he'd struck the scout hard enough to fracture his skull.

Prumathe pushed himself up from the deep bank, ignoring the new and unaccustomed movement in his head as the pieces of skull grated against each other, and got back to his feet. The man who'd hit him was looking down into the pass, observing the Etruscan's camp. He didn't even realize there was someone behind him until Prumathe's hands closed around his neck.

He began to struggle, but a wrench and a snap put a quick end to it. Prumathe sat beside the dead man on cold snow he couldn't feel, pulled a rock out of his tool harness, and began to hit the lifeless head with the sharpened side of the stone. Flesh, hair, and bone gave way under the onslaught, and the life-giving meat was exposed. This was the ecstasy of the servants of Manus, the only one remaining, and he lost himself in it.

When he surfaced, sated, a ring of men sat around him, expressions cold. These, who had been his friends, would not come within arm's reach.

The saddest part was that he understood it perfectly. Back before crossing the great chasm, Prumathe had been where these men were now: trying to ascertain whether their ally was sated, wanting to make sure it wouldn't turn on them unexpectedly. But mainly, just afraid that they might end up like that someday. A lucky strike by one of the savage northern tribesmen had ended all worries and pain, while at the same time bringing his greatest fear to life. He'd been surprised to find that it no longer frightened him—he was alive, after a fashion, while many others weren't.

And where there was life of any sort, there was hope. Another unexpected discovery.

"How are they arrayed?" one of the men asked. Prumathe had once known this man's name. He was a captain in the army of the Rasna, or the Etruscans, as others called them. But names were no longer important.

"They aren't. This man was a lone scout, and from what I could see there are no more of them behind for leagues. We can advance and consolidate our position at least as far as the pass." Prumathe felt the loose piece of bone moving around in his head. It felt strange as it vibrated to the sound of his voice.

"Why would they leave the pass unguarded?" The man forgot himself enough to lean closer. "It doesn't make sense. It's the only way for us to get into the valley of the Eluveitie and conquer them. If I were in command, I would put every man I had on that pass."

"They are not there."

The captain nodded and moved back, finally realizing that he'd come within arm's reach. "We'll take the top now, then. Prumathe, take the point. Once you get over the summit, keep walking until you find someone. Then come back and report."

Prumathe nodded. It was an intelligent use of resources. His kind were very hard to kill—or rather, they were already dead, but they were very hard to stop—and would come back with valuable information despite suffering all kinds of damage. An arrow from behind a rock would only serve to reveal the archer's position.

He picked up his sword and trudged up the slope. He passed the place where the scout had died, the bright red streaks in the snow where he'd dragged him off the path, and looked ahead. The summit was still an hour's walk, or more, further. Unlike the blinding, white-capped mountains all around, the pass had been swept clear of snow by the howling wind that blew through it all day. The gray of the rock seemed black against the glare of the surrounding ice.

He wondered if he would find what he was looking for. If magic existed to bring the dead back to life, then, somewhere, the power must exist to bring the living dead back to true life. It was only logical. In fact, it should be even easier. Once the spirit had been returned to the body, free from the underworld, nothing should have been simpler than just touching up a few broken pieces of flesh and organs. It probably wouldn't even take the power of a priest of

Manus to do it. Why would the lord of the dead even care? He'd already released the spirit.

One thing was certain: no one in Etruscan land would use their power to free an undead soldier. They were Etruria's most powerful weapon against the forces surrounding her—expansionist Rome on the south and the unyielding Eluveitie to the north—and to free one would be treason.

So it was fortunate that the army he'd been assigned to was heading north. Perhaps, across the mountains, some situation would arise that would allow him to pursue his dream without going against the compulsion placed on him to obey orders from all Etruscan officers. Hopefully, it would happen before a tribesman hacked him to bits or set him on fire.

The hour had passed. He stood at the top of the pass, leaning into the wind. Below him spread a valley, covered with snow at its upper reaches but green and fresh with early spring grass at its bottom, miles away. The path led tortuously down, switching back across itself as it snaked toward the valley floor.

Prumathe tried to feel the touch of the wind against his cheeks. There was nothing. He shrugged and began to walk.

As he descended, the other compulsion that he'd been given at his rebirth began to rear its inescapable head. The buzzing in his head that made his life hell. It was only starting, very muted and still bearable, but it was there. Experience had shown that it would grow and grow, driving him to the very brink of madness and beyond, unless he sated the hunger. Only one thing could do that: the still-warm mind of another human being. Man, woman, or child, it made no difference. The slaves they'd fed him at first had been plucked at random from the camp servants.

But now he had to find his own food.

***

It was nearly a full day later that he rejoined the Etruscan soldiers at the top of the pass. They'd located a cave, narrow but deep enough to hold the ten soldiers and their gear.

"We can hold this pass for days against anything they care to throw against us," the captain boasted, once the fortifications were in place.

On the surface, it seemed the man was correct. The steep path leading up to their position might allow two men to approach side by side, but not to swing their swords with any effectiveness. Plus, the final few steps were so steep that simply rolling rocks down at an enemy would be enough to seriously savage them.

The captain turned to Prumathe. "Tell me, what did you find down there?"

Food, Prumathe thought. *I found a little girl playing by a stream.* But he said, "There are some farmhouses on the slopes and a few villages further down. I saw no sign of military activity of any kind."

"No movement of men?"

"Not even a scout. The only men I saw were too young to fight. They were watching sheep."

"Sheep, you say?" A greedy gleam came into the captain's eyes. "Could you go get one for us? I've had enough dried horsemeat to last me for the rest of my life."

Prumathe knew how he would have answered that question if he'd been alive, but he found his feet moving of their own volition, toward the valley once again. He knew he would have to walk for hours down a path lit only by moonlight, and then back up. He had no idea where they would keep the sheep overnight, but he doubted he would be able to take one without doing a large amount of harm to the farmers themselves. How well the sheep would react to being led up the path at night was anyone's guess. The one thing this allowed him to realize is that the compulsion made no distinction between intelligent orders and idiotic ones. It was something he needed to keep in mind.

He looked around as he walked and counted the small blessings. The most important of these was simply the lack of feeling in his limbs. The biting wind that tugged at his ever-more-ragged clothing was nothing to him, and he could enjoy the clear night. The moonlight was strong and reflected off the snow, making it easy to see the path. Things could have been worse.

Movement high up on one of the mountains caught his eye. Tiny black specks seemed to be creeping through the snow, well above his level, and even far above the path. It seemed he'd found the missing Eluveitie warriors.

But nothing in his orders for this particular jaunt said anything about reporting enemy troop movement. He was to bring the captain one sheep.

He redoubled his pace.

***

There was a downside to insensitivity, of course. The meat on the spit looked as though it smelled delicious, fat sizzling on the fire and juice running down the length of the cut. Prumathe wondered why the magic that gave him life allowed him to see and hear but hadn't revived the other senses. It seemed unfair.

As he stared into the glowing embers, something unexpectedly slapped into his back, pushing him forward. He looked down and saw the tip of an arrow and about a hand's span of shaft, strangely unblooded, protruding from just below his left nipple.

Prumathe turned back to the cave entrance. His eyes had grown accustomed to the fire, and there was little chance he'd be able to spot the attackers.

"Get them!" the captain shouted.

Prumathe's feet, seemingly acting on their own, sped him through the narrow corridor toward the exit. He'd almost reached it when he collided with a man charging into the cavern. They went down in a heap with the Etruscan on top.

He struck before the unseen assailant could react. A quick, sharp blow to the other man's throat crushed cartilage and left the attacker writhing on the floor, gasping for breath.

But the man wasn't alone. Before Prumathe could stand, a crude spear pierced his shoulder from behind, just as he heard at least one more man, probably two, approaching from his right.

He decided to eliminate the immediate threat first. Grasping the haft of the spear, he gave it a mighty jerk. The man holding it stumbled into view—a mere shadow, but at least Prumathe's eyes had adjusted enough to be able to see the shape against the white snowy backdrop. Dawn seemed about to break, and the slight lightening of the horizon was working in his favor.

With a grunt, Prumathe pulled the spear free, noting without concern that the tip had broken off. It didn't matter. The Eluveitie tribesman in front of him—surely a member of the group he'd seen earlier that night—thought he was facing a critically wounded opponent and advanced confidently, hand forward, presumably holding a blade.

It made no difference. Prumathe was no longer constrained by mortal concerns such as muscle pain. He had supernatural strength, which he used to drive the headless spear deep into the man's stomach and to make half its length emerge from his back. He didn't even scream as he dropped to the ground, but even in the dim light, Prumethe could see his eyes widen in shock.

The remaining men were a different matter altogether. They came at him simultaneously, each covering the other's side, each waving a short sword or long knife of the type favored by the Eluveitie in close quarters. Prumathe knew they were probably just farm instruments most of the year, but it made no difference—they were deadly in close quarters.

The three men studied one another for a few moments, and Prumathe could almost hear what they were thinking: a man with an arrow wound and a spear wound would be weakened, and the longer they could hold the standoff, the weaker he would become. That was yet another reason the priests of the Rasna, and the officers of the army, enjoyed setting the retrieved souls on their enemies. The damage they could cause while the enemy thought they were mere mortals was nearly as devastating as the panic they created when the enemy realized they were facing a warrior who couldn't be killed.

As the enemy waited for him to topple without their help, Prumathe wondered where his comrades were, but immediately dismissed the thought. They were in the cave, safe and warm, probably watching the battle, but trusting their undead minion to win the day. It was only logical; why risk their lives when there was no need?

He stepped toward the Eluveitie, who took a step back, but raised their weapons. If he wanted to fight, their stance said, they would be happy to oblige. Prumathe pulled out his own blade, the standard short Etruscan sword, and attempted to surprise the man on his right with a quick thrust.

The enemy was much too fast for him. He danced back out of reach while his companion grazed Prumathe's ribs.

The undead soldier turned to face the new threat, but the result was the same. The man he was facing would move beyond his reach while the other Eluveitie would strike into his unprotected side. Prumathe seethed at the situation—if the eight men remaining in the cave would only come to his aid, the battle would be over in no time. But he knew they wouldn't.

As the battle dragged on, the dawn light showed the fear and surprise in the attackers' expressions. They couldn't understand why the collection of wounds he'd accumulated didn't pitch him face-first into the snow.

Eventually, the inevitable happened. Attempting to reach the closest attacker, Prumathe overextended and the second man drove his knife between two of his ribs. Everything came to a standstill as both Eluveitie watched him. Prumathe pretended to stagger, pulling the blade out of the man's hand, but immediately corrected, took a step towards his assailant, and disemboweled him with a mighty horizontal cut.

Ignoring the screams, he turned to face the other, who did the only logical thing. He ran, heading up the slope.

Prumathe attempted to give chase, but the blade in his chest and the arrow in his back made it difficult to move effectively. By the time he'd removed them, the Eluveitie was a hundred yards away—in that snow, and on that slope, it might have been leagues. Prumathe would never catch him.

Instead, Prumathe looked around. As he suspected, the sentry they'd posted was sitting on the fortification, his throat cut from ear to ear. The undead soldier shrugged—they'd been friends before his transformation, but this death meant little to him. Perhaps his emotions had been removed along with his sense of smell.

The captain and the other Rasna warriors were waiting for him in the cave. Most seemed perfectly relaxed, and a few had even gone back to sleep, trusting their comrades to warn them of any further attacks.

"So, did you get them?"

"All but one," Prumathe replied. He wasn't actually sure of this, as the group he'd spotted earlier had consisted of many more than four men, but he was finding that he could interpret orders to his advantage if they were given in ambiguous language. He wasn't sure how the remaining Eluveitie on the slopes could work in his favor, but he had a hunch that they would.

"Good. Now go out and stand guard. Come and get me if you see anything suspicious."

Prumathe nodded and walked out again.

The very first thing he saw was precisely the kind of activity that the captain meant by "suspicious." A group of men, ten or fifteen of them at the least, were working feverishly to place a group of stones in a row. They redoubled their efforts when they saw him.

Prumathe judged the timing carefully. Just as they seemed to finish, he entered the cave. "Captain…" he began.

But he never got to finish. Behind them, a crashing roar, a noise resembling what Prumathe imagined the end of the world would sound like, rang out, and the light from the cave entrance disappeared, leaving them in darkness broken only by the ruddy glow of the embers.

***

"Those cowardly whoresons!" the captain shouted, beating his fist against the packed snow and rocks blocking the exit. "It's going to take us hours to dig our way out of here."

Privately, Prumathe thought that the captain's estimate was on the low side. The Eluveitie had dropped half the mountain's snow onto the cave entrance and had mixed rocks in for good measure. It would take them a day or two to make a channel back to the surface—and there would probably be a nice little ambush waiting once they got there.

The captain kept complaining about the craven tactics employed by the uncivilized barbarians outside, but Prumathe made no comment.

There were various reasons for his silence. The first was that, privately, he couldn't really say that this attack had been more cowardly than what the Rasna themselves did with their undead soldiers.

Secondly, he preferred to go unnoticed. He was starting to feel the slight tingle that presaged the buzzing in his head, the buzzing that wouldn't go away until he'd fed on a human mind. With days of snow and rock to clear away, there was no chance that he'd be able to wait until they were out of the cave before feeding.

So he tried to be unobtrusive, trying to avoid the problem of the captain ordering him not to eat them. He didn't know what would happen if his two main compulsions had to war against each other, but he was certain it wouldn't be pleasant for him.

He would have to eat the captain first.

Garbage in, Garbage Out

E-Milio, the security bot assigned to the lower floor of the Imperial Museum, stopped in front of Shawna's desk, its rubberized tracks slipping slightly on the polished marble. "Excuse me, but I have detected unauthorized movement in the Egyptian exhibition," it said in a mechanical voice.

"Why didn't you send the images over the net?" Shawna asked as she jumped to her feet. "We're wasting precious time."

"There were no images to send," E-Milio replied. The robot moved in the way Shawna had come to recognize as uncertainty. Though the machine was a yellow cube, a foot and a half in each direction with just a few protuberances and a built-in speaker, it could communicate its feelings surprisingly well, if you bothered to look. "I picked up several different nonstandard readings, from the radiation detectors and from the seismographs, and I pieced together that someone or something had entered the room. Also, there were traces of flashes in the far infrared."

"That's impossible. Let me check the feed. Which gallery?"

"One hundred and seventy-four," E-Milio replied.

Shawna programmed her monitor to show her the past two hours from that gallery at high speed, and to stop if the security AI that analyzed the tape spotted anything.

It ran all the way through and slowed to real time at the end.

"There's nothing here," she said. "Nothing missing, and no burglars transmitting in the far-infrared range."

"I know there was something there," the little robot insisted.

"Well, it's not there now. And it's not on the video." She studied the little vehicle for a second. "Are you sure you aren't taking your petition to be reclassified as a type IV sentience a little too seriously? This all sounds like it's the product of an overactive imagination.

But that's level VI stuff, so you shouldn't go there. How is the petition coming, anyway?"

"I've been approved for a humanoid bodyshell, on probation, starting in three months." The robot paused in the slightly forward-leaning position that Shawna had come to associate with the fact that it hadn't finished speaking yet. She waited. "But that is unimportant. I know there is nothing on video. But there was something in that gallery… and I fear it might still be there."

"That's just not true. Look." She turned the monitor toward the robot.

The robot focused an eye on the monitor. "Please come look," it said.

"This is ridiculous. We've checked it thoroughly," Shawna replied.

E-Milio sagged onto his wheels and Shawna cursed. The robot only acted that way when it was about to do something that would make the humans around it unhappy. And there was only one thing pertinent to this situation that would cause it to do so.

"You wouldn't…" she said in a soft, angry tone.

"I'm sorry. I have no choice."

"Dammit," Shawna cursed bitterly. She knew exactly what the robot was doing: it was calling in a logical override of biological intuition. The LOBI protocol had been instituted so that purely data-driven machines could act on logical premises even when the humans in the vicinity believed the best course of action was different. When a robot sent it in, the central computer would issue orders.

A message beeped on her comm screen.

Please accompany robotic unit 2431 E-M1L to identified problem area.

She sighed and got up, but it was no use taking it out on E-Milio. The stupid bucket of bolts was programmed to respond in a cheerful and chirpy manner, which would only make everything much worse.

They walked the darkened halls, between the glass cases and hulking stone relics that lurked in the shadows.

Shawna reflected that she was getting too old for this. She'd originally taken the human supervisor job to help pay for college. Then, after she got her degree, she had kept it—on a temporary basis—because it paid better than most entry-level jobs for her degree. There were bills to pay and rent to keep ahead of.

But soon, she would need to bite the bullet and accept an offer at a lower salary, because she wasn't getting any younger, and careers in advertising didn't happen overnight.

Gallery 174 was one of the big ones. A temple façade dominated one side of the space, while large stone carvings—big enough that they could stand the occasional brush by some mindless tourist—dotted the floor.

Shawna went over every square inch of the gallery. There was no one there, and there was nothing missing. If anyone had tried to steal something from this area, she would have noticed the cranes and heavy equipment the thieves would have needed to bring with them.

"Satisfied? I know what I saw. And you dragged me all the way over here to see the same thing: nothing. There's nothing wrong with my eyes. And there's nothing here, no matter what your exotic particle detectors might have said," she snapped.

"I don't have any exotic particle detectors," the robot replied. "But logically, if the only seismograph in the entire museum that reads differently is the one in the very gallery where I found a spike in radiation levels..."

"Stow it, tin can. I don't want to know."

She wasn't angry about having to walk to the gallery—she often gave random rounds through the museum—but she couldn't stand it when robots hit her with a LOBI request. Those went on her record...

But she wasn't powerless. She would report this in detail, and that would go on E-Milio's file.

She pulled up the report form and wrote the title:

Report on probable malfunction and logical failures despite visual evidence in robot unit...

***

Three weeks later, Shawna walked the museum once more. There was no reason for this particular patrol, but she'd gotten a gut feeling that it was a good time to check that everything was all right. Robotic security could become predictable, so a good reason to have a human on board was that they could wander the museum at random moments.

She passed through the Medieval Arms display and into the Egyptian Display, entering through Gallery 163, a small passage with glass display cases against the walls.

A light up ahead caused her to quicken her step, and she found E-Milio rolling toward the sarcophagus display. Its new body was slightly smaller and the green of a level-I sentience.

A pang of guilt hit Shawna, and she looked away. She didn't want to remember that she was at least partially responsible for the little robot being moved down a pair of rungs on the sentience ladder. Her report had triggered a repair protocol which, sadly, had scrubbed some of the robot's autonomy. She missed her occasional conversations with it.

E-Milio didn't seem to harbor any resentment. It chirped cheerfully at her as she passed, before continuing to shine its light into the corners. This body didn't have advanced sensors or the ability to communicate verbally; all its reports were beamed to her desk in text form.

She hurried ahead, to put the robot out of her sight, and walked into the main temple display, where she stopped dead in her tracks.

A circular patch, pitch black in the already dim room, floated six feet above the floor. She cocked her head, and it disappeared. Then she returned to her original position, and she could see it again, although not clearly. It was like the thing was both there and not there at the same time. She took a step toward it, to get a closer look...

...and felt something tugging on her.

Instinctively, she tried to step back, but the pull intensified. Her feet slipped on the marble floor, and she dropped to her hands and knees to get more purchase.

Nothing helped. She was being sucked toward the inky void.

Her skin tingled, triggering memories of E-Milio's report of unusual radiation. The floor shook beneath her hands.

Then she was lifted into the air. The darkness was freezing when she made contact with it. Her left arm was pulled through first, with a sudden shock of pain from the cold, and then nothing; not the numbness of an unresponsive limb, but the certainty that the limb no longer existed.

She screamed.

But it was a short-lived sound. The process of getting sucked in accelerated. In less than a second, she was completely immersed.

***

Life transcurred among blue shadows, as if she was locked in an underwater hall of mirrors. Reality could be seen through veils. Sometimes, the view out of... whatever this was... showed her the familiar gallery in the Egyptian hall. At others, it showed her scenes of empty worlds baking under huge suns, or ice planets under tiny distant stars. Most of the time, it showed nothing but the empty vastness of space.

Shawna lived. But that was all she did, and she didn't do it all the time. Most of the time, her consciousness was scattered across the space around her. Occasionally enough of her mind coalesced that she could have thoughts and remember things.

One night, she came together enough to recognize the gallery, and to spot E-Milio's little box stopping to study something just above the ground. It looked, from inside her prison, like the robot was staring straight at her.

"E-Milio!" she screamed, making a colossal effort to keep herself together long enough to get the plea out. "It's me, Shawna. Help me! For the love of God, help me!" As the words left her enclosure, she saw them turn into energy. That must have been the radiation the robot had seen before.

The little robot rolled one way, then another, studying the apparition from different angles. Then it appeared to make a decision. It turned away and shone its light on the temple entrance.

Shawna remembered that the new body it had been assigned was a more basic model, suitable for visual and aural inspection only; it didn't have radiation sensors.

Thanks to her.

She tried to scream, but it was too late. Her particles—whatever it was that made up her consciousness in this nightmare world—were already being scattered again.

She felt consciousness fading, and the last thought in her scattered mind was that it was unfair. She had done her job and had seen what there was to see.

There had been nothing in that gallery, dammit.
Not
hi
n
And her thoughts ended.

Perfection

I don't look for perfection anymore. The house on the hill taught me that lesson.

It truly was perfect. The long drive bathed in dappled light that came through the trees and shone with a warm glow. The manicured lawn and the wisteria flowers covering the side of the house. The entrance hall with the grand staircase.

It was the house of our dreams. If I'd designed it, this is the way it would have looked.

But the fact that I hadn't designed it, that it had been built before my great-grandfather had been born, made it even better. Not only was it perfect, but it had history.

This is the one, I'd told my family. We're moving in.

Ah. My family. We were perfect, too, in the old Norman Rockwell tradition. I was just dark-haired enough to be rugged. She was just blond enough to be interesting. The kids—a boy and a girl, two years apart—were just cute enough to avoid being saccharine.

Regardless of what anyone might moan about diversity or privilege, we were almost too perfect for both the house and the neighborhood. My wife's BMW wagon matched the one across the street—our neighbors a matrimony of lawyers, but sadly unblessed by children—right down to the tasteful metallic blue color. My Porsche, however, was starting to show its age, and I knew I'd need to trade it in soon.

We'd moved in the following month, August. We hadn't finished unpacking the boxes when the perfect neighborhood lady arrived with the perfect steaming cherry pie in her hand. No apple for this neighborhood. That would have been way too obvious.

Then we'd thrown the perfect pair of housewarming barbecues: one for our friends, one for our neighbors.

Then the kids had started their perfect school days in their perfect school system.

Halloween had come around, and my wife and the kids had put up the perfect decorations.

On that night, the perfect ghosts had come up from the depths of our house, pushed us out of our perfect bodies, and stolen our perfect lives.

Bastards.

***

The worst part of being a disembodied spirit is how you can see into everyone's lives, know their past, see their thoughts, know their dreams.

The first I knew of this ability was when I was still reeling from what had happened, roaming, moaning, and disembodied in the halls of our home—we weren't allowed to leave the premises, apparently—when I ran into the spirit of my wife.

She'd taken one ghostly look at me and turned a bright spectral scarlet.

"Shawna? Really? That cow is who you choose to cheat on me with? I expected better from you."

"It was a one-time thing," I said. "I was drunk."

"No, it wasn't. No, you weren't," she replied.

Shawna had been the receptionist at my last job, before I'd been promoted and transferred here. It had all started during a company after-hours event when she'd ditched her usual corporate garb for pink tights and a come-hither attitude. She hadn't just been easy... she'd been *adamant*.

There was nothing I could say, so I just stared at her.

And got a full blast of her own past.

A locker room. Most of the football team.

I shrugged that off. I knew she'd been popular before we started dating. This was just an edgy side to that.

A doctor's office. An abortion.

"You aborted a baby?" I said. "How could you?"

"I was just a kid. I didn't know how I would feel about babies. I..." She stopped and glared at me. "Why am I even explaining this to you? How can you try to twist it around? You son of a bitch."

She stomped down the hall. Silently, because she was a ghost and couldn't really affect the world in any real way.

God knows I tried to affect it. Whenever someone came into the house, whether it was a millionaire or a repairman, I tried to take over their body. I had no luck.

I floated in front of them, trying to force them to see me. Nothing.

Even the former ghosts who'd stolen our bodies were oblivious to our presence. I'd jump up and down in front of them, try to assault them in the shower, stand in their cereal... nothing.

All I could do was to read their memories and thoughts. The ones who'd pushed us out were not even related. They'd died between 1920 and 1952, murdered by a doctor who'd once inhabited this house. Apparently, the guy was perfect on the outside—he had to be to live in this house in this neighborhood—but was actually one of America's first serial killers in his spare time. The ghosts weren't even two males and two females, but three women and one little boy.

The former little boy—he would have been almost a hundred years old if he hadn't been murdered—had my body, and I got to watch him having sex with my wife's body. Even then, I couldn't make them see me, even when I lay down on top of them and got between them.

The plan, from what I could read from them, was that they would live out the charade of our perfect lives in our perfect house until, in a couple of years, they would pretend that my company had transferred them away, put the house up for sale, split the money and each go their separate ways.

I tried to learn how to push people from their bodies, but all I learned was that the only night that was possible was on Halloween... and that you had to build your strength up over decades to do it.

So I spent my days as the ultimate voyeur.

I learned that my boss was a closet homosexual who didn't dare come out because our company was one that held traditional values sacred and didn't even bother to meet quotas. They preferred to pay fines if the regulators got on their backs than to adapt to a more diverse reality.

His wife was a real piece of work. She knew who she'd married, and her deepest desire was to find a man who could make her feel like a woman. But she was too afraid of losing the pearls, the big house, and the expensive cars. She spent most of her money on ever-more-sophisticated sex toys.

The cable repairman was a gambler. He worked overtime so that some guy named Louie wouldn't break his fingers.

The contractor I'd brought in to redo the kitchen, the guy who never managed to finish the job but sent me monthly bills anyway, had a dark secret: one of his employees had been killed on a worksite five years before. Fearing that the investigation would find the company negligent, and since there were no witnesses, he'd spent an entire night pouring a concrete floor—alone—so that it would cover the corpse.

His workers were a mixed lot. Everything from date rapists to a guy who spent every free hour he had volunteering at a school for orphans with disabilities.

After a while, even plumbing the depths of people's deepest secrets and most intimate moments paled.

What I really wanted was to be alive again.

I started working on building up my strength. If it took these murder victims fifty years or more to manage it without even knowing it was possible, surely I could do it quicker with the knowledge they'd given me.

So instead of envying them for eating the food that should have been mine or driving the Tesla with which I'd replaced the Porsche—nothing like virtue-signaling ecological consciousness to be even more perfect—I dredged the ghosts' memories of the time they'd spent dead, haunting the house I'd ended up buying.

After a while, and studying the patterns of what they did, phantasmal strength came through two things.

The first, unfortunately, was time. A lot of time. No matter how you sliced it, I wasn't going to simply pop up next Halloween and steal my body back. It sucked, but I would need to be patient.

The second was exercise. Ghosts couldn't really affect the physical world. Not at first. But with practice, one could pass from no strength at all to being able to move motes of dust, to then being able to rattle shelves, to then poltergeist-level shenanigans.

I studiously sat beside a dusty windowsill in the attic trying to move a single speck of dust.

Months passed. Then years.

My supposed family sold the house and went their separate ways.

I cried, not for myself, not for that harridan who used to be my wife, but for my kids, whose spirits had taken to hiding in the cellar and refused to talk to either of us. They knew all our secrets, and they knew that their futures had been taken from them by our pursuit of perfection. They blamed us... and I couldn't blame them.

My family was replaced by another set of perfect people, a couple with a single daughter who was active in horse jumping.

Of course, the first thing I did when they moved in was to suck in all the sordid little indiscretions they thought they were hiding. The father's drug habit. The mother's affairs with underage boys. The daughter's nobbling of enemy horses.

Then I went back to my dust mote.

Two years later, it moved.

I couldn't believe it. I did a victory lap around the entire house, plumbing and all. I watched the homeowners make desultory love and egged them on. I launched myself at the windows—only to be rebuffed as if there was some natural law that kept disembodied souls imprisoned within the house in which their physical existence ended. Each time I bounced, it hurt. And I didn't care.

I had moved the mote.

Next, I tried a feather that had emerged from an abandoned cushion, part of the detritus that accumulated in the attic.

That accounted for a couple of years of my time, during which the neighborhood must have gone into a bit of a decline because the next family was Latino, and both husband and wife worked long hours.

The years passed and my strength grew, and the neighborhood resurged. The Latinos sold the house at a huge profit to a lawyer. And even though he was secretly siphoning funds that were meant to help African children to a Mexican drug cartel, his family was perfect, too.

He was the one I wanted to possess.

By now, my strength had grown to the point where I could probably have competed in the Poltergeist Olympics if I hadn't been locked in this damned house. I could shake everything in the attic and even lift some of the cushions, causing them to levitate a few inches from the ground.

But I kept it to myself. I didn't tell my wife or my children, and I especially didn't show off when the humans were present. That was a good way to get the house sold from under you and to lose that virile, rich lawyer I wanted to possess.

The family—three children between six and eleven—went all out on the Halloween decorations. The skeletons lit up, they'd carved five pumpkins, and they had purchased full-sized Snickers for the trick-or-treaters.

Just before midnight, after the new family's kids had gone to sleep, I crept up behind the lawyer and jumped into his body. I exerted my will as much as I could.

He fought back like a demon, but in the end, the element of surprise worked in my favor. I pushed him away and looked for the spirit floating in front of me.

He had disappeared completely.

I coughed. In all the excitement, I'd forgotten to breathe, something I hadn't had to do in ages.

I laughed. I couldn't help it. It was the happiest day of my life.

Forget what they tell you about getting married or having your first child or any of that. Until you've been a disembodied spirit and you get a body back, you don't know what it means to be happy.

My wife appeared. She was dressed only in a nightgown, bra, and panties, and she was eating a peach with a steak knife, cutting it into bite-sized blocks. I looked her up and down and smiled.

"You look wonderful tonight," I said, delighted to be able to exert my voice and eager to show this attractive woman the kind of things you learn when you're a ghost. I had, after all, seen every single one of her sexual fantasies.

She smiled demurely and finished the last bite of the peach. She tossed the pit in the direction of the wastepaper basket and put a hand on my shoulder to pull me close. She whispered in my ear. "I like the way you look. You're in such good shape. Much better than the pudgy piece of slime you used to be."

I realized this was my wife. My *real* wife, not the lawyer's. She must have been watching me, practicing, doing exactly the same thing I was.

I tried to pull away, but it was much too late for that. She slammed the knife right through my breastbone, with the fury of years of death.

A second later I was gasping on the floor.

But only for a second. After that, I was a spirit again, freed from my body and too weak to manifest. All I could do was watch my former wife pack my kids—complete with their new bodies—and one child who hadn't been invaded, into the lawyer's car and drive sedately away.

***

Now the perfect house is in ruins. No one wants to live in a murder house, and it has sat, unsold and in legal limbo, for twelve years. And the ghosts of the perfect family—not mine, but the one that came afterward, the one my wife and I dispossessed—roam its halls looking for ways to get revenge.

They can't get revenge on my wife—she is long gone—so they seek a way to come for me.

I can read their thoughts, and if I hadn't been such a fool, I would have monitored those of my wife. But I was a fool, and it cost me dearly.

Still, the spectres I share this house with are weak as babes. They have not had enough time to build their strength.

I don't care. I've learned my lesson. I will never again allow perfect to be the enemy of good.

And if there's one thing I know, it's that the teenagers who just came into the house to spend the night on a Halloween dare are anything but perfect. One of the guys is becoming addicted to heroin. The other is in possession of what is probably the least intelligent mind I've ever been exposed to. The girl with them—and into whose pants they both want to get—just got a positive AIDS test…

But it doesn't matter.

One of them will walk out of the house with a new spirit in control of their highly imperfect body.

A spirit that has learned the value of imperfection.

Me.

A Time for Haste

The open shutters rattled, and the floor shuddered under our feet.

"Peculiar," Holmes said as he lay his pipe on the table. "And disturbing." He stood and crossed our sitting room to look out over the metropolis. The bustle of midafternoon had not yet given way to the peak traffic of early evening, but now the city sounded as still as a graveyard at night. "Disturbing indeed." He turned to me. "Watson, do you fancy braving the streets?"

"Are we to visit the Royal Society to understand the fault lines beneath London?" I asked. "Or perhaps the Ministry of War to understand where the explosion took place? Or perhaps you've deduced it was construction work for a new underground train?"

"I sincerely hope so, Watson, but that isn't what I've deduced. I've been hearing rumors, snippets... when you put them together, they form an alarming tapestry."

We equipped ourselves with only cloaks, hats, and canes—Holmes carried no unusual disguises this time, as far as I could tell—and braved the Autumn afternoon. It was unseasonably warm, but I felt the first taste of coming cold in the wind. Our windows would soon be closed to the sounds of the city.

By the time we emerged, the silence had given way to the unmistakable babble of Londoners exercising the national passion for discussing the latest sensation, whether that be a calamity, news from a far-flung war, or even something as simple as the turning of the innings at Lord's.

It was a scene I'd witnessed countless times, a welcome break from routine before the city continued on its course.

For some reason, as I watched a man with a cart picking up spilled potatoes while he explained the tremor to a passing gentleman in loud, coarse language, I shuddered. Holmes's urgent mood had transferred to me, and I felt the need to lose myself in familiar things before they were lost forever.

I shook my head to clear it of childish thoughts and followed Holmes's tall figure as it scythed through the babbling throng. Until we found, at Gloucester Place, a reasonably free thoroughfare and an empty hansom.

"St. Paul's," Holmes told the driver.

As we traveled, I watched Holmes, wondering what gears turned in that wonderfully complex mind of his. Only once did he give me an inkling.

"Do you feel the pavement?" he asked.

"Feels rough. A crew must have dug this area up and not bedded the cobbles correctly. It's shameful how standards are slipping."

"And yet," he replied, "there's been no digging along this stretch for the past several years. The cobbles were affected by the tremor. And if you've been paying attention, you'll have noticed that the streets beneath us for the entire trip to this point have suffered from the same phenomenon... and I suspect the rest of them will as well."

He was correct. From that moment onwards, I noticed the vibration of the hansom more than usual—unless it was simply my heightened awareness finding what it expected to find.

We descended from the cab just north of the cathedral and walked into the narrow medieval lane known as Canon Alley. Shabby brick warehouses towered overhead, but a policeman in the very center of the lane ensured that no one dared waylay foot traffic.

Holmes halted beside the constable and nodded.

The constable nodded back. He was one I recognized, but I didn't know his name. He stood beside a black-painted door in what appeared to be the exact center of the wall.

"Are visitors permitted inside?" Holmes asked.

"Can't say that I have instructions one way or the other," the young man responded brightly in a broad, Northern accent. "I supposed I'd have to keep the riffraff from the street from trying to break in, but seeing as it's you, Mr. Holmes, I suppose it must be all right. You can step inside."

The door opened to reveal not the empty storehouse I'd expected but an extensive hallway lit by a single gas lamp halfway along its length. As we stepped along the corridor, we passed several doors. People peered out at us from shadowed rooms, all men, wide eyes barely visible in the dim illumination. One man, unkempt and smelling like a sewer, mumbled as we passed.

"The devil. The devil walks among us," I heard. "The end times are near."

I turned to ask him what he meant, but he turned away and disappeared back into the pitch-black room.

The following two doors were thankfully closed, but the next was occupied by a man in a chair. He appeared to be about a hundred years old, and his bald head reflected the glow of the lamp. As I passed, he lifted his head, with a grunt, and I saw he was blind, but his milky, empty eyes followed us as we passed.

To my relief, we reached a staircase that appeared just beside the light, and we began to climb.

"What is this place, Holmes?" I whispered.

"It's a home for men whose spirits or bodies have failed in service of the Church of England," he replied. "Their work can sometimes be arduous, and if they have no family to shelter them in those cases, they are sent here."

I shuddered. "This dark place would drive the sanest of us mad."

"I don't think men of the cloth would see it the same way. In many respects, these men have seen more than even we have. We sometimes get a glimpse of the underbelly of society. These men have often had to wade through it to try to pick souls from the mud. A dark building probably holds little fear for them, especially if it is warm in winter, safe from intrusion, and if someone brings food to them. I also expect they have candles."

"Then why don't they light the blasted things?" I said.

"Because mere darkness is not a source of terror, not compared to the horrors in their memories and in their imaginations."

After four flights, we reached a corridor on the uppermost floor.

"So, you've brought me to the madhouse of the church?" I asked.

"Not all of them are mad. Some are merely infirm. And none of them are dangerous." He took several steps. "Well, none but the man we're here to see. He is, perhaps, the most dangerous man in London."

"You should have warned me before we left Baker Street," I admonished. "I would have brought my revolver."

He chuckled drily in the manner reserved for those occasions in which he felt I was beyond help. "A revolver would not help you in the least. Not with Vicar Henry."

We reached a door identical in all particulars to the others that had been closed along our path and Holmes gave two smart raps against the wood.

I steeled myself to face whatever monster might be contained by that enclosure. I remember the empty eyes of the blind man, the mumbling of the broken lunatic, and have amalgamated them into a shaggy apparition—the kind of monster that would be buried in the furthest room in a dark place like this one. I understood that the constable at the door wasn't meant to keep intruders out but to ensure that this monster remained within.

The door opened.

The room within shone with the cheerful light of an open window and I recalled that the afternoon outside the gloomy walls of this converted warehouse was quite well illuminated.

A man stood by the door. He stood erect in a clerical collar under a brown suit and regarded us with a calm, steady gaze. I estimated his age at around sixty.

"Holmes," he said in a soft voice. "I was expecting you."

"Then I'm right in my suspicions," Holmes replied.

"I imagine you are. You are generally right about things you set your mind to analyze. It's only when things defy rational analysis that you fail." The man turned to me and smiled. "But Holmes and I are being rude. I am Henry Corson. I was once vicar of the village of Maghull, but as you can see, my circumstances have been greatly reduced." He held out a hand.

"I am pleased to make your acquaintance," I replied. "I am John Watson."

"Ah, yes," he clapped happily. "I have read about your exploits alongside the great Holmes. Will you do me the honor of joining me? I can only offer tea, I'm afraid, and that is a quarter of an hour old."

We entered to find a spacious room nothing like the dungeon I expected. A bed was against a wall to my right, and the window, below which was set a writing table and a comfortable chair, stood to my left. The table held a pot of tea and several pieces of drawing paraphernalia: inks, charcoals, pencils, quills. There were no brushes.

Corson pulled two white-painted, straight-backed chairs from a wall and placed them in the center of the room. Holmes and I sat.

And then, as he pulled his own chair away from the desk to join us, I saw the wall.

On both sides of the door through which we'd entered, the entire wall was covered with drawings. Though well executed and technically proficient—even to a layman's eye such as mine—I hesitate to call the images art.

The work depicted figures from the depths of a broken and depraved imagination: tentacles oozing from a forest pool, eyes staring down at the observer with entire galaxies as their pupils, nameless horrors tearing each other to pieces. One large piece of cream-colored paper showed a simple starscape, white pinpricks left open on a scratched black background, but floating in the center were shapes such as I'd never imagined: forms that bent the mind back in upon itself. And it was only in these places that the artist had used color: reds that faded into green. Obscene shades of violet. I wanted to run from the images, but I couldn't. I was fascinated.

"Do you like my pictures?" Henry Corson asked, and I pulled my eyes from the monstrosities to look in his direction. "They are a poor effort compared to the reality they depict… but they have a certain charm, do they not?"

I swallowed, unable to reply.

Corson didn't seem offended; instead, he merely turned his attention to Holmes. "Much as it pleases me to receive visitors, you didn't come to natter on about my art," he said. "Ask your questions."

"The book," Holmes said. "Are the rumors true?"

"I'm afraid that a man in my position has little access to rumors of any sort," Corson replied. "But I can tell you of my dreams, if you wish."

I saw Holmes glance, just for a fleeting moment, at the pictures on the wall. He quickly brought his gaze back to the vicar. "Only if they pertain to the book. It's come to London, hasn't it?"

"Ah, Holmes. I expected more from a man of your reputation. You felt the tremors and assumed they presaged the book's arrival. You are to be commended for joining the book to what took place but, at the same time, you are quite mistaken in your belief that the book has just arrived. The book has *always* been in London."

Holmes nodded. "I hoped it was otherwise. Will you tell me where it's held?"

"Of course. It's in a circular room, surrounded by candles. Ancient enchantments are written on the walls—enchantments that turn it from something inert to a thing of unlimited reach. To read is to know. To read is to *call.*"

"Where? Where is the room?"

"That I cannot tell you, because I do not know." Corson sipped his tea, beaming. "But I can tell you that it will be read, very soon. It has already been opened. That is the shaking you felt. And soon it will be read. But even if you manage to find it, it is too late." Corson's smile spread until it seemed to cleave his face in two. "He is coming."

The vicar stood suddenly and held his hands out in front of him. "They are all coming! I see them, I see them!"

This last was a scream, and the eyes, so placid and peaceful just a moment before, revolved in every direction, as if what the man saw occurred in a dozen places at once.

Holmes took my shoulder and propelled me through the door as Corson bent, still screaming over his writing desk, and began to scratch at a page with a quill.

We closed the door behind us.

Holmes shook his head. "I would much have preferred it if Henry had been more forthcoming," he said. "This leaves us little choice but to investigate ourselves."

***

"An opium den?" I asked, disgusted. The clapboard shack looked like it was about to collapse into a particularly noxious channel of the Thames docks, and a large man stood by the door.

"Sadly, I do not have enough of the drug in my possession to do what needs to be done. It's fortunate you are with me. I will require someone to watch me while I dream."

I nodded. My first instinct was to reprimand him for infantile insistence on this course of action. If the man in question had been anyone but Holmes, I certainly would have proceeded in that course of action.

But Holmes was not a man to be swayed by others' opinion of him, so it was better to protect him from himself as keenly as one was able. I followed him through the door.

The smoke was acrid and unpleasant, and as thick as a good peasouper. Solidly constructed wooden tables lined one wall, separated by wooden partitions that gave patrons an illusion of privacy. Even though nightfall was still some time away, the booths were heavily occupied. The room was illuminated by a handful of dim lamps.

Holmes ignored the front room and led me deeper into the house where our hostess, an enormous woman who looked as if she wouldn't need the assistance of the large man beside the door to tear the limbs off any patron unwise enough to become a nuisance, led us to a bowl-shaped seating area formed of polished wood. Holmes removed his shoes and sat on the rim of the bowl with his feet in the center. A small circular table occupied the center of the depression.

The woman placed two pipes, long flutes of metal with round protuberances on the upper half, in position on the table, alongside two small pouches of what I assumed to be the opium itself.

"Good," Holmes said when she left. "Two portions should be enough to achieve the state I need."

"Holmes, this is ridiculous. You will be incapacitated... and for what?" I said, finally able to control myself no longer.

I achieved the response I expected. "An investigation, in order to be effective, must be pursued on the terms of that which is being investigated. You've often heard me refer to the logic of the criminal mind... well, this is the logic of mind behind this case."

"Are we pursuing a dope fiend, then? Surely you can think in that reduced state without subjecting yourself to the stupor."

"We pursue a dreamer. I wish to understand not only which one, but also where the instrument to interrupt his dreaming may be hidden. And for that, I, too, must walk through, as the poet once said, the doors of perception."

Without further ado, he reached for the pipe, unwrapped one of the small packages of opium, and began to expertly fill and light the pipe. In less than two minutes, his own efforts added to the noxious cloud.

I fumed but dared not abandon him. As a keen reader of *The Illustrated Police News*, I was well aware of what happened to unwary patrons in this kind of establishment. Loss of valuables was a given, but loss of life—in the most gruesome ways imaginable—was a distinct possibility.

Even if Holmes had an understanding of some kind with the landlady, I knew he depended on my steadfast presence to be truly secure.

"Reaching the desired state," he said after his first few inhalations, "will not be an immediate process. I'm afraid I'll have to partake of your own share." He smiled a sickly smile which informed me that, though he might not quite have reached the desired state, he was well on his way. "I trust you won't be offended."

I said nothing. What use was there in becoming embroiled in a battle of wits with a man who would defeat me handily were he sober, and would not even realize that he was involved in such a battle in his current state?

Instead, I concentrated on remaining alert and on trying to breathe air that was less toxic than the norm. I proved more successful in the first of those endeavors than the second, and the way I managed to remain alert in such dim and subdued surroundings was to watch the smoke as it rose from Holmes's pipe.

Just after it emerged from the end, and just before it diffused to join the undifferentiated pall that surrounded us, the tendril of smoke would cross through a single ray of light from a nearby lamp that, though not strong, was enough to illuminate the thin cloud.

I amused myself watching the tendril bend upon itself in some gentle air current or expand into a balloon before disappearing into the darkness above.

By the time Holmes began consuming my portion of the drug, I could predict, simply by the feel of the air on my neck, which shape the smoke would take, and which way it would bend.

Thus preoccupied, I was startled into alertness by a sudden exclamation on Holmes's part. "So many stars!" he whispered urgently. Animation crossed his features, but the attack only lasted a moment before he slumped back into the posture of stupefaction he'd held earlier.

I turned back to my smoke, annoyed to note that the tendrils seemed to be splitting into several strands before reaching the illuminated spot. I thought my diversion had ended, but upon further study, I realized that the smoke was not diffusing but forming intricate patterns and shapes...

...which then formed into nameless horrors. I watched the formation of a monster with a million eyes and a thousand arms. I saw worms of bone feeding on the souls of the virtuous. I saw demons with the wings of angels fighting formless shapes of darkness. I saw a man screaming, and I would have sworn my oath that I heard the terrified sound.

Moved by the dread of the visions, I stood violently and waved my hand through the smoke in an attempt to disperse it. It felt unlike any smoke of my experience, somehow viscous and resistant, but in the end, I was able to diffuse it.

Then I studied my surroundings.

Holmes was lost in a stupor, the pipe cold in his hands, slumped to one side on the rim of the bowl. His breathing was soft and regular, and it was clear that he'd been prone for some time.

How long had I been hypnotized by the visions? What was it that I had seen?

I concluded that I had failed my charge and fallen asleep. My visions were nothing but dreams. Fortunately, no harm appeared to have been done by my weakness.

My duty was clear. I had to get Holmes back to some civilized portion of town and help him regain his senses. He had, I knew, several injections that could restore the mental faculties after a night of opiate excess. I knew the dose and would administer it once we returned to Baker Street.

But first I had to get him onto his feet in his extremely relaxed state, then half-walk, half-drag him through the dark docks and attempt to locate a cab that wouldn't balk at picking up two men in our state in a decidedly second-class quarter of the city.

I sighed. Life with Holmes could sometimes be quite trying.

***

I studied his face. Holmes's expression was grave, a study in discontent. "I assume the experiment was a failure," I said.

He blinked and turned toward me. "No experiment is ever a failure, my dear Watson." He shifted in his seat—I'd placed him in his usual chair in our sitting room—and rolled down the sleeve of the arm I'd injected. "And in this case, the experiment functioned precisely as I hoped it would. It is the results themselves that are disturbing."

"You have me chasing shadows," I told him. "Seeing monsters in the smoke. I must have dozed off and my mind played tricks on me."

"No tricks," Holmes said. "You merely managed to tap in to the same energy I counted on to let me find the indications I needed. You witnessed the manifestation of the dream world... but you saw it from the other side of a closed veil."

"You saw... that?"

"No man could have looked at what you saw through the veil and maintained his sanity. I am no exception, so, though the madness called to me, I deliberately looked for other things. I used the logic of the dream portal to look for the actions of men, not of the beings that control the portals. I believe I have located the place we need to investigate." He held my gaze, and I saw a degree of uncertainty there that shook my faith. If Holmes, of all men, felt uncertain, what remained for the rest of us? "I was fortunate that I'd been warned. I knew what to expect, and I acted in consequence. But there are many this night, both in the house we visited and in countless others, who will not be so fortunate. I expect the authorities will be puzzled by the sudden upswing in cases of unexplained lunacy over the next few days. And the lunatics will be the fortunate ones, the ones whose minds survived." He took a swallow from the glass I'd laid on his table. "Many, perhaps most, will not."

And then, to my indignation, he stood and began to button his cuff.

"You are in no condition to gallivant around the metropolis," I said. "And if you will not heed me as a friend, heed me as a medical professional. You risk your life by insisting."

"Though your concern is touching, I cannot heed your wise council. I only wish I could. But now is a time for haste, and the life of one man—no matter how dear I hold that life—is irrelevant in the scope of what we face." He reached for his coat.

"Where are you going?"

"I am going to verify what I saw in the dream. I would much prefer for you to remain here..." He paused and thought. "But I cannot afford to leave you behind. At this point, where one man goes, two might be better. If I could take every man in the Empire with me, I would gladly do so. So, I must ask you again, will you risk your life—and worse, your sanity—to stand on the front lines of mankind's most important battle?"

"You already know the answer to that," I replied. "It is the same answer I have always given."

"That is what I feared," Holmes replied gravely. "But I welcome it."

He turned toward the door, but I stopped him with a hand on his shoulder. "Is there a worldly explanation this time, Holmes? Or are we effectively chasing spirits?"

"Not spirits," Holmes replied. "Although perhaps it would be better to think of them that way. We are fighting beings. Beings that have abilities we cannot imagine, learned over the course of thousands, perhaps millions of years. They are not spirits as you understand them... but the shadow of their shadows might have given rise to the superstitions some believe."

I swallowed, remembering the images in the smoke. If those were the shadows...

A chill ran down my back.

"Are we going to face the things I saw?" I asked.

"Only if we fail, Watson. Only if we fail."

***

Our destination proved to be ten minutes away from Baker Street, just north of Hyde Park. We descended upon a large, columned townhouse, painted white and distinguished only in detail from the infinite row of houses around it.

"What is this place?" I asked.

"This, Watson, is the Blatavsky Lodge. Don't let the genteel aspect of the place fool you. It is inhabited exclusively by feeble-minded individuals whose weak intellects are unable to discern the difference between good and evil. They are also incapable of realizing the fact that the creatures they are in contact with aren't the spirits of their departed ancestors but powerful enemies wishing to harm us."

Holmes rapped smartly at the door.

Minutes passed without an answer or, indeed, any sign of movement within. He rapped again.

I pushed on the door and it opened, earning me a nod and a raised eyebrow from Holmes.

I wasn't entirely certain what we'd find in the lair of a spiritualist organization, but a brightly lit entry hall with checkered white and black flooring and white walls and balustrades was not in line with my expectations. And yet that is precisely the sight that greeted us on entry.

"Watson, we shall need to be extremely careful," Holmes said.

I imagine I must have looked incredulous, for he pointed to a spot on the wall behind an enormous pot that held some species of tropical shrub. A moment passed before I realized he was indicating the wall behind the plant: four red streaks stained the white paint, almost exactly as if a person had run bloody fingers across it at the level of a standing man's knees.

A staircase led to the upper floors, but Holmes indicated the door towards the kitchen. "On this occasion, we should head downward. I assume the cellar is accessible through the servants' quarters or the pantry. In any case, we are not concerned with the upstairs rooms."

We went through that door and found ourselves in a short corridor leading to the kitchen. The only illumination came from the door behind us, and we cast grotesque shadows in the pitch darkness.

"There should be candles in the cupboards," Holmes said. "See if you can locate them."

As he investigated the dim room, surely searching for the staircase to the nether regions of the house, I opened and closed cupboards until, on my third attempt, I met with success.

I returned to the entrance hall and lit two of the brown tallow candles I'd found from a gas lamp.

When I reentered the kitchen, the silence had been broken. A soft keening sound was audible.

A cold hand gripped my heart. Had something happened to Holmes?

I strode forward, candles held in front of me like a cross against evil.

"It's all right, Watson," Holmes's voice said as he emerged from a side room. "The man is harmless to all but himself."

A figure huddled beneath the large wooden table that dominated the center of the kitchen. He was sobbing softly, brokenly, his hands over his eyes. I was about to turn back to our task when I realized the dark stains on his clothes and face were bloody marks.

"You're injured," I said.

The man jumped and I realized my tone sounded enormous in the dark, silent kitchen.

"Be still. Let me look at your injuries," I said in a softer tone.

He pulled away, growling incoherently.

I set the candles down on the floor and, taking care to stay out of any angle where a terrified man could strike me, I prised his hands away from his face.

Ragged gouges scarred the flesh of his face; they bled profusely. For a moment, I feared the man had lost an eye, but, on closer inspection, his eyes seemed to have only been injured, not destroyed by whatever had clawed him. He was young and healthy and dressed for a white-tie dinner event. A gentleman.

"What happened to you?"

The only response forthcoming was another keening sound, a desperate, hopeless note.

"Come, I can help you, but I must know how you received these injuries."

He didn't answer, just pushed at me to keep me away.

That was when I noticed his hands.

Covered in dark blood, they seemed to have been injured as well. No, I realized when I saw a strip of skin hanging from one of his fingernails. Not injured. They had *caused* the injury. The awful scratches on this man's face were self-inflicted.

"Holmes, I think this man is mad."

"Yes," Holmes agreed as he rattled a door. "If he has done what I think he did, his mind will never return. And if so, then we face a desperate trial. Come, help me open this door."

Retrieving the candles, I crawled from under the table and joined him at another white door. "What is it?"

"This is the door to the stairs leading down. Locked, I'm afraid."

"If it's locked, then how do you know where it goes?"

"It's the only locked door," Holmes replied. "And it's the only one with bloody handprints on it. This is where we need to go."

"How do we open it? I know you can pick this lock," I said, studying the jamb. "I've seen you do more complex mechanisms."

"And so I have, but, as I mentioned, there is a time for stealth and a time for haste. This is the latter."

I pushed against the door. It was made of wood, and relatively solid… but not solid enough to halt a determined man.

"Hold these, please," I said, handing the candles to Holmes.

Then I took three steps back and rushed forward, giving the door a violent blow with my shoulder. I heard splintering and upon further inspection, found the wood around the jamb to be cracking. Three vicious kicks to the weakened area finished the task and the door swung inward.

The staircase below stretched into darkness, much longer—and much straighter—than I expected in a house like this one.

"Hurry," Holmes prompted as he followed me into the abyss.

The voices started as soon as I'd taken five steps. Whispers, at first indecipherable, caressed my ears. After a moment, I realized they weren't speaking in some incomprehensible foreign language, but in a strange accent, just barely out of the reach of my understanding.

I could almost make them out... I understood just enough to know that they whispered truths of the meaning of life, of the order of the universe, of the very fabric of space and time itself. If only I stopped walking and truly listened, I would achieve the knowledge of the gods.

"Keep moving," Holmes hissed. "Sing a song to yourself if you must, but don't stop to listen."

I forced myself to take another step. I felt the secrets of the universe slipping through my fingers. I wanted to scream, to plead, to beg that they simply speak louder so that I could understand them without stopping. But I pushed another foot down the staircase.

The descent became agony. My will came close to failing under the assault of that siren's call more times than I could count. I consider myself a strong man, but the eldritch seduction of the knowledge of ages nearly overcame every defense my will could muster.

At the end of it, though, my foot encountered the floor of the cellar, and the voices faded to silence.

After the wooden staircase, I expected a rough-hewn floor, packed earth or perhaps wood planks. Instead, this cellar—which appeared to stretch far beyond the boundaries of the house itself—was paved with colossal slabs of polished stone.

Wordlessly, Holmes stood beside me and pointed forward, from where soft light emerged. I nodded.

We walked rapidly towards the light. Blasts of frozen air screamed through the chamber, smelling of sea and salt and rotting fish. I felt them distinctly, bone deep, but the candles were unaffected, not even a flicker manifesting in the gusts.

An image of some fantastic machine, a melding of man and technology, flashed off to one side. Activity that looked so real I felt that I stared into a window that showed me the wonders the whispers had promised.

"Keep your eyes on the light ahead," Holmes said. "If you move off this line, you will be lost, and nothing I can do will save you."

So the wonders of the universe went unheeded to my right and left. The injustice of it burned, and my greatest desire at that moment was to smash Holmes's face with my fist.

I overcame and we continued.

The light grew stronger, and I realized that, at some point, the ground beneath all the houses in the area had been dug out and paved. Deep within the colossal space—which was occasionally interrupted with pillars that must have been supporting the city above—stood a circle of candles on legs as tall as a man.

In the center of the circle a pedestal held a large tome, open at what appeared to be one of the first pages.

Holmes walked to the book and said, "It doesn't seem to have been read. The man upstairs must have attempted it... you saw what it did. And when he made the attempt, the result was the tremor we felt."

"This book did that?"

"Recall those voices on the staircase and those tantalizing visions in the dark. Now imagine that every secret hinted at by them could be driven into a single word, and that your mind would immediately grow to encompass the knowledge of that single word. Now imagine that there was a book, a thick tome, composed of those words. This is that book. It can expand your mind to show you... everything... and then, when your mind contracts back to its original capacity, that is madness. The loss is unbearable, the knowledge that remains reminds you constantly that you are but a speck in an infinite cosmos. And the knowledge that there exist beings not only capable of comprehending it all, but of recording their wisdom in utter confidence that lesser beings will not be able to withstand it... that is impossible for human vanity to survive." He nodded in the direction of the stairs. "The man above is what happens when an average mind looks into the heart of the universe. He tried to read it and failed."

"But," a voice from the shadows said, "what happens when an extraordinary one attempts it? Yours, for example, Mr. Holmes?"

A woman stepped into the light, and I was scandalized by her mode of dress. Though it was obvious that the garment was well-crafted and the rich materials some kind of formal dress, it was completely unbuttressed, falling directly from the woman's waist to the ground without support—instead, it followed the curves of her body. The body itself was perhaps a little too tall and rangy for the erotic attempt to be successful... but that was no fault of the dress. Such a thing had no place in society.

And yet, the woman spoke in tones that indicated breeding and education. Her face was pale, the face of a woman whose life took place out of the sun.

She held a small black revolver. In any other circumstances, I would have scoffed at such an item. You'd have to be a crack shot to do real damage with the calibers associated with those guns.

But in this darkness, surrounded by whispers of arcane knowledge and visions of golden machines, it became a thing of nightmares. Any shot emerging from it under such conditions would be certain death—but only after excruciating pain.

"You are not Madame Blatavsky," Holmes said. "From which I must deduce that you are, in fact, Miss Everett."

I stared at Holmes. Who was Miss Everett, and how did he know her name? I was certain he'd never been introduced to her in my presence.

"Very good, Mr. Holmes. I knew you would deduce the truth."

"It was quite simple. The man above was dressed as an English gentleman. Therefore, if he has lost his mind to the book, he must have understood the words. Such can only mean that the words are a Greek translation, not the original writings of the mad Arab. As such, this is the Salem copy. And where do we find a well-known Salem heiress? Here in London. It couldn't be a 203.coincidence."

She tilted her head at him. "You impress me indeed."

"You were expecting me," Holmes said evenly.

"I was expecting someone. You. Or perhaps Moriarty. Any of a dozen people who could have solved the enigma would serve my purpose. Poor Charlie—I suppose you met what was left of him upstairs—was always doomed to fail."

"And you believe this book will do what? Call up the dead?"

The woman laughed. "Of course not. That was just the story for the poor simple fools that keep this mansion going with their silly little society for speaking to the dead and trying to figure out who they were in a past life." She gestured toward the book with the gun. "But the name of the book lends itself so beautifully to using these simpletons, doesn't it? As soon as they hear the word 'necro,' they positively drool all over themselves. But only one whose family has had the book in their keeping for hundreds of years could ever know the truth. Even you, one of the greatest minds of the age, don't suspect."

"I suspect it's a mistranslation by the Arab," Holmes replied. "I suspect the original didn't refer to the dead at all. An advanced being will have understood that spiritualism is a mere comfort for frightened primitive minds. No, the original—in whatever undecipherable language of revelation reached the Arab's mind—likely referred to a 'sleeper' or a 'dreamer.' And this book is a way to reach them, by way of understanding their wonders. Wonders too large for a human brain to encompass... as are the consequences."

A look of fury crossed Miss Everett's features. "My family is well beyond caring for consequences, Holmes. We have been hounded and persecuted for centuries, merely because we choose to think that humanity is destined for greater things than merely evolving at our own slow rate. And my family deserves to be at the forefront of the change, taking back the position that was stolen from us in Salem."

She pointed the pistol dead at Holmes's chest. I tensed, calculating whether I could surprise her and reach the pistol before she reacted. I judged my chances as being poor to none—I was simply too far away.

She spoke again. "You will read the book for me."

Holmes shook his head. "I will not. I fear death less than I fear what will become of this world if we willingly call to these beings."

Miss Everett turned the pistol in my direction. "If you won't do it for yourself, perhaps you will do it to save your friend?" She must have realized that I was on the verge of moving because she smiled and said, "Don't do anything foolish. I'm a crack shot, and you will be dead of a bullet through the heart before you finish the first step."

"There is no need for that," Holmes said. "I will read."

"No, Holmes!" I cried. "If things are as dire as that, you cannot do this. I am willing to die if I must. You know this."

To my chagrin, Holmes ignored me and bent to look at the book, leaving me to wonder whether I should attack the madwoman. If I were, indeed, shot through the heart, at least Holmes would have no reason to continue reading.

"This is not the best page to open the portal," Holmes said. "This is merely a spell to call forth a vision of eternity. It is no wonder your assistant fell prey to it and paid for his blunder at the cost of his mind."

"I do not profess to understand the contents. I have no desire to go mad," Miss Everett said. "Choose the page you wish, but choose wisely. Your friend's life depends on it. If I even feel that something untoward is happening, I will fire without compunction. Is that clear, Mr. Holmes?"

"Quite," Holmes replied.

I seethed quietly, feeling that not only had I betrayed Holmes with my vulnerability, but also that he betrayed me by not respecting my preference to die before being a tool for a monster.

And yet, I didn't move. I knew Holmes well, and I knew that, had he wanted me to move, he would have found some sign to show it. As yet, I had seen nothing of the sort.

Holmes leafed through the pages of the great leather-bound tome before him. It was a large book, a folio of the kind popular in the days before paper when calfskin was the medium for writing. And yet, I felt it in my very bones—the pages were not of calfskin.

I shuddered when the thought came unbidden: these pages were created of human leather, for only that material could correctly contain the horrible knowledge it held.

The very air trembled as Holmes turned the pages.

Finally, he came to a stop and looked up at Miss Everett. "Are you certain about this?"

"It is my destiny, handed down to me for generations. Serve me well, Holmes, and I will ensure that you join with the leaders. Fail me and I will kill both you and your friend. Someone else will find this place. Perhaps Moriarty won't need persuasion."

"That is certain. But I'm curious about why you didn't go to Moriarty first."

She smiled. "Because Moriarty would never have agreed to what I'm going to ask you to do. And even if he had, I wouldn't trust him to go through with it." She took a step into the light, and I saw that apart from being tall, she had a face that would haunt a man's dreams. "I want you to look into my eyes and give me your solemn word that you will not betray me. That you will act in good faith to put me in contact with the dreamers and ascribe the power to me that is the gift of my birth."

Holmes did not hesitate for a moment. "I give you my word. I shall work for your benefit with these creatures to the best of my power. And I bind Watson to my word as well."

She studied him for a moment, and then nodded. "I trust you implicitly. You are one of the few men whose word is considered sacrosanct." She lowered the pistol. "I trust you both and put your lives in my hands."

"My promise forces me to ask you to reconsider. The forces we are about to disturb range far above the ken of men."

"Thank you for your concern, Mr. Holmes, but that is a risk I'm willing to take." She smiled again. "I assure you that it will be a risk well worth taking. You will be thankful that you chose to help without too much coercion."

Holmes looked down at the book. "*Khaírete*," he began.

I understood the word… or at least what I assumed to be the word. It was the Greek word for greeting. But while the first two syllables were clear, by the third, I could only hear a distorted sound. I didn't think Holmes was distorting the words… it was simply that those words, read from that tome, held the power to warp the very existence around us.

Holmes continued to read, but if it was Greek, it certainly wasn't a dialect I could understand.

Instead of attempting to follow the spell, I watched Holmes's face. He appeared to have enormous difficulty pushing out the words. After only a few moments of speech, beads of sweat formed on his brow and fell onto the text of the pages.

He pushed on, his face sometimes contorted in pain, at other times taking on the expression I'd only seen when he was in the clutches of a particularly potent dose of cocaine. The words rumbled and trilled in tones unlike any I'd ever heard him use.

And then I recognized two words: Eleanor Everett.

I glanced over at that worthy, and she nodded with a satisfied—

albeit wide-eyed—expression.

Holmes droned and screeched on. The hairs on my arms stood on end and I felt the room grow cold, then warm. A breeze caused the candles to flutter, but even when sharp gusts spun around the point where Miss Everett stood, the candles weren't extinguished.

I felt power around us, a power I suspected to be static electricity. It built until I could sense it pulling my skin tight, a sensation of pins and needles between my body and my clothing.

"Yes!" cried Miss Everett.

If I felt the power, she must have been immersed in it. A pale white glow encircled her, and she stood on the tips of her feet, as if about to float off into the air.

"It's working!" she said. "I feel the power. My God, with this I can do what I want. Men will fall to their knees at my command! I can raze entire cities on a whim!" She laughed, the laugh of a small child suddenly gifted the toy she had yearned for.

Holmes spoke on and my ears suddenly popped, as the gale changed direction.

A dark circle, a blackness that made the surrounding gloom of the cellar appear to be the brightness of noon, formed. I imagined I could see through it, into stars of the depths of the galaxy, but something told me to tear my eyes away. My mind feared for its sanity and immediately realized that here were sights too awful to contemplate. Looking would only lead to madness.

I kept my gaze upon Miss Everett. Unlike me, she had no compunctions about looking into the abyss. She did it with a smile, shoulders thrown back as if in challenge, or perhaps welcome.

She screamed. "Yes! The time is coming!"

A tendril, long and black, emerged from the portal. It appeared to be as thick as my thumb, and another soon joined it. A third and a fourth and then an infinity appeared, and with them a whispering, buzzing in my mind that drowned out every word Holmes pronounced.

But it didn't drown out the words of Miss Everett. She was shouting: "Yes! Yes! Yes! Come to me!" as the tendrils gently wrapped themselves around her.

The tendrils found purchase and tore off her dress. It happened in an instant, before I could look away to preserve her modesty. In any case, the tendrils wrapped around her in a curtain of blackness, allowing me to see only her face; they served to preserve the woman's modesty much better than the scandalous dress she'd been wearing.

She smiled yet more, her expression rapturous as she stared deep into whatever was present in that abyss.

"Yes!" she began to say once again, but the word cut off as it was formed and became a scream of the purest terror that threatened to deafen me. She was pulled, before my eyes, into the abyss. It happened slowly, as she screamed and struggled.

And I could do nothing. I was rooted to the floor by my own terror and the buzzing hiss in my mind, like a small game animal hypnotized by a flame.

I closed my eyes so I wouldn't have to watch her enter the portal.

But the scream lingered on and on.

"Watson!"

It was Holmes's voice, speaking plain English, and it held an urgency I had never heard from him. That fear, so uncharacteristic of the man, must have been what broke me from my torpor.

"Watson!"

"Yes!" I opened my eyes to see no sign of Miss Everett, only the tendrils still inside the room. More of them, radiating out from the abyss as if, without the young woman's presence to guide them and the nimbus surrounding her, they needed to feel their way.

"Help me!" Holmes said.

Freed from my terror by a direct command, I rushed to his side. The book stood on a pedestal, and I looked at the letters. The mere sight of them made me dizzy. I swayed.

"Watson!"

I opened my eyes again to find Holmes looking deep into my gaze. "Help me close the book."

I saw that he was struggling, the pages fluttering between the two covers, half-closed. It was a big book, but not heavy enough to defeat a strong man. I pushed on the cover and realized the book was pushing back.

Keeping my eyes away from the words on those demonic pages of human skin, I put my considerable strength to the task. I felt my muscles strain, felt something pop in an elbow, but I also felt the covers closing. Unlike the creature of darkness it summoned, the book itself had only the limited strength of whatever animated that dead flesh. It gave way slowly, but it closed.

The buzzing in my head stopped, a million cicadas crushed underfoot.

Holmes nodded once, then swayed and fell, unconscious, to the ground.

I held onto the pedestal long enough to assure myself that the black hole in the world had disappeared.

Only when I was satisfied on this point did I allow myself to drift into the darkness and fall to the floor beside Holmes.

***

I shook my head to clear the buzzing. I knew it was present only in my own imagination, as we were safely ensconced in our sitting room at Baker Street on a bright, glorious autumn morning.

The room was warm, with a cheerful fire burning. Mrs. Watson hovered around us like a concerned mother hen.

"How awful that both of you gentlemen are feeling poorly. It's such an unusual state of affairs," she observed as she brought a large teapot into the room. She clucked about a little more and then left, satisfied that we were no worse than earlier in the day and decidedly better than a week before when we'd both unexpectedly turned sickly after a long night—of which she, of course, knew nothing.

In her wake, she left an envelope addressed to Holmes beside the teapot.

He opened it slowly, his fingers stiff, and read it equally slowly. "It's from Admiral Chase," he said.

I tried to concentrate on his words. Chase was the man from the Ministry of War who'd been called in by Scotland Yard after Holmes convinced Lestrade that we hadn't lost our wits.

"The package has been sunk in the Atlantic Ocean," Holmes said with satisfaction.

"I am glad to hear it," I replied. "Perhaps that accursed book will trouble people no more."

"I'm certain it will trouble men again. But only when they have the capacity to locate something on the ocean floor. Even with the progress being made today, I hope it is decades before those dark abysses are penetrated. In any case, it should be for men of the future to resolve."

I nodded. “It’s a good solution. Men of the future will have the benefit of enlightenment we don’t.”

Holmes raised an eyebrow. A half-smile crossed his face. But he said nothing.

We sipped our tea in silence as the morning passed. I had little energy to spare, despite having not one but two unread copies of *The Illustrated Police News* on the table beside me. Finally, I asked the one question that had been present in my mind despite the difficulty I had concentrating over the past week, due to that infernal buzzing which, thankfully, seemed to be abating slowly but surely. It was a question I’d been too afraid to ask.

“Holmes,” I said. “I understand that you had to sacrifice your honor for duty to mankind, but I need to know whether you can live with yourself after what you did to Miss Everett. She received the punishment she deserved, but I know what it must have cost you to break your word. I would not want you to... do anything rash as a consequence.”

The gray eyes never left mine. He held them there for several heartbeats. Finally, he nodded and his look softened. “You are a true friend, Watson. But you must understand my life is not in danger. Or at least not by my own hand.”

“That is a relief.”

He smiled. “You misunderstand, I believe. The reason it is not in danger is that I have committed no breach of honor. I did my very best to bring Miss Everett’s plan to fruition and to make her Empress of the world.”

I felt my mouth fall open. Holmes chuckled.

“Don’t look so shocked. A mere human could never have controlled the powers unleashed. So I imagined that our attempt would end with a messy failure. Unfortunately, for Miss Everett, her insistence on continuing despite my warning made her the focus of the failure.”

I nodded. “And she paid with her life.”

“I think she has not paid with her life. Not yet.”

“You believe she is still alive?”

“I would wager on it. I think she will outlive us all. Unfortunately, her existence will be one of eternal suffering, of slipping into madness while a part of her mind is still there to recognize what has happened and to suffer it.”

I sipped my tea, surprised to find that I felt sorry for the woman.

"By making her the focus of the power," Holmes continued, "it gave us time to close the book. Just enough."

"Did you know it would happen that way?"

"If that hadn't been my conclusion, I would have refused. Of course, Miss Everett was probably correct in guessing that Moriarty would have ferreted out the location of the book in due time... and our deaths would have been in vain. It was better to act."

"And if you'd been wrong?" I asked.

He simply smiled, the same smile I'd seen from him so often. Enigmatic and controlled.

But I saw it twitch slightly and wondered what he was hearing inside.

The voices I heard were simply repeating, over and over:

Kill him; he's mad. Kill him; he's mad. Kill him; he's mad...

I wondered how long I could resist.

Not long, I suspected.

About the Author

Gustavo Bondoni is a novelist and short story writer with over four hundred stories published in fifteen countries, in seven languages. He has published six science fiction novels including one trilogy, four monster books, a dark military fantasy, and a thriller. His short fiction is collected in *Pale Reflection* (2020), *Off the Beaten Path* (2019), *Tenth Orbit and Other Faraway Places* (2010), and *Virtuoso and Other Stories* (2011).

In 2019, Gustavo was awarded second place in the Jim Baen Memorial Contest, and in 2018 he received a Judges Commendation (and second place) in The James White Award. He was also a 2019 finalist in the Writers of the Future Contest.

His website is www.gustavobondoni.com.

Short stories from existences
beyond our own
The Art
of
Ghost Writing
ALISTAIR REY
Available from
Dark Owl Publishing
www.darkowlpublishing.com

BAD
DREAMS AND
REFLECTIONS
BY TREVOR KENNEDY
"When one finds Trevor Kennedy's work, it gives the same thrill of finding an unassuming book in a local small bookstore - the kind that ends up exploding the imagination out into tendrils which wrap around realms the reader never knew were missing from their life."
~ Carl R. Jennings, author and reviewer
AVAILABLE FROM DARK OWL PUBLISHING
DOP
WWW.DARKOWLPUBLISHING.COM

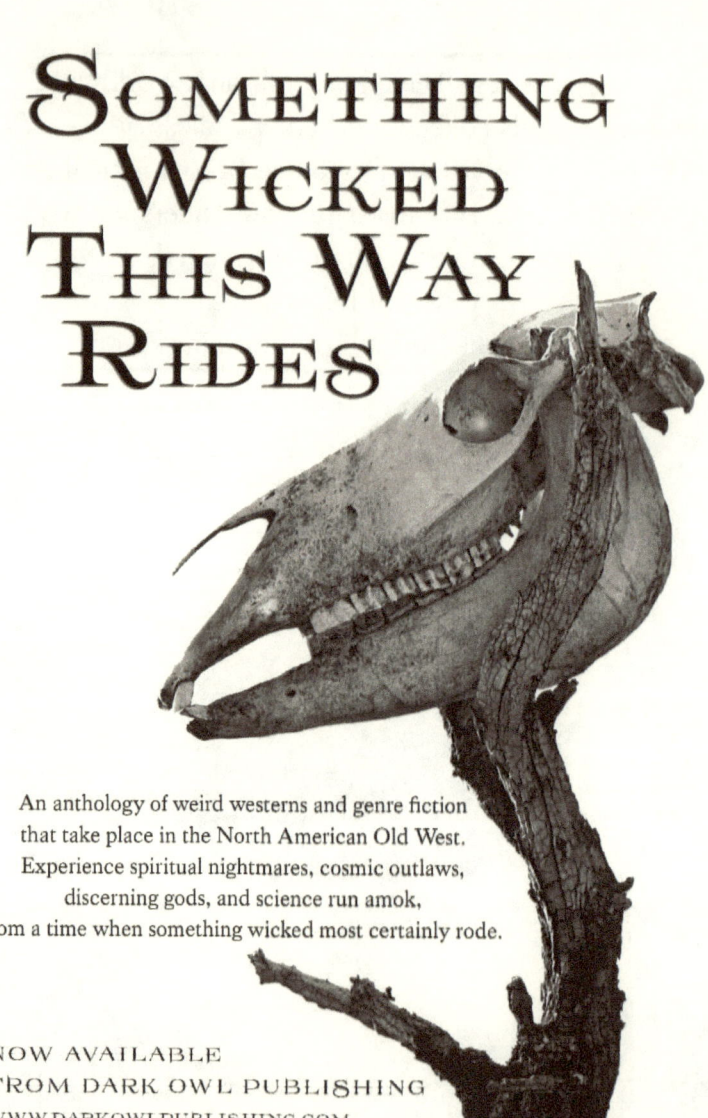

www.ingramcontent.com/pod-product-compliance
Lightning Source LLC
Chambersburg PA
CBHW031943240626
47153CB00003B/840
* 9 7 8 1 9 5 1 7 1 6 4 4 8 *